"What u... ...

It's lust, ...

Zeke's eyes gleamed. "Three out of four isn't bad."

"I won't settle for three out of four this time," Tara said. "You didn't trust me enough to know what was best for me then, and you obviously don't now."

"I'm a reporter. I deal in facts. Trust is an intangible."

"So is love," she reminded him. "But you need both to make a relationship work."

"All this talk about love and trust is a blind, isn't it? You wanted an excuse to stop seeing me, and I provided one by accepting a job overseas. If I'd rejected the offer, you would have invented some other reason to walk out."

"You make it sound as if it was my decision alone."

"Wasn't it?" he demanded. "Can you deny you were already pregnant when I asked you to come with me?"

She felt her spine crumble. *He knew.*

Dear Reader,

As always, Intimate Moments offers you six terrific books to fill your reading time, starting with Terese Ramin's *Her Guardian Agent*. For FBI agent Hazel Youvella, the case that took her back to revisit her Native American roots was a very personal one. For not only did she find the hero of her heart in Native American tracker Guy Levoie, she discovered the truth about the missing child she was seeking. This wasn't just any child—this was *her* child.

If you enjoyed last month's introduction to our FIRSTBORN SONS in-line continuity, you won't want to miss the second installment. Carla Cassidy's *Born of Passion* will grip you from the first page and leave you longing for the rest of these wonderful linked books. Valerie Parv takes a side trip from Silhouette Romance to debut in Intimate Moments with a stunner of a reunion romance called *Interrupted Lullaby*. Karen Templeton begins a new miniseries called HOW TO MARRY A MONARCH with *Plain-Jane Princess,* and Linda Winstead Jones returns with *Hot on His Trail,* a book you should be hot on the trail of yourself. Finally, welcome Sharon Mignerey back and take a look at her newest, *Too Close for Comfort*.

And don't forget to look in the back of this book to see how Silhouette can make you a star.

Enjoy them all, and come back next month for more of the best and most exciting romance reading around.

Yours,

Leslie J. Wainger
Executive Senior Editor

Please address questions and book requests to:
Silhouette Reader Service
U.S.: 3010 Walden Ave., P.O. Box 1325, Buffalo, NY 14269
Canadian: P.O. Box 609, Fort Erie, Ont. L2A 5X3

Interrupted Lullaby

VALERIE PARV

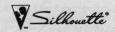

INTIMATE MOMENTS™

Published by Silhouette Books

America's Publisher of Contemporary Romance

To all the babies lost before or soon after birth,
who are still very much loved and remembered

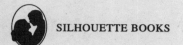 **SILHOUETTE BOOKS**

ISBN 0-373-27165-4

INTERRUPTED LULLABY

Copyright © 2001 by Valerie Parv

Visit Silhouette at www.eHarlequin.com

Printed in U.S.A.

VALERIE PARV

lives and breathes romance and has even written a guide to being romantic, crediting her cartoonist husband of nearly thirty years as her inspiration. As a former buffalo and crocodile hunter in Australia's Northern Territory, he's ready-made hero material, she says.

When not writing about her novels and nonfiction books, or speaking about romance on Australian radio and television, Valerie enjoys dollhouses, being a *Star Trek* fan and playing with food (in cooking, that is). Valerie agrees with actor Nichelle Nichols, who said, "The difference between fantasy and fact is that fantasy simply hasn't happened yet."

SILHOUETTE MAKES YOU A STAR!
**Feel like a star with Silhouette.
Look for the exciting details of our new contest
inside all of these fabulous Silhouette novels:**

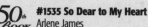

THE
CALAMITY
JANES

FIRSTBORN
SONS

How To Marry A Monarch

Family
Revelations

Prologue

When the baby's lusty cry tore the air in the small private hospital, the new mother burst into tears of relief and joy. Seeing the midwife rush the newborn baby into the resuscitation room, the mother had been frantic with fear. Now, hearing her baby's healthy cries as the midwife placed him into her arms, the mother knew everything would be all right.

It had been a difficult night. The doctor was to have been here long ago, but had stopped to help at a horrendous accident between two crowded buses at a major intersection in the city. According to the midwife, staff had been borrowed from all over the hospital to help deal with the victims pouring into the emergency room, a scene being repeated at hospitals throughout the city.

Admiring the new baby, Rosemary Fine felt triumphant. As a midwife she was accustomed to coping without a doctor most of the time, but when a baby needed resuscitating, she normally called for backup. This time she couldn't call anyone because the mother, Jenny Fine, was her sister-in-law, and it was against hospital rules to deliver a relative's baby. With everyone too busy to ask questions, Rosemary had decided to go ahead on her own. She had nearly regretted it when the baby was born, but everything was all right now. Rosemary had seen to it.

Jenny quickly counted tiny fingers and toes. "I suppose everybody does that," she said, her voice sounding thin.

Rosemary mustered a smile. "Probably. He looks pretty good to me. Vaughan, isn't that the name you chose for him?"

"Sylvia for a girl and Vaughan for a boy." Jenny brushed damp hair out of her eyes with her free hand, her gaze blurring. "Did I hear Ross tell you that the nice woman in the next room lost her baby?"

The midwife hesitated. "You weren't supposed to hear that. Her baby's cord prolapsed, causing oxygen starvation. There was nothing Ross or anyone could do."

Jenny's arm automatically tightened around her baby. "How terrible. She told me her name is Tara, and she's so beautiful. A model, I think. We checked in almost at the same time. Her partner couldn't be with her, either, so I hope he gets here soon. She'll need him to comfort her. After I lost Josh, they told me it was crib death and nobody's fault, but I kept asking myself how I could have made a difference. Tara's probably doing the same right now."

Rosemary brushed her sister-in-law's hair out of her eyes. "You mustn't distress yourself about it."

Jenny sighed. "You're right. But I couldn't face Ross if anything went wrong this time. He wants a son so much. How much longer is he going to be tied up? Except for a few minutes here and there, I've hardly seen him since I arrived."

"You've been married to a midwife long enough to know that nothing ever goes to plan. He'll stop in as soon as he can, but like me, he's had to extend his shift until more staff can get here,'' Rosemary said. ''Apparently half the city's still at a standstill. They're swamped in emergency.''

The new mother peeled back the cover swaddling the baby. ''Hi, Vaughan. Your daddy's going to be so proud of you.'' She lifted her head, her eyes bright. ''I'll have a word with poor Tara later. She must feel devastated. ''

Rosemary shook her head. ''It's not a good idea. She's best left to deal with her grief in her own way. We'll see she gets professional help when she's ready.''

Jenny looked uncertain. ''If you think so.''

''Trust me, I do. Ross is arranging to move her to a ward away from the other mothers and babies, so you're unlikely to meet her again. You concentrate on getting your strength back and taking Vaughan home. Let Ross and me look after Tara. There's nothing for you to concern yourself about, nothing at all.''

Chapter 1

As soon as she walked into the meeting and saw who was sitting in the front row, Tara McNiven felt tension coil inside her like a snake waiting to strike. What was Zeke Blaxland doing here? He could be here for the same reason as the rest of the audience, to hear about the children's charity she represented, she told herself shakily, but somehow she sensed he had another agenda. Zeke always had another agenda.

She had heard that he was back in Australia, and his column had been carried by the Australian papers while he was living in America so she was used to seeing his photograph on the editorial page three times a week. She had managed to convince herself that she was immune to the sight of his ruggedly handsome features but being confronted by him again in the flesh made her all too aware of the reality. She would never be immune to Zeke, no matter how much time they spent apart.

Other members of the audience, all executives from the city's fashion retailers, were casting him curious glances. As

Australia's best-known newspaperman, he was instantly recognizable by sight as well as by reputation. His mane of collar-length black hair was as much a trademark as the challenging spark in those pewter-grey eyes.

He was taller than most other men but managed to look relaxed even coiled into a chair a size too small for his impressive frame. It was a wary kind of relaxation, she couldn't help noticing. He was probably assessing every detail of her appearance and demeanor.

Well, let him. She schooled herself to not show that his unexpected presence had unsettled her. She had changed since they'd been together, but knew she looked good. She weighed a few pounds more these days but it suited her. Her hair was straighter, curling under onto her shoulders where it had once tumbled midway down her back in a torrent of curls. Zeke had liked to run his fingers through it, she recalled, a shiver of memory rippling over her scalp and down her spine.

She was glad she was wearing her best power-dressing cerise jacket and navy skirt, the colors flattering her honey-gold complexion. Business-like but still feminine, she had decided as she'd checked the mirror before leaving home.

The shorter hairstyle emphasized the features that had made her a successful model before she became spokesperson for Model Children, the foundation she and a group of fashion designers had established to help children in need.

She sighed inwardly. Try as she might to play down her model looks and focus attention on the work of the charity, it didn't help. Like Zeke Blaxland, she was recognizable wherever she went.

She could hardly complain. Her background had helped her to recruit some of the biggest designers in the industry to support the cause, and her fame ensured the charity got the publicity it needed to help as many children as possible.

Now she wanted to broaden the foundation's base to include other arms of the fashion industry.

She felt her brows arrow into a frown. Zeke Blaxland's name hadn't been on tonight's guest list, she would swear to it. But demanding to know what he was doing here would only show how much his presence disconcerted her and she had no intention of giving him such an advantage. She had given Zeke far too much already.

Just thinking of how much sent a pang through her so sharp it was almost physical, but she fought the sensation. Deliberately she pulled herself together, for once thankful that she stood five-ten even without the slender heels she wore for speaking engagements. Zeke used to say she was one of the few women who could meet him eye-to-eye— almost.

He liked the almost part, she recalled with a surge of bitterness. Near equality wasn't the same as true equality, something he had never wanted from a woman, or not from her, anyway. He liked to kid himself that he was a New Age man when truthfully, he hadn't a New Age bone in his magnificent body.

Tara's heart picked up speed. Once his caveman approach had thrilled her. She had enjoyed the feeling of being protected and, yes, loved by him. She swallowed hard, remembering the feel of his arms around her, so strong and dependable, as his sensuous mouth shaped hers to his will, while his clever hands manipulated her body with a skill worthy of a virtuoso violinist. She had been a willing instrument and Zeke the bow. Lord, what magnificent music they had made together.

Her heart thundered and her palms moistened as she thought of the end result of their lovemaking she had carefully kept from him. Once she wouldn't have dreamed of keeping anything from him, especially something as important as the child they had conceived together, but his decision to work in America had made it impossible for her to tell him the truth without looking as if she were trying to manipulate him.

Their baby had been stillborn so there had been no need for him to find out. No need for them to both endure the nagging sense of loss she'd lived with for so long. There was nothing he could have done, and she couldn't have borne forcing him to give up his dream to remain with her, only to have their life together end so disastrously.

A choking sensation gripped her. So much had happened in a year. A year, seven months and a handful of days, she amended inwardly. She hadn't been aware of counting the days but now she found that part of her had logged every minute since he had left.

She made herself take deep breaths, conquering wire-taut nerves with an effort of will. She owed it to herself and the children not to reveal how much Zeke's presence bothered her. "Fake it," the photographers used to tell her during her modeling days. Why were these things invariably easier said than done?

She stepped forward. "Good evening, ladies and gentlemen. Thank you for inviting me to address your group about the projects we're currently undertaking at the Model Children Foundation. I'm told you choose a different charity to support each year and since Model Children was started by people in the field of fashion like yourselves, I hope to persuade you to choose M.C.F. this year. Are any of you familiar with my work?"

She saw Zeke's hand shift as if he meant to raise it. "I mean, the work of the foundation?" she restated, and saw his arm relax. But his eyes continued to flash a challenge at her. "You can't ignore me forever," they seemed to say. As if she could ignore him for one single minute. But she didn't have to let him know it.

Another man raised his hand. He seemed younger than

most of the men in the room, probably his early twenties and less outwardly confident. A very junior executive, she couldn't help thinking. "The foundation helped my wife and me when our first child was born. A fire in our house destroyed every stitch of clothing my wife had prepared for the baby as well as the beautiful new nursery we'd prepared."

This time her smile was genuine as satisfaction surged through her. She was able to stop thinking about Zeke's eyes on her for all of thirty seconds as she turned to the man. "You're Todd Jessman, aren't you?" He nodded. "I remember seeing the fire reported on the evening news."

"I wondered how the foundation managed to step in so quickly. I doubt we'd have had the courage to ask for help but after the news story, your people appeared out of the blue with everything we needed. My wife was overwhelmed. We did write, but it's great to have a chance to finally thank you in person."

She shook her head. "I can't take the credit. A large group of fashion designers and others in the industry are behind the foundation."

"And they are getting excellent publicity in the bargain," came a soft interjection.

At the sound of Zeke's gravelly voice, an involuntary shiver shook her. It reminded her too vividly of compliments freely given and lapped up like mother's milk, of whispered suggestions in the moonlight, and promises made over the phone.

Promises ultimately broken, she made herself remember. From what she knew of him, Zeke hadn't changed. In his syndicated column, Difference of Opinion, he took potshots at everything that was good about people. She had once asked him why he preferred to write about the negative side of human nature. He had responded that good news didn't sell papers.

It was where their outlooks reached a fork in the road. She

believed that what goes around comes around. Zeke believed you had to fight for what you wanted. He hadn't fought for her, she thought, wondering what else he could have done to make a difference. No, she wasn't about to start making excuses for him now. With his cynical attitude, they couldn't have lasted anyway, even without the baby.

She pulled her thoughts sharply back to the present. It wasn't easy. She had never loved another man the way she had loved Zeke and she was staggered at how much it hurt to see him again, surveying her with hard-eyed intensity as if she were meat in a butcher shop window.

Not meat, candy, she remembered him saying once. He had told her how, as a boy, he had pressed his face against a candy store window, his eyes eating up all the goodies inside. With not a cent to his name, that was all he could do. *With you, Tara, I feel as if I've finally been given the keys to the store,* he had told her the first time they'd made love.

Too bad he had eaten her up then spat her out, she thought, feeling anger flash through her. She subdued it and made her fingers unclench, forcing herself to concentrate on her task. Normally she could assess her audience in a couple of glances, enough to decide exactly what tone to take in her presentation, but tonight her thoughts were in chaos. Although the audience was two-thirds male, Zeke could have been the only man in the room for all the attention she had paid the rest, she realized with a shock.

Zeke would turn up when the meeting was being covered by *Australian Life* magazine, she thought furiously. The journalist and photographer had already set their equipment up at the back of the room as they had done for a number of the foundation's fund-raising activities. Accustomed to performing for the camera, she hadn't let the visitors distract her unduly. The dress-for-success outfit was her only concession to the coverage. Zeke's presence was another matter.

The visiting journalist was bound to recognize him and

would no doubt want to interview him, as well. No matter. Maybe they could find out what his motives were and save Tara the trouble. She only hoped he would behave himself well enough not to spoil the story for her. No matter what he thought, the publicity was intended to help the foundation far more than any individual.

"It's true the fashion designers benefit from the publicity," she carried on, amazed that she could sound so unruffled given the turmoil inside her. "But children in need are the real beneficiaries and tonight I'd like to show you how you can join us and help make a difference in their lives."

She had their attention, she saw with satisfaction as she warmed to her subject. Business people responded to factual information, she knew from previous experience. Appealing to their emotions was the fastest way to scare them off, so she deliberately made the presentation very practical, with lots of case histories like Todd's so they could visualize their efforts playing a real part in improving the lives of the children the foundation was intended to help.

She couldn't imagine having the same impact on Zeke, she thought. His own experience had made him cynical about charity. Her breath caught as she remembered the night she'd learned about his background. She had wanted him to accompany her to a fund-raiser for a foster family program. He'd objected but wouldn't go into details.

She'd pressed. He had always been reluctant to discuss his family and now she wondered if she'd hit on the reason when she'd asked that night, "Zeke, do you have some experience of foster care?"

"Bitter experience," he'd snapped, his eyes becoming shadowed. "My mother was only seventeen when somebody spiked her drink at a party and she woke up in bed with an older boy whose name she never knew. When she found herself pregnant, her family disowned her. She couldn't cope alone."

Tara's heart had leaped into her throat. "She gave you up for adoption?"

"It would have been better if she had. She left me with a foster family long enough to settle in, then she took me back to live with her."

"At least she loved you enough to come back."

"I might have believed it once, but three times is a little hard to swallow."

"Oh, Zeke." Her heart went out to the small boy whose trust had been so badly betrayed. No wonder he was reluctant to show affection after learning that it could be snatched away at a moment's notice. "What about your mother's family?" she'd asked.

He'd looked away. "Her father was a religious type who didn't want to know her or me. I only tried to see him once, to tell him his daughter had died in a car accident. It was made clear that I needn't have bothered."

"It's his loss," she'd said firmly, wrapping her hand around his. His fingers had felt cold. "I'm sure he regrets it now that you're so successful."

"Too late. So now you know why I object to supporting something that did me more harm than good. If a parent puts a child up for adoption, at least everybody knows where they stand."

To Tara, things weren't always so simple, but she had known it was futile to argue with Zeke when his mind was made up. And who knew, she might have felt the same if her early life had been as disrupted as his. She had also understood why he'd resisted making promises to her. Their life was wonderful as it was, he'd insisted. Why tamper with perfection?

As a result, when she found out she was pregnant she had known she couldn't force him into a commitment he didn't want. Nor could she go with him, for the same reason. She had hoped he would stay in Australia of his own accord, but he hadn't. From his comments tonight, it seemed he hadn't changed at all.

Awareness of him played through her thoughts like background music as she went on to explain how the foundation had started when a woman on her own had unexpectedly given birth to triplets without the resources to clothe and equip them.

Tara had been a patient at the same hospital, although she avoided mentioning that part, especially with Zeke in the room. She had expected to be in the maternity ward and her heart had been torn in two when she had been moved to a surgical ward instead, with a woman who coughed all night. It was a long way from a baby's healthy cries, she remembered thinking.

The single mother with the triplets had been the talk of the hospital and as soon as she was discharged, Tara had buried her aching sense of loss while making telephone calls to colleagues and persuading them to donate clothes for the babies. One of her favorite designers had gone further, creating an adorable miniature wardrobe for the triplets. The resulting publicity had led more of Tara's colleagues to offer money and assistance, and before long the foundation was a reality.

She had never expected to become the charity's spokesperson. At first she could barely be around children without falling apart, but slowly it dawned on her that there was healing here, too. Seeing so many babies and children being given hope for the future had renewed her own sense of hope. Her pain had slowly eased to a distant ache that only caught her unawares every now and then.

In helping others, she had helped herself to go on. She called on that strength now to keep her voice steady and her body language serene, describing work the foundation had done and the work still to do, and how the audience could play a part.

When they broke for coffee she was immediately surrounded, but even as she answered questions she was aware of Zeke across the room, a coffee cup untouched in his hand, his gaze on her. His look felt like a flame, licking at her body.

Time to take the bull by the horns. Excusing herself, she strode up to him, her own coffee cup held like a shield in front of her. "Hello, Zeke."

"Nice talk. Very persuasive," he said evenly.

"Wasted on you."

"I didn't come to be recruited," he denied. "You know my philosophy—charity begins at home."

"Then why are you here?" she demanded.

In the confined space, his body brushed hers and she felt her pulses leap in instant response. When they were together, his hard body hadn't always been encased in expensive tailoring. More often, it had been encased in nothing at all and the image sent shards of desire spearing through her.

Chemistry, that's all it was, she told herself desperately. Zeke had never had to do much to send her into orbit. Sometimes merely touching her was enough. This time she owed it to herself to keep her feet firmly on the ground.

"I want to learn about your work," he insisted, his deep voice close to her ear.

The warmth of his breath curling around her nape made the room seem to recede.

"Isn't it a bit late?" she managed to whisper around a throat as arid as the Australian Outback. They both knew she wasn't referring to her work.

"According to our speaker, it's never too late to do your bit," he murmured. He shot a deliberate look at the reporter taking notes at the back of the room. "Unless you don't practise what you preach."

Of all people, Zeke should know she did, she thought with a sinking heart. "I suppose you hope to make a fool of me in front of the magazine people."

He looked mildly insulted. "I don't need *Australian Life* as a mouthpiece. My column has as many readers a week as they do in a month."

Her spirits sank even further. "You're writing about the foundation in your column?"

His smile twisted her insides in an instant, an unwelcome response but she forced it away as he said, "It's possible."

"For your series on charities that help themselves more than others."

It wasn't a question. The leaden feeling in her stomach told her she was right even before his smile became wolfish. "Since starting that series, I've visited charities whose head-quarters would make the Taj Mahal look modest. Debunking them has been a pleasure."

"Model Children isn't a publicity stunt," she denied, keeping her voice low although it was an effort. "We've saved whole families by helping the children."

"Too bad our family wasn't one of them."

Stopped in her tracks, she stared at him. "You can't blame me for what happened. You were the one who went to America, then moved in with someone else." His eyebrows lifted and she added, "Gossip travels fast in the media. How is Lucy, by the way?"

"You'll have to ask her new husband," Zeke said flatly.

For the first time she saw genuine pain cloud his startling pewter eyes. "I'm sorry, I didn't know."

A cynical smile tilted his full lips. "If you'd come with me to the States you would have known. Of course, if you'd been with me in the States, I wouldn't have turned to Lucy."

She felt anger flash into her gaze and didn't care if he saw it. "You're saying it was my fault?"

"Wasn't it?"

"I couldn't go with you." She was well aware that the desire to keep this between them wasn't the only reason her voice came out as a strangled whisper.

"You never did say why."

"I told you—"

He cut across her savagely. "You gave me excuses but no real reason."

"I had my work."

He glanced around the room, part of a technical college by day. There was little of glamor about it and she saw his gaze absorb the fact. "Nineteen months later you're not modeling at all. You're stumping around the country talking business people into parting with their cash. Yet you couldn't take the time to come with me where your career could have really taken off. Were you afraid of failing or succeeding?"

"Neither," she insisted, feeling her heart gather speed. She hadn't been able to share her reasons with him then, and there was no point now. "I had other priorities."

His mouth twisted into a sneer. "Evidently I wasn't among them."

"Must we always bring this back to you?"

His finger stabbed the air. "This time it's to you. You were the one holding the reins. You could have come with me but you refused."

"So you drowned your sorrows in Lucy. It took what? Just over a year to love her and leave her. You didn't pine for very long." Not nearly as long as Tara herself had.

At his startled look she wondered what she had said wrong. "I didn't leave her, she left me," he stated, astonishing her. "It seems I wasn't sufficiently in touch with my feelings."

The cynical way he said it turned it into a denial. Bitterness threatened to swamp Tara. "You actually care what a woman thinks? This is certainly new behavior." Her opinion never carried much weight with him, she recalled.

"I make a point of learning from my mistakes."

Tara felt her breath rush out. What did he consider a mistake—his behavior toward the other woman, or—she could hardly bear to think it—leaving Tara?

Signs of the coffee break winding up caught her attention. "We can't talk now. What about after the meeting?"

His slow smile, alight with masculine interest, instantly made her regret the suggestion but it was too late to retract it now. "Going to make a personal appeal to me, Tara? I could get to like this foundation of yours."

"You don't have to like it. You only have to give it a fair appraisal," she snapped, and stood up purposefully to move to the podium again. It was just as well she had already given this talk many times before, because her concentration was well below par. She was too aware of Zeke Blaxland leaning back with his arms folded across his broad chest, his expression daring her to put a foot wrong.

Potent with memories, the scent of her perfume lingered in the space around Zeke and he inhaled slowly, cursing himself for a fool, but unable to stop himself. *Poême,* he thought, automatically putting a name to the heady fragrance with its reminders of the foolish satin and lace scraps she called lingerie. Did she still wear that stuff?

From where he sat, the new Tara McNiven looked all business. She had never been skeletal, like some models, but her new curves were a definite improvement. The glimpse of satin skin and hint of décolletage her businesslike jacket afforded him set his pulses hammering. His imagination began to work overtime on the rest.

Her hair was shorter, too, brushing her shoulders in a waterfall of gold he knew from experience would feel like silk. His fingers twitched with the need to touch her. He turned it into a drumming gesture on his knee, saw her notice and frown, and stilled his hand.

What had possessed him to gate-crash the meeting? His lack of faith in charities was no secret, but he didn't really believe Tara's foundation belonged in his series. He'd researched them, and had no doubt that they were on the level. It didn't mean he believed in what she was doing, but neither did he think she was in it for her own benefit.

So why was he here?

If he was honest, the answer was pacing up and down in front of him as she urged the group to put themselves in the children's places. "It's easy to say that one person can't make a difference, but all it takes is the willingness to try."

Amid the rueful nods, Zeke felt himself frown. Was Tara sending him a message? When they were together Zeke had been guilty of shutting himself away in his study for long periods. The only place she had had his undivided attention was in bed.

Her gaze bored into him. "We've all heard the saying about charity beginning at home." She took a breath. "Tonight, I want you to go home and look at your own children, and imagine their lives if you couldn't provide for them. Then when you're in bed tonight, spend five minutes imagining what it would be like not to have that bed."

Zeke felt a growl well up in his throat. He didn't have to imagine what it would be like. He knew from his own experience, and no charity had come along to rescue him. He pushed the unwelcome memory aside, preferring to picture himself in Tara's bed. Arousal throbbed through him at the very thought. Considering that it felt like a lifetime since he'd been with Tara, he was amazed how clearly he remembered every moment together, starting with the day he'd met her.

She had been the celebrity attraction at a car show where he had gone to check out the latest model Branxton convertible. He had barely been able to find the car for the spotlights and cameras aimed at her as she posed alongside it.

Irritated at having to wait until the publicity shoot ended, he had voiced his disapproval to a colleague he spotted in the throng. "Do they still have to sell cars by draping them with bubble-brained women in low-cut clothes?"

"Depends whether you're selling the lowered sports suspension or the viscous drive differential," came a throaty voice in his ear. Startled, he'd noticed that the photographers had been dismantling their gear and trying not to grin as the model cornered him with fire in her eyes.

He'd felt himself flushing. "You heard?"

"Enough to know that you're wrong about me on at least one count."

His gaze had slid over her breasts swelling so tantalizingly in the low-cut gown that his throat dried in automatic response. "It obviously isn't the dress."

Her lips had begun to twitch. "Obviously."

"Doesn't it bother you to be used as a prop to sell cars?"

She had shrugged, somehow imbuing the gesture with grace and beauty. "Doesn't it bother you to write about chicken farming?"

"Battery hens," he had corrected her, unwillingly pleased that she had connected him with his latest piece. "It's my job."

"For the moment, this is mine." She'd offered her hand. "I'm Tara McNiven."

Her fingers had felt cool in his and he found he didn't want to let her go. So he hadn't. "Zeke Blaxland. Shall we continue this discussion over coffee?"

To his relief she had nodded. "There's a Green Room behind the main stage. We can go there. It's more private."

Private had sounded good. "My place is even more private."

She had given him an old-fashioned look. "I already told you I'm not bubble-headed."

He soon discovered it was true. Apart from a masters in business, she had a burning curiosity about everything including him, he was humbled to find out. He was still astonished by how good a team they made, out of bed as well as in it. Her refusal to come with him to America had been all the more devastating because he had finally thrown caution to the wind and started to trust her. He had even started imagining a future together.

His memories weren't only of the good times, either. He recalled nursing her through a bad bout of flu, the first time he'd done such a thing for anybody. He'd been worried about getting it wrong, and had probably gone overboard with the chicken soup and the funny videos, not to mention watching over her while she slept.

When she awoke and found him there, she had protested that she looked awful. He couldn't convince her that he found her beautiful even when her nose was as red as a beacon and her glorious hazel eyes were streaming with cold.

She was all fire and brimstone now as she urged her audience to be aware of the world outside their own, and Zeke's body responded to her passion automatically. He was glad he had a folder of notes to hide the reaction. He could almost see the headlines if his response was noticed—Charity Spokesperson's Most Upstanding Convert. When had he started thinking in headlines? Maybe he'd been writing the darned column too long.

He tried to focus on her words. Despite what she evidently suspected, he had come with an open mind, knowing that if anyone could give him another slant on the charity story, Tara could. He'd been open-minded in approaching all the groups he'd included in the series. It hadn't been his fault that, upon closer investigation, they had been found wanting.

He'd meant it when he told Tara that he learned from his mistakes. He was starting to suspect that one of them had been accepting the offer to file his column from the paper's parent publisher in America. What had seemed like the chance of a lifetime was beginning to look like the biggest mistake of his life.

After the emotional tug-of-war he'd endured as a child, he had never wanted anyone to become as important to him as Tara had. Was that why he'd headed for another country? He hated to think so, but the longer he was in the same room with her, the more he was forced to question his decision to leave.

When she'd let him walk out, he had convinced himself he was doing the right thing. Love was a fool's paradise. Relationships never lasted. His disastrous involvement with Lucy was further proof if he needed any. So why was he back here, hanging on Tara's every word? Was he some kind of glutton for punishment?

Must be, to have agreed to stay and talk after the meeting, he decided. He resolved to make it brief, snare a few quotes for his column, then get the hell out.

Remembering why he was here, he dragged his attention back to what Tara was saying, although it wasn't necessary. Even while he was thinking about their relationship—former relationship, he amended inwardly—the journalistic side of his brain had absorbed every word. His mind had always worked that way. Compartmentalized. Tomorrow if he had to, he could give her entire speech himself.

That left the greater part of his thoughts free to focus on Tara herself, noting the graceful way she moved on the podium and the innate sexiness she projected like a beacon. Part of it was her training as a model but mostly it was natural. She was totally unselfconscious. Except when her eyes rested on him, then she tensed in a way he didn't like at all. As a result, she didn't look at him half as often as he found himself wanting her to.

He was annoyed to find his thoughts straying to their talk after the meeting. Maybe he wouldn't hurry away, after all. They had a lot to catch up on, purely as friends. Perhaps they could do some of it at his new apartment overlooking Sydney Harbor. By night, the view was truly spectacular.

His body stirred again and he knew the view had nothing to do with it, other than the one right in front of him now. Remember what Tara had always said, he ordered himself angrily. "Modern women want more from a relationship than sex." He had to remind himself again that he and Tara didn't have a relationship anymore. She probably didn't want anything from him except the sight of his back as he left.

She had been happy to see it once, when he went away, he reminded himself. When she refused to discuss coming with him, he had been so furious that he had gone without a backward glance, sure that there must be someone else. When he demanded a name, she had gone quiet, leaving him to draw his own conclusion.

It was partly why he'd turned to Lucy. She was all the things Tara hadn't been, malleable, loyal, deferring to him in everything. Until he got exhausted doing her thinking for her, and demanded that she develop a mind of her own. Then she changed into a tigress who was never satisfied with anything he did. Coming from a wealthy family, she couldn't understand his need to take care of himself, and that his job sometimes took him away from her at inconvenient hours. Her daddy could take care of them, she insisted, refusing to accept that Zeke might prefer to make his own way.

So the relationship had ended and he wasn't particularly sorry, except for having to face the rare fact of his own failure. Lucy had a new partner, her daddy's right-hand man, who had none of Zeke's pigheadedness when it came to accepting a house, a job and support from her daddy. Zeke wished them well.

When he let the paper lure him back to Australia with the promise of the chance to write features of his own choosing, he hadn't meant to see Tara again, at least not consciously, but some part of him must have planned it all along. When he read about this meeting, it had seemed like fate. He had already started the charity exposé so it had seemed logical to add Tara's group to his list of targets.

Except that this target was proving elusive. He knew if he wrote up the foundation as worthwhile, he might be accused of going easy on his former lover. But he wasn't sure he could condemn her work as bunk, either. Too many things she'd said touched an unwelcome chord with him. There was nothing for it but to investigate further before he made up his mind. But first there was the talk she had promised him. Zeke was amazed how much he looked forward to it.

Chapter 2

Zeke took his time clipping his notes and Tara's handouts into his folio while the room emptied around him. The journalist and the photographer had left, disgruntled by his refusal to be interviewed. Now only one other man remained. Todd Jessman, Zeke thought, his brain automatically supplying the name. Tara's foundation had helped him and his family, he recalled. From old journalistic habit, he tuned his ear to their conversation.

"I'd love you to send me photos of the baby," he heard her tell the man. A slight catch in her voice made Zeke frown. Didn't she know she shouldn't get emotionally involved with the people she was supposed to help? Zeke had always prided himself on his objectivity. Emotional involvement was a weakness that clouded judgement. Another point they disagreed on.

"I'll be sure and send some. Thank you again." The man touched her arm and Zeke tensed, surprised by the force of his instinctive reaction. The man was married with a kid, for pity's sake. On the other hand, maybe he needed reminding of the fact. If he wasn't getting enough attention at home, he could mistake Tara's professional concern for something more.

Before he had completed the thought, Zeke was at the front of the room, coming between them physically. He was a big man and while he didn't deliberately use his size to his own advantage, he didn't mind if it occasionally had that effect. His actions annoyed Tara, he realized when he saw her take a step back. From him? He didn't like that, one bit.

"I have to go now," she said to the young man, and Zeke swore he heard a tremor in her voice.

The young man looked from her to Zeke and swallowed, getting the message at last. "Okay, I'll be in touch."

She raked Zeke with a look. "Do you enjoy intimidating people?"

"It never worked with you."

"Perhaps you should keep it in mind." She began to gather up her things. "You didn't say much to the magazine people."

So she had noticed. Good. "I told them this was your show and they would have to get their quotes from you. What did you expect? A hatchet job?"

She tried to keep the pain out of her eyes and suspected she failed. "Isn't it what you came to do?" He couldn't deny it, she saw as his expression fleetingly revealed the truth. She pushed files into her briefcase. "I have to go."

"You promised we would talk."

It was out before she could stop it. "Why am I the only one who has to keep promises?"

He took a deep breath. "I never made you any promises I didn't keep, Tara."

It was true, he hadn't. He had promised she would be the only woman in his life and she had been, while they were together. He had promised her the sun, the moon and the stars and she had found them all in his arms. But he had never promised her forever because he didn't believe in it.

She understood that his upbringing argued against it, creating a barrier around his heart that he allowed no woman to penetrate, least of all her, but it didn't lessen the hurt. Had Lucy managed to break down the barrier? Tara doubted it.

She had always suspected that if Zeke let her into that secret place deep inside him that he guarded so fiercely, he would be a lover without equal. He very nearly was already. But his reserve remained as a silent warning to come close but no closer.

"Why did you come back to Australia?" she asked, hearing herself sound hollow with the strain of the evening.

"You sound regretful."

Probably because she was. "We hardly parted on good terms."

"Your terms," he said with sudden coldness. He looked around the empty room and beyond it to the corridor where a janitor was turning off lights. "You're right, we do need to talk, but not here. I could use some coffee."

"And I could use some sleep," she shot in quickly before he could suggest going to a café. "We can talk on the way to my car, then I have to go."

"Kind of you to offer me a lift," he said, although they both knew she hadn't. "I sold my car when I left the country and haven't replaced it yet. I live at Neutral Bay so it's on your way if you still live in the same place."

How had she ended up driving him home? she wondered as he shadowed her to the lift and down to the basement car park. Her compact car looked lonely in the cavernous space and she was unreasonably glad Zeke was with her, although she refused to recognize any reason other than security. "I hate these places at night," she admitted, not sure why.

"When I'm not around, you should have a security guard escort you in future," he instructed.

It was good advice, but she had trouble thinking past the first part of his statement. "What do you mean, when you're not around? You haven't been around for a year and a half and I've coped perfectly well. Isn't it a bit late to tell me what I should and shouldn't do?"

"I never could tell you what to do," he said as he folded himself into the passenger seat. Normally she loved her car with its reminders of a similar model she had purchased in her late teens. Now she wished for something more spacious to put greater distance between herself and the man beside her.

When she reached for the hand brake, she couldn't help brushing against him and a riot of sensual thoughts raced through her head, none of them the least bit welcome. Or so she told herself. Convincing the parts of her that suddenly ached for his intimate touch was another matter.

"It didn't stop you trying," she snapped, throwing the car into gear with less care than usual and steering on autopilot.

"I never stop trying," he said so softly that she wondered if she had heard correctly.

Concentrating on easing out into the traffic, she kept her startled glance to herself. "Two confessions in one night? Working in America can't have changed you that much?"

"I've had a lot of time to think about what's important in my life. I want us to try again, Tara."

It was just as well she had both hands on the wheel, giving her something to hold on to, she thought. The traffic streaming along Military Road made it impossible to do what she really wanted, and that was to pull over and demand what in blazes he thought he was doing. She couldn't simply pick up where they left off.

He sensed her resistance. "Leaving was a mistake. When you said you couldn't go with me, I should have turned the offer down and stayed in Australia." As soon as the words were out, he knew they were the reason he was here. The real reason.

Her heart ached. Nineteen months ago, hearing him say that would have made all the difference in the world. It wouldn't have saved their baby. Nothing could have done that. But it would have meant everything to have his support through the nightmare of losing their child and facing life afterward. At the same time, she had recoiled from using her pregnancy to blackmail him into staying when he hadn't wanted to for her sake alone.

Pain fueled her anger. "So you made a unilateral decision to return and claim what's rightfully yours. Did it occur to you that I might not want to be claimed?"

He chuckled ruefully. "I've never been stopped by a challenge before."

"I'm not a challenge, Zeke. I'm part of your past, as I'm sure you told the magazine reporter."

"I didn't tell them anything except that it was your show and I was there to observe."

She glanced away from the traffic long enough for him to register her surprise. "And are you?"

"I'm not the enemy, Tara. You may think I am because of my exposé on charities that help themselves more than other people, but so far your foundation doesn't seem to be one of them."

It was more than she had expected from him and she felt heat blaze a trail through her. "Thank you."

In fairness he had to say, "Don't thank me yet." He paused, then added, "Save it until I have enough material to write the column."

She felt her pulse jump. The thought of him investigating her was almost more than she could handle, but she refused to let him see it. "Then you'd better get yourself a car," she said through gritted teeth. "I don't make a habit of driving audience members home." Especially not this one.

"Turn left here. You can pull into the driveway at the end of the road," he said.

She did so, not sure whether she was glad or sorry that they had arrived at his apartment building. The street was a steep one, leading down to the harbor foreshore, with the city ferry terminal only a short stroll away. In front of them was a swathe of parkland, then the water sparkling like black velvet strewn with diamonds. Zeke explained that his apartment occupied the entire ground floor of the old Federation terrace house that had been converted into a duplex. The view must be sensational, she thought.

"Nice place," she commented tensely.

"It came with my new job," he said. "Would you like to take a look at the view?"

"I can see it perfectly well from here."

"Scared, Tara?"

His softly voiced challenge was all it took. She wasn't scared of him, nor of her ability to deal with the situation. In comparison with what she'd been through since he'd left, Zeke Blaxland was a piece of cake. "Very well, but I won't stay long. I'm starting on a book, and the only time I get to work on it is early in the morning."

"About the foundation?" he guessed. She nodded. "You always said you wanted to write, but I thought it was going to be a torrid romance."

She was painfully aware that the vision had been fueled by their affair. This time she would have to look somewhere else for inspiration. "I changed my mind," she said flatly.

"Pity. But I'm glad you're following your dream."

She could say the same for him. According to the same media grapevine from which she had learned about his marriage, Zeke's column was now published in a dozen countries in several languages. He also did an op-ed piece on a national morning television show. She had first seen it in hospital after the baby was born and it had almost been her undoing. But after a year or more of being confronted with his image everywhere she turned, she was immune to the effect, or so she tried to assure herself.

Liar, she taunted herself silently. She would never be immune to the sight of Zeke on television or anywhere else. She had only to glance sideways to remind herself of how vulnerable she still was to his brand of charm. Charisma was an overused word, but he had it in spades.

Even when she looked resolutely away, his presence radiated toward her like a beacon. You're a moth to his flame, she told herself scathingly, forcing herself to remember what happened to moths when they flew too close to the light. It didn't stop her from getting out of the car, locking it and following him inside.

She might have known his apartment would be spectacular. He never did anything by halves. From a plant-filled atrium, he led her into a vast living area furnished with Corbusier chairs and sofa separated by a mirrored coffee table. Her high heels clicked against the white Italian tiles covering the floors.

Beyond the living room, a dining area contained a fruit-wood table surrounded by a dozen rope-seated chairs. A handcrafted boat sat atop a trestle side table, and above it a brass mirror was angled to reflect the view. Kelim rugs and softer natural elements, terracotta pots and baskets of plants, relieved the coolness of the tiled floors.

"It's lovely," she admitted, impressed in spite of herself. Home-making hadn't been among Zeke's inclinations when they were together. His previous apartment had been beautifully but impersonally furnished by the simple means of buying several room lots complete with accessories from a fashionable furnishing store. This apartment was another matter. It exuded a feeling of home that she wasn't accustomed to associating with Zeke. "Did you hire someone, or is this your own work?"

''A bit of both,'' he conceded. ''I had good advice, but I knew what I wanted.''

He usually did. She accepted the glass of sparkling spring water he offered her, foolishly pleased that he had remembered she never drank when she was driving. It bothered her to think she might be what he wanted, because she already knew how hard it would be to refuse him. She wasn't sure she wanted to, only that she had to. Having ridden the emotional roller coaster with him once before, she'd be crazy to climb aboard it again.

She tensed as he moved up behind her, but it was only to steer her closer to the spectacular view. His hands on her shoulders felt warm, strong. A molten sensation flowed along the length of her spine and pooled beneath the curve of her stomach.

''You wouldn't believe how much I missed this.''

She found her voice with an effort. ''The harbor view?''

He turned her again until he was looking directly into her eyes. ''This view.''

The raw emotion in his gaze made it clear the harbor wasn't in the race. She had half expected it, she told herself, forcing herself not to move. It was the test she had set herself by agreeing to come with him.

When she said nothing, he began to massage her shoulders with gentle but persuasive movements until she wanted to melt. ''No comment, Tara?''

She shook her head. ''It is the approved journalistic phrase.''

He frowned. ''In my experience it's used by people who have something to hide.''

She jerked away from his hands as if stung. He couldn't know her secret, but conscience made her react. Or else it was the unnerving effect of his nearness. Both, she suspected. She was mad to put herself through this. As a test of her indifference to him, it was already a failure.

He studied her intently. "What is it, Tara? Did I say something?"

She fought the urge to wrap her arms protectively around herself, and walked to the wall of windows looking onto a vast terrace. The view might as well have been painted on for all the impact it had on her. She was far more aware of the man behind her. "This wasn't a good idea."

"On the contrary. It's the only good idea I've had in a long time."

Turn and face him now, or you never will, she commanded herself, but found it almost impossible to do. Almost as hard to say lightly, "Am I hearing things? Zeke Blaxland is a positive fountain of good ideas."

"You know I was speaking personally."

As much to remind herself as him, she said, "Not an area I have a right to go into."

His gaze hardened. "Because you don't feel anything for me anymore, or because you do?"

How did one answer the unanswerable? She picked up her bag and started for the door, but he was there before her. "You can't leave yet. I asked you a question."

"I can leave anytime I please," she said, not at all sure that it was true.

He saw it, too, she noted, and pressed home his advantage. "Tell me to go to hell right now, and I'll know I'm wasting my time. I won't bother you again, ever."

"You'll stop investigating the foundation?"

He shook his head. "Not until I get what I came for, but I guarantee I'll be a model observer. You won't even know I'm around."

And the sun didn't have to rise in the morning. As long as Zeke walked the earth she would be aware of him. In the same room, she could no more ignore him than she could fly. "It won't work," she denied, her hair haloing around her head as she shook it. "You'd find some way to make your presence felt."

"You make me sound like a glory-hunter," he said, sounding wounded. "But you're probably right, it is a big ask. However, there's another solution."

"What is it?"

"We make love here and now, and get it out of our system."

His so-called solution was so typically Zeke that she almost choked. "What makes you think that will solve anything?"

His smile was infuriatingly cocky. "Maybe it won't, but it's a lot more fun than standing at the door, arguing all night."

Too late, she remembered that Zeke thought falling into bed could solve any argument. Unfortunately, he had been right more often than she cared to remember. But not anymore. "Sorry, Zeke, I'm otherwise committed."

His eyes narrowed. "Committed as in another man? The same man who kept you from coming to America with me?"

"There was no one else then and there isn't now," she said tiredly. "Given the complications that go with being in love, I've decided I'm better off celibate."

She saw no point in letting him know she had been since he'd left. Pregnancy had imposed its own limitations, but in truth no other man had interested her since Zeke. Whatever his failings, he was a tough act to follow.

Evidently you weren't, she told herself. He hadn't waited long before rushing into another relationship. Pain blistered through her. Jealousy. Anger. Other emotions she refused to identify. All of it on a level only Zeke aroused in her. Still did, she recognized in panic. She had to get out of here.

He read the urge to flee in her startled movements. "What's so all-fired important you have to rush home to it?"

"My life."

"Your writing and your precious foundation?"

When she nodded dumbly, he looked skeptical. "Can they keep you warm at night, Tara? Can they enfold you in love and comfort the way my arms can? Like this?"

Before she had time to martial her defenses, he took her in his arms. She tried to stiffen but it was useless. He knew exactly how to hold her to turn her to putty in his embrace. Almost of their own accord her arms went around him. As soon as her fingers traced the muscular contours of his back she knew she was lost. For eighteen months she had dreamed of being right here, resting her head against the hollow of his shoulder and feeling the steady drumming of his heart reverberating through her.

Except that it wasn't steady at all. It beat as rapid a tattoo as hers did, as his lips traced a pattern along her hairline then descended with lightning swiftness to claim her mouth. "Now tell me again how you prefer celibacy," he insisted.

The moan she heard escape from her throat was part passion and part despair. Why did he have to come back just when she was getting her life back on track? She didn't blame him for the baby. The doctor said her contraception had failed during a bout of flu, so it was nobody's fault. But she did blame Zeke for rushing off to the States without a backward glance after she refused to go with him. She hadn't been ready to tell him about the baby then, but she would have, given a little more time. Instead, he had slammed the door shut on further communication.

She had wanted to break the news in a way that made it clear he didn't owe her anything. Knowing how he resisted family ties because of his own chaotic childhood, she wouldn't have imposed them on him. Barely recovered from the flu, she hadn't bargained on feeling so wretchedly ill in the first weeks of pregnancy, unable to deal with her own emotions, far less Zeke's.

By the time she was ready, he had gone without leaving

a forwarding address. She could have contacted him through
the newspaper but it wasn't a message she had wanted to risk
falling into the wrong hands, so she had decided against it.
Thinking she would never see Zeke again, it didn't seem to
matter. Now she wasn't so sure.

The thought didn't stop her body from responding of its
own accord. After so long, his touch shocked her system into
overdrive. Every inch of exposed skin felt alive in a way that
terrified her. He was right, celibacy had nothing to compare
with the way he made her feel.

It didn't help to remind herself that forever wasn't in his
vocabulary. He was here. Nothing mattered except the demands he made on her mouth as his hands roved over her
body, exploring, pleasuring, exciting. As he eased her jacket
open and slid his hand inside, her heart almost stopped. When
she felt him cup her breast, she went weak. She moaned
again, shifting closer to him to press his hand against the
spot where he would feel her rapid heartbeat.

He was aroused, too, she felt as their altered positions
made it apparent. Seeing how quickly she had made him
want her brought her senses close to overload. How could
she have forgotten what they were like together?

She hadn't forgotten for one single moment, she understood in the instant, eye-of-the-storm moment she had for
clear thinking. She had accepted his invitation knowing what
would happen. Wanting it. Wanting him.

His tongue began a sinuous dance with hers, sending
spears of sensation lancing through her. She wanted to deny
everything he made her feel, but the words stalled inside her,
unable to compete with the way her heart pumped in erratic
rhythm, hazing her mind and filling her with yearnings. As
they kissed, he massaged her nipples, sending her into a spiral of desire that could end in only one way. "Oh, Zeke, it's
been so long," she heard herself murmur.

''Too long,'' he said in a voice like broken glass. ''I want to make love to you.''

It was enough to break the spell. ''No, Zeke.'' She placed a hand against his chest, the gesture too ineffectual to push him away but symbolic enough that he understood her meaning. Self-preservation was the only thing urging her to refuse him. He knew every inch of her body as well as she knew it herself. He was bound to notice the changes in her and ask questions.

Questions she was far from ready to answer.

She found she ached to say yes more than she had wanted to do anything for a long time. To know the mind-shattering pleasure of his possession and to surrender utterly to his will, even as she commanded him, was a heaven she had dreamed of all the time they'd been apart.

Not that she hadn't tried to put him out of her mind. Awake, she had almost succeeded. About her dreams she could do nothing. Instead of dulling her need for him, the long months of abstinence had sharpened her desire until it registered as an exquisite pleasure-pain sensation that ached to be satisfied.

But not tonight.

Not ever, if she had any sense. Her breath escaped in a sigh of frustration. When had she shown any sense around Zeke? This time she had little choice, she thought as she closed her jacket with shaking fingers and took an unsteady step away from him. It was only a few inches, but it felt like a vast gulf of emptiness opening between them.

''Am I going too fast for you?'' he asked, sounding as strained as she felt.

If you could count the months of abstinence as fast, she thought ruefully. ''No, it's just...I don't know how I feel about us anymore.''

His expression turned cold. ''As I recall, you never did.''

The accusation in his tone shocked her out of her remaining torpor. "I wasn't the one who went away and found someone else."

Light broke across his strong features. She had forgotten the full force of his attractiveness, she thought distractedly. His dark hair was thick and full, curling slightly at the ends where it wanted a barber's touch. In anger, his eyes looked like the sea in storm but the glint of gold reminded her of how they could sparkle wickedly at her, usually just before they made love. She closed her own eyes against the reminder. It would be a long time before she saw that look again, if ever.

"Is that what this is about?" he demanded, sounding furious. "It's okay for you to send me away but not for me to find comfort somewhere else. What was I supposed to do? Wait until you made up your mind that I was worth making a few temporary sacrifices for? Or did you hope I'd come rushing back, unable to exist without you?"

Both options had occurred to her. Evidently only one of them to him. She dragged her fingers through her hair, mussing it. Her scalp felt tight and tense, good company for the rest of her. "I didn't want anything from you that you weren't prepared to offer freely, and I still don't. You did the right thing finding someone else. I'm only sorry it didn't last." Then she wouldn't have to deal with this.

Instead she would have to deal with knowing he was forever beyond her reach. She wasn't sure which was the worse torment.

"Well, I did come back," he said, startling her. "I tried moving on and it didn't work. You can't give to one person something you've already given to another, and Lucy sensed it. I decided to come back and find out if you felt the same way about me. Was I wrong?"

Say yes and end this now, she urged herself. Instead, what came out was a lame, "I don't know."

"You don't know if you still care about me?"

He sounded so bitter that she wanted to weep. She kept her head high. When their baby died she had shed all the tears in the world for their child, for him and for herself. She had thought she had no tears left. Now, feeling her eyes grow heavy, she knew she did, but shedding them in front of him would be far too revealing. To herself or to him? The question caught her off guard, silencing her until she realized he was waiting for an answer.

''We can't pick up where we left off,'' she said with an honesty he couldn't possibly understand. There were too many layers under what he thought he heard.

His generous mouth tightened into a hard line. ''Can we pick up at all?''

''No.''

She hadn't intended to be so forthright, but survival demanded it. If she said so much as another word, she would break down and admit that there was more than a chance. After what she had experienced in his arms tonight there was a bedrock certainty. And it was a luxury she couldn't afford. One night with him would undo all the months of silence.

How could she tell him she had conceived and lost their baby? How would he react to being excluded from something he had every right to expect to share? Even now, she had trouble justifying it to herself. No matter how difficult he had made it, or how ill she had been at the beginning, she should have found a way to tell him. Now it was too late. Would he even believe the child had been his? He had been ready enough to blame her refusal to come with him on another man. She wasn't sure he believed her denials even now.

There was only one thing she could do. It cost her almost more courage than she possessed to retrieve her bag and touch a hand to the side of his face in silent homage to what might have been. ''Goodbye, Zeke,'' she said, and made herself walk through the door.

Chapter 3

Three days later, Tara knew she had done the right thing in walking away from Zeke, but couldn't make herself feel good about it. She was babysitting for her sister-in-law, Carol, when the sound of the front door opening and closing told her that her sister-in-law had returned. Carol came into the room and dropped her briefcase on a side table. "Children asleep?"

"Finally." Tara's tone suggested it was an achievement.

Carol gave a wry smile. "I hope they didn't give you too hard a time."

"Of course not," Tara assured her. "Cole might be at the Terrible Two stage, but he always makes me laugh. And Katie's so sweet, calling me Tawa through the gap in her teeth. How can you refuse them anything?"

"I remind myself it's for their own good." Carol paused at the kitchen door. "Join me for lunch?"

Tara nodded. "I'm seeing a publisher this afternoon and having dinner with a potential benefactor for the foundation, but I'm free till then."

"Another schmoozy dinner. How do you stand spending so much time with people whose only attractive feature is their bank balance?"

"It isn't always the case. Some of them are sweet, and when it's for the kids, it's worth it," Tara said.

"We've never really discussed it, but it can't be easy for you, dealing with children every day. Even minding mine must be a strain."

Tara let out a long sigh. "When I'm bathing them or playing with them, I sometimes feel such a longing for what might have been. Then I think how lucky I am to be an aunt to your two. They help in the healing process."

"Children are like that," Carol conceded, adding realistically, "especially when they're asleep."

"Then they're positive angels," Tara agreed, laughing.

"I don't know why dramas always have to coincide with the nanny's day off," Carol went on. "Although if Mrs. McCarthy changes her will one more time, I swear I'll hasten her end myself."

Tara laughed. Her sister-in-law was a lawyer who had set up a practice at home while her children were young. The client in question was bedridden, but still feisty enough to enjoy the power her fortune gave her over her family. According to Carol, the woman changed her will at regular intervals to keep her clan under her thumb.

Tara perched on a stool and watched Carol prepare sandwiches with practiced ease. Her sister-in-law was one of six children, all younger than herself, so she was incredibly domesticated. She was also a good friend. Tara's brother, Ben, reminded her frequently, that marrying Carol was an example of his dedication to pleasing his little sister.

Pleasing himself had nothing to do with it, she thought with humor. Ben was a doctor and had met Carol professionally when she defended a colleague in a malpractice lawsuit. Love at first sight, Ben had called it, when he wasn't claiming he chose Carol so he'd have his own private lawyer on tap. Tara knew which reason she believed.

"This is the first chance I've had to ask you how Monday's talk went?" her sister-in-law said, levering the top off a mustard jar.

Tara traced a pattern on the granite counter. "The usual."

Carol's hands stilled. "No matter how many times you do this, you never describe it as usual. In fact you assure me every presentation is different. So out with it, what's the problem this time?"

"Zeke Blaxland is investigating the work of the foundation."

Carol caught her breath. She knew about Zeke and had been incredibly supportive during Tara's pregnancy and the shattering aftermath. Other than Tara's doctor, her brother and sister-in-law had been the only two people Tara had confided in.

Tara knew that Carol still felt badly about being out of Australia when the baby was born, but the family had been in England, settling Carol's elderly mother into a retirement place. They had flown back as soon as they could, but it was too late. Tara had assured Carol she understood. Their presence wouldn't have changed the outcome. And they had supported her through everything else, including the baby's memorial service. Carol had shed almost as many tears as Tara herself, and had held Tara's hand through the days that followed.

Now she frowned in sympathy. "Oh, honey, how awful. Did you hate him on sight?"

Tara laced and unlaced her fingers until she regained her voice. "Worse than that, I didn't hate him."

Carol covered Tara's hand with her own. "You didn't do anything foolish?"

Tara knew her laugh sounded hollow. "You mean like go

home with him and let him make love to me? Does one out of two count?''

Reading between the lines, Carol shook her head. ''Sounds like your sense of self-preservation kicked in just in time.''

What self-preservation? Tara asked herself. Zeke had been in her audience for only a few hours before she'd thrown caution to the wind and driven him home. She hadn't been reckless enough to go to bed with him, although it was close. But he still managed to dominate her waking thoughts. Her dreaming ones, too, she had discovered, only in her dream they had been a family of three. This morning she awoke with tears drying on her cheeks.

''I didn't have him figured as the charitable type,'' Carol said.

''He isn't. He's writing a series of columns about charities that help themselves more than the people they're set up to help.''

Carol looked shocked. ''He must know the foundation is genuine or you wouldn't be involved.''

Tara nodded. Carol knew that after ending her relationship with Zeke and losing the baby, Tara hadn't wanted to face the world at all, far less be involved in a cause that brought her into daily contact with young children. She hadn't wanted to return to modeling, either, so had retreated behind closed doors to lick her emotional wounds.

But the storm of publicity surrounding her efforts to help the single parent with the triplets had refused to abate. Gradually she had been drawn into similar projects until it had become a full-time job.

She sighed. ''I hope Zeke agrees with you. The publisher I'm seeing wants me to write a book about the foundation's work, so he must think it's on the level.''

Carol rested her elbows on the counter. ''So why are you letting Zeke undermine your confidence? I can hear it in your voice and see it in your body language.''

Tara straightened, chagrined at being read so easily. Reading body language was part of a lawyer's stock-in-trade, she told herself, but it didn't change the fact that Carol was right. "How can I be the children's spokesperson when the proof of my own failure as a mother was sitting in my audience last Monday?"

There, it was out. Tara had barely articulated her reasoning to herself, but as soon as she said it, she knew it had been nagging at her from the moment she'd seen Zeke in her audience.

"Losing the baby wasn't your failure any more than it was Zeke's," Carol stated. She retrieved a jug of homemade lemonade from the refrigerator and added it and two glasses to a tray with the sandwiches. "Let's go outside. It seems I have a pep talk to give."

"I don't need a pep talk." But Tara followed her sister-in-law out to a table and chairs placed underneath the weeping branches of a crepe myrtle. From somewhere in the greenery, a Little-Wattle Bird gave its distinctive rusty-hinged cry. "It's beautiful out here," she said.

Carol wagged a finger at her. "Don't change the subject."

"Can I make a statement in my own defense, counselor?"

"Only if it doesn't incriminate you."

Tara poured them both a glass of lemonade. "Everything I can think to say fits that category."

"Because you're not as over Zeke Blaxland as you tell yourself."

Tara felt her eyebrows lift. "You're supposed to be on my side."

"Sometimes defending a client involves making them deal with facts they'd rather not face." Carol held out the plate. "Have a sandwich. They're good if I do say so myself. Then we'll discuss Zeke."

About to refuse, Tara saw Carol's expression. It was easier to eat than to get into an argument with someone who made a career out of it, so she took half a sandwich and bit into it, although her appetite had deserted her.

Was she avoiding facing facts? Perhaps so, Tara thought on a silent sigh. She was still attracted to Zeke, but it didn't mean she had to give in to it. "Whatever he and I had is over. All I'm hearing are echoes from the past," she said firmly.

Carol looked unconvinced. "As long as you're sure."

Tara wasn't, but decided to let it lie. She appreciated Carol's and Ben's support, but there was nothing they could do. At some stage Tara knew she had to learn to deal with a world that included Zeke. Now was as good a time to start as any.

"You haven't told me how the insider trading suit ended," she said, seizing on the fastest way to divert her sister-in-law.

Her tactic worked. "We won. My client was completely exonerated. Didn't you read this morning's paper? We made the front page and the editorial."

Tara had avoided looking at the paper. She choked back an instinctive protest as Carol went to fetch the paper. Seeing Zeke's byline and knowing he was writing his column practically on her doorstep was another thing she must learn to deal with.

Carol came back and spread the paper across Tara's knees. "Read the headlines then the editorial. I get a mention in both."

Tara dutifully scanned the story, feeling pride in her sister-in-law's accomplishment. "So the unwinnable case wasn't as unwinnable as everyone predicted," she said, a note of pleasure in her voice.

Carol nodded. "That's pretty much what the editor says, too."

Tara flipped pages until she came to the piece in question. It painted a glowing word picture of Carol's handling of the difficult case. About to congratulate her, Tara's eye strayed to the photo at the top of the next column and her heart almost stopped. A new photo of Zeke accompanied his column. It showed him seated behind a desk, making him look much more commanding and handsome than the previous head shot. More like the man she remembered so well, she thought.

Like someone drawn to touch a hot stove to prove it really can burn, she began to read and her blood turned to ice in her veins. "How can he do this?" she stormed after a few paragraphs.

Carol looked surprised. "I thought it was pretty flattering myself." She glanced over Tara's shoulder and saw what she was reading. "I didn't mean to put that in front of you. I didn't have time to read beyond the editorial this morning. Sorry."

Tara shook her head although her muscles felt stiff and unresponsive. "I would have seen it sooner or later."

Under the heading, Not-So-Sweet Charity, Zeke urged his readers to consider carefully where they donated their hard-earned money, suggesting that some organizations were designed as much to provide for their organizers as to help the underprivileged.

"How dare he suggest that I'm a do-gooder," Tara demanded hotly.

Carol scanned the column and she frowned. "He doesn't mention your name, or the foundation's."

"He doesn't have to. After *Australian Life* publishes their piece and notes that top-gun reporter Zeke Blaxland was checking us out, it won't be hard for people to put two and two together."

Carol read on. "Are you sure you aren't reading too much into this? Zeke may not flatter some of the fund-raising activities people do, but he doesn't say anything that could give rise to legal action."

''He only suggests that we're in this for our own benefit.''

Carol gestured dismissively. ''Nobody in their right mind will think he means you. You gave up a fortune in modeling fees to help set up and run the foundation.''

''Because I want the bulk of the money to go to the children. He doesn't mention that part.''

''Maybe he doesn't know it,'' Carol suggested.

Tara stood up, adrenaline surging through her body. ''Then it's time he did, counselor. I may have no legal redress, but I can give that son-of-a-columnist a piece of my mind.''

''Wouldn't it be better to cool down first?''

It was the last thing Tara wanted to do. ''I'd rather tackle him while my blood is so hot I could burn him by bleeding on him.''

In spite of the situation, Carol laughed. ''Poor Zeke. I wouldn't want to be in his shoes when you get hold of him.''

Tara looked affronted. ''How can you say 'poor Zeke'? He's the one using his position to take a cheap shot at me just because I didn't leap into bed with him the moment he showed up.''

Carol shook her head. ''I meant poor Zeke after you get through with him. From the look on your face, that cheap shot may turn out to be a lot more expensive than he bargained on.''

The Publishing House was a curious hybrid. Built behind a century-old sandstone facade, the new tower rose seventeen floors above Sydney's historic Macquarie Street. Tara's publisher was headquartered there, as was the editorial division of Zeke's newspaper. When she parked outside, she wondered how she was going to cope with coming here on a regular basis, knowing that Zeke was only a few floors away.

Today it wasn't a problem. She not only wanted him back in town, but seated behind the desk in his office so she could give him a large chunk of her mind.

Naturally, because she was fired up to confront him, he wasn't there. His computer screensaver featured an animated figure walking through a never-ending series of doors that closed behind him one after the other, accompanied by cheerful sound effects. Across the screen scrolled the words, "Missed me by that much."

It was an in-joke, related to Zeke's love of classic television shows, she remembered, thinking of the hundreds of tapes in his collection. She wasn't a fan but her pleasure had come from watching him while he watched the tapes. Some of them he knew practically by heart. Unwillingly, she found herself remembering long, rainy Sunday afternoons when they made huge bowls of popcorn and watched marathon sessions of old series.

Sometimes he had turned the sound off and made up his own dialogue, urging her to join in until they had both been helpless with laughter, she recalled. Inevitably, she had ended up in his arms, her laughter turning to passion as his kisses deepened. From the sofa, they invariably slid to the floor and made love while some old superhero flickered in the background. She couldn't be certain but she suspected that their baby had been conceived at such a moment.

She made herself turn away from the screen, unwilling to be reminded of those days.

"Looking for Zeke?" came a familiar voice behind her. "He's out."

She spun around. "Matthew Brock. It's great to see you. Still working for this newspaper then?"

He looked rueful. "Until the right man comes along to take me away from all this, I don't have much choice. I finally stopped chasing Pulitzer prizes and settled for a steady paycheck and what little security this business has to offer."

Matthew was a photographer and Tara had worked with him many times during her modeling days. "You never chased Pulitzer prizes, although you have the talent for it," she said. "You always preferred security. A plateful of do-nuts and you're anybody's, you used to tell me."

He rolled his eyes. "I never could put anything past you, Tara. You look great. I know you're pretty involved with the kids thing, but if you ever want a modeling assignment..."

"I'm after blood, actually," she cut in, remembering her mission.

He looked interested. "Zeke's blood, by any chance?"

"Blood, bones, whatever."

"'Hell hath no fury,'" he quoted, adding, "I gather you saw the column?"

She affected an expression of innocence. "Did he write a column concerning me?"

"Zeke knows better than that, but reading between the lines, it wasn't very kind, considering the two of you used to be an item. Maybe that quote should be about a man scorned."

"I didn't scorn him, he left me," she snapped then caught herself. Matthew was an old friend, not the enemy.

She jumped as her cell phone played the first few notes of "Jingle Bells." Matthew grinned as she answered it. It was early for Christmas, but the tune was easy to hear in a noisy setting. By the time she flipped the phone shut, she could feel her face muscles tightening. She relaxed them with an effort.

"Problem?" Matthew asked.

"Only a potential benefactor calling to cancel our dinner engagement tonight. Apparently something came up. I'll bet I know what."

"You might be reading too much into this. Not everybody reads Zeke's column."

"There may be a corner of the African veld he doesn't reach, but I happen to know this lady never misses it. She told me she's thinking of supporting one large charity rather than a number of smaller ones but she'll get back to me. In a pig's eye.''

"Oh.''

"Yes, oh. When I get my hands on Zeke…''

"Maybe it's just as well he isn't around. He's doing wonders for our circulation.''

She laughed in spite of herself. "You and your insecurity. The paper survived while Zeke was in America. It will survive again without him.''

"Wow, you really are out for his blood.''

"When is he due back?''

Matthew looked thoughtful. "He's following a lead, something about a baby farming racket he's working on.''

Something tightened inside her. "Baby farming? Isn't that a bit out of Zeke's line?''

Matthew shook his head. "Before agreeing to come back to Australia he negotiated the right to work on features of his choice. This is one of them.''

She kept her tone carefully neutral although every instinct shrilled a warning. "It sounds fascinating. What's it about?''

Matthew shrugged. "I don't know much. I only took a couple of pictures that Zeke wanted. A mother being united with a year-old baby that was apparently stolen from her, for one.''

Something inside Tara wound even tighter. "Really?''

He nodded, glad of her interest. "Yeah, it's all very cloak-and-dagger. Zeke needed a shot of the hospital involved, so I used a long lens to avoid tipping them off. It's a place with a flowery name. The Roses Private Hospital, that's it.''

She could hardly breathe. "How fascinating.''

Concern flashed over his features. "Keep it to yourself, Tara. If anyone else breaks the story before Zeke is ready, he'll kill me. It's his baby.''

She felt faint. His baby. Matthew couldn't know how his words stabbed her to the heart, but not because of a newspaper feature. Zeke's infuriating column was nothing compared to what she had just learned. He was investigating the hospital where she had given birth less than a year ago.

She knew better than to hope that her baby had been stolen and given to someone else. She had only to remember her son's lifeless form when the midwife brought him to her after attempts to revive him had failed. So she held no hope that things might be different for herself. But if Zeke managed to access the hospital records, and he was more than capable of doing it, he was bound to learn the truth.

Matthew regarded her anxiously. "Are you okay? You've gone chalk-white."

She made herself nod and say shakily, "I've only eaten half a sandwich today. My blood sugar is probably in my boots by now."

He took her arm. "Let's grab some coffee and you can have a snack."

She didn't really want food, but she needed to occupy herself until Zeke returned, and she *did* feel shaky. Besides, the photographer was one of her favorite people. "Okay but I can't stay long. I have a meeting in the building in less than an hour."

"That's just long enough to tell me more about what you plan to do with Zeke when you catch up with him."

It was more a case of what he would do with her if he uncovered the truth, she thought as she allowed Matthew to steer her out of the office. The unkind things Zeke had written in his column would pale into insignificance beside his reaction when he knew she had kept from him the birth of his own child.

Chapter 4

A tense half hour later, Tara rode the elevator from the cafeteria back to the editorial floor. "Thanks for the coffee. It was great to catch up," she told Matthew.

"Considering you hardly heard a word I said."

She shot him a rueful look. "Was it that obvious?"

He nodded. "I've known you a long time. Zeke was the man for you from the moment you set eyes on him. It doesn't look as if anything has changed."

She kept her gaze on the floor indicator. "Everything has changed. He stopped being the man for me the day he left the country."

Matthew shrugged. "If you say so."

She took a sharp breath of frustration, not sure whether she needed to convince him or herself. "Matthew..."

But the elevator doors swished open onto their floor and Matthew gestured her ahead of him. "Age before beauty."

She laughed. "At least you never change."

Her laughter died when she saw that Zeke still hadn't returned to his desk, evidenced by a growing pile of messages. "Doesn't he believe in keeping regular hours?"

Matthew shrugged. "The office is made available to him as a courtesy. Officially he's a consultant, free to set his own hours." His expression said that some people had all the luck.

Frustration gnawed at Tara as she glanced at her watch. "I can't wait any longer. I'm due at a publisher's meeting."

"Shall I tell Zeke you were looking for him?"

"Tell him..." She hesitated. What could she have Matthew tell Zeke second hand that wouldn't suggest she had wanted an excuse to see him again. Matthew obviously believed it. She didn't want Zeke to draw the same conclusion. "Don't bother. I'll catch up with him later."

Matthew feigned disappointment. "Pity. The showdown promised to be entertaining."

Not if she had had anything to say about it. "But messy," she said shortly.

"They're the best kind. Now all I can look forward to this afternoon is processing prints of some society woman riding her horse in Centennial Park."

Matthew might complain about working on the society pages but Tara knew he loved the whole scene. "Maybe she'll have a rich son," she consoled him.

He pouted. "Could be, although with my luck he'd be straight."

Murmuring supportively, she left to keep her appointment, more disappointed than she had let Matthew see how anxious she'd been to see Zeke. The feeling made her pause reflectively, her hand poised over the elevator button. Was her anger over the column merely an excuse to see Zeke again?

As her sister-in-law had pointed out, he hadn't written anything that he hadn't told Tara face-to-face when they were together. And she could be reading too much into the potential benefactor's phone call. If so, it was just as well she had missed Zeke. The more distance she kept between them the better, she assured herself, although she was aware of stabbing the elevator button with unusual ferocity.

When the doors opened, she stepped inside, making an effort to focus on the meeting ahead. She looked forward to getting her teeth into a new project, and she wasn't about to let anything—or anyone—spoil it for her.

Furlong Press was on the fourth floor of the same building. The firm had been established by Colin Adeel, a retired jockey who had started out publishing racing industry fare, then gone on to publish other books when he found he had a flair for picking bestsellers.

Tara had been pleased and flattered when he'd approached her to write a book about Model Children. Zeke had been right when he said she had always wanted to write. Like him, she had assumed that when she did it would be a novel. She had a file bulging with ideas, and had tried to write in the days following the loss of her baby, but the timing had been hopeless. Now her step lightened as she approached the publisher's office. Other writers told her she should write about what she knew, so this might be the start she needed.

"Go right in, Ms. McNiven," the receptionist said before she could introduce herself.

Tara pushed open a frosted-glass door with Colin Adeel's name in gold on it, then stopped in her tracks, her heart automatically picking up speed at the sight of the man behind the publisher's desk. "Zeke? What are you doing here?"

"My job. I own a slice of Furlong Press."

She felt as if all the breath had been squeezed from her body. "Colin didn't say he planned to sell the business."

Zeke tilted the black executive chair so far back she expected him to crash to the floor at any minute, but as usual his sense of balance was perfect. The angle of his body brought him into disturbingly direct eye contact with her. "He hasn't sold out. He needs capital to expand, and I want something more than a column to write, so I let a mutual friend broker a partnership between us. You're not the only one with dreams, Tara,'' he said softly.

She struggled to deal with the overwhelming reality of his presence. It was hard enough when she was prepared for it. Unprepared, she felt alarmingly vulnerable. "You never talked about wanting to go into publishing.''

"We never talked about a lot of things and we took far too many things for granted.''

What was he saying? "It's too late,'' she found herself whispering.

"It's never too late while we're still breathing.'' He gestured to a chair opposite the desk. "Sit down and stop looking as if you're going to run out of here at any moment. This is us, remember?''

Was her discomfort that obvious? She had come to the newspaper looking for his blood, sure that she could deal with her memories while she gave him a piece of her mind. But she had envisioned having the showdown with other people around. No part of her plan had included being alone with him. For a moment she debated turning and fleeing, but everything in her balked at giving him the satisfaction. She sat.

"This isn't supposed to be about…us…'' Strange how hard she found it to force the single syllable out. "This meeting is supposed to be about a book Colin wants me to write.''

Zeke thumped a palm down on a folder in front of him. "Don't worry, the whole deal is spelled out here. But Colin's a romantic at heart. He knows you and I share a lot of history. When he briefed me on the company's future projects and I heard that your book was on the list, I asked if I could sit in on the meeting. He said he'd let me handle the contract as a way of easing me into the business. I suspect he thinks we're about to rekindle our romance.'' He spread his hands wide. "So here I am.''

His expression of innocence didn't fool her for a second. "Colin might believe what we had can be revived, but you don't."

He abandoned all pretense of ease and let the chair clatter to the floor as he leaned toward her. "What do you think?"

Her gaze flew to his face. On Monday night, she hadn't believed him when he said he wanted to try again, thinking he was only saying it to lure her into his bed. The very idea made her throat feel dry but she refused to swallow and confirm his effect on her. However skilled he was as a lover, and she knew he was spectacular, she needed more from him than sex.

Nine months of imagining her future as the mother of his baby had shown her how much she yearned for a real home and a family, the kind of future Zeke refused to believe in. "It's over," she said flatly. "We've both moved on. You to Lucy…"

"And you?" he put in, his voice hard.

"It's hardly any of your business."

"But there is a man?"

She wished with all her heart that she could say yes and end this now, but it wouldn't be true. She hated to think it might never be true, because Zeke had spoiled her for other men for life. "I didn't say so."

His eyes flashed fire at her. "You haven't said there isn't."

She made a move to rise. "This will get us nowhere. For some reason you wanted to believe I had another man in my life before you went away, and you're still obsessed with the notion although it never was true. It still isn't."

She saw him digest this. "I'm trying to understand what happened between us."

"What happened was, we needed different things. You don't believe in happy-ever-afters and I do. It's that simple."

He made a show of glancing around. "You haven't found your happy-ever-after yet."

"It hasn't stopped me from looking."

She wasn't surprised when his expression turned skeptical. "What if you never find it?"

"You have my permission to say 'I told you so.'"

He shook his head violently. "It won't give me as much satisfaction as you evidently think. I want to believe in happy endings, but experience has taught me they're a myth."

Her sigh whistled between them. "You see? How can you hope to find something if you're not prepared to concede it exists?"

"I came closest when we were together," he said softly.

Shock poured through her like a paralizing drug. She felt frozen into immobility, knowing she should leave but unable to make her body obey her mind's commands. Unwillingly, she remembered the long, dark nights when he had whispered that she was the best thing that had ever happened to him. No one else had been there for him the way she had, he had assured her.

She had taken pride in being what he called his anchor, forgetting that anchors could be cut adrift if the winds and tide were strong enough.

She felt cut adrift now, at the mercy of a tide of desire so powerful it threatened to deluge her. "Don't do this, Zeke. It isn't fair."

"All's fair in love," he reminded her.

"What we have isn't love. It's..." Her voice trailed off as words failed her. War was hardly the right description. So what was between them?

He looked intrigued. Too late she realized she'd used the present tense and knew it was too much to hope that he hadn't noticed. "What would you call it?" he demanded.

"Lust, infatuation, sex. Never love."

His eyes gleamed. "Three out of four isn't a bad start, considering that a moment ago you were writing us off completely. At least now I know there's something to work with."

"I'm not prepared to settle for three out of four this time," she said flatly. "I won't let you use sex to control me anymore, Zeke."

He looked genuinely shocked. "I never used it to control you. You enjoyed our lovemaking as much as I did and you were more than willing to take the initiative on occasion."

Her blood throbbed through her veins as she remembered only too well how much she had enjoyed it. He had taken her to heights she had never dreamed were possible. And he was right, she couldn't claim to have been passive, either. He had said he liked a woman who was prepared to go after what she wanted.

He had spoiled her for any other lover, she conceded unwillingly to herself. As with the best of anything, once you had known it, there was no settling for less. "You can hardly doubt how I felt," she reminded him, blushing as she remembered how he had carried her to climax after shuddering climax until she was left raw and aching, but fulfilled beyond her wildest dreams.

He was not above exploiting his effect on her to get his own way, she remembered. She had never made any secret of wanting a deep and lasting commitment, but had settled for what she could have with Zeke because his passion was so addictive that she had allowed it to drown her deeper needs. Well not anymore. "You didn't trust me enough to know what was best for me then, and you obviously don't now."

"I'm a reporter. I deal in facts," he said. "Trust is an intangible."

"So is love," she reminded him. "But you need both to make a relationship work."

He let his gaze settle on her for a long time until she felt her skin growing hot under his scrutiny. "We managed very well with what we had."

She leaned forward, placing her palms flat on the desk, feeling a need for something solid beneath her touch. "We didn't manage, as you put it. As I recall, we broke up."

"It wasn't for lack of trust, at least not on my part."

Her blood cooled as she remembered the story he had been out working on when she'd come looking for him. Was he trying to tell her that he knew her secret? Dear Lord, not so soon, she prayed silently. She had feared that she couldn't keep the truth from him forever, but she had hoped for more time to prepare herself. "What are you saying?"

"All this talk about love and trust is a blind, isn't it? You wanted an excuse to stop seeing me and, fool that I was, I provided one by accepting a job overseas. If I'd rejected the offer, you'd probably have invented some other reason to walk out."

She knew confusion showed on her face. "You make it sound as if it was my decision alone."

"Wasn't it?" he demanded with the sound of a trap snapping shut. "Can you deny you were already pregnant when I asked you to come with me?"

She felt her spine crumble and only years of modeling discipline kept her upright in the chair as the room whirled around her. "Oh, no."

She saw his face turn ashen and realized she had just confirmed what had probably been little more than suspicion before. "Then it's true." His voice came out like the sound of a winter gale whipping over a barren landscape. "I'm investigating a baby farming racket at a private hospital. A source on their staff gave me access to their computer files and I found your name on a list of women who'd been admitted to the maternity section of the hospital during the time I'm investigating. We were interrupted before I got the whole story, so I didn't know what to think. At first I thought it was a mistake, or someone else with the same name, but it was neither. You had a baby, didn't you?''

She hesitated. Since he'd left, she had replayed over and over in her mind the moment when Zeke found out. Much as she yearned to, she had never been able to imagine him simply taking her in his arms and holding her in understanding and support. It wasn't going to happen now, she judged by the cold fury on his face. His hands were balled into fists and he looked as if he had trouble keeping them at his sides.

His even features twisted in anguish. ''Dear sweet heaven. All these months you let me torture myself, wondering if I should have stayed, when you were already pregnant by another man.''

The thought that he had actually regretted his decision to leave gave her a small measure of comfort, but it was quickly overtaken by the white heat of anger, giving her the strength to fight back. ''You're doing it again, aren't you?''

''Doing what, for pity's sake?''

''Pushing away good, honest emotion by turning it into something else.''

''You're not making any sense.''

''I think I am. You never wanted closeness, Zeke. Not with me or anybody. After the way you were brought up, it makes you feel too threatened, too vulnerable. The longer we were together, the more that feeling grew. I know because you weren't the only one feeling the closeness, the longing for forever. But it isn't going to happen as long as you respond to closeness by pushing me away. Accusing me of seeing someone else is part of that.''

''I'm not accusing you, dammit. You just admitted to being pregnant by another man.''

''I admitted to being pregnant,'' she said in a voice barely above a whisper.

She had reached him at last, she saw when his hard expression started to crumble. If he had considered that the baby might have been his, he had dismissed it as impossible. "You had *my* baby? But how? We took precautions."

"The doctor told me they failed after I had that bout of flu," she said hoarsely. "It was nobody's fault, just one of those things."

"A child is hardly one of those things," he said in a tone that could have cut glass.

She shook her head. "I didn't mean it like that. Our baby meant everything to me. You must believe that."

He heard the catch in her voice but the dark fury that ignited his gaze showed that he had put his own interpretation on it. "Meant? Oh, no, Tara, you didn't…you wouldn't…"

In a blinding flash, she understood what he thought she was trying to say and felt mortified that he would consider her capable of such a deed. "Of course not. How can you possibly think I could do such a terrible thing?"

"I apologize," he said stiffly, but with heart-wrenching sincerity. "I do know you better than that, or at least I thought I did. You'd better tell me everything."

Despite all the pain he had caused her, she wished there was some way to spare him the agony she knew she was about to inflict. "Our baby was a little boy. I called him Brendan. He…he was stillborn."

She saw him summon years of reporting experience to maintain control, but after all they had meant to each other, she recognized the facade for what it was and her heart lurched. He asked, "What went wrong?"

It almost broke her to hear the crack in his voice that belied his hard expression. "The umbilical cord caught around his neck and he couldn't get oxygen. It simply wasn't meant to be."

"I had a son."

The simple statement tore through her like a knife aimed straight at her heart. "We had a son," she corrected softly.

His eyes blazed havoc at her. "No, *you* had a son. You

didn't see fit to include me, even though the baby was as much mine as yours.''

She held herself from flinching beneath the angry words he hurled at her like lightning bolts. She had drained herself of anger months before, the fury of it gradually giving way to numb acceptance. To Zeke, the pain was new and raw. He would need time to come to terms with what, to him, was a fresh loss. And he was right, she had denied him the experience. Bearing the brunt of his anger was the least she could do. It couldn't fully make amends, but it was all she could offer him.

''Why?'' he demanded. ''If you had told me, I'd have stayed with you, been there for you.''

She lifted her head. ''It's precisely why I didn't tell you. I didn't want you to feel you had no choice but to stay.''

''So you gave me no choice at all.''

Unable to sit still a moment longer, she stood and began to pace. ''I'm sorry for what I did. It was wrong to shut you out at such a time. But I can't go back and undo it.''

''Are you sure you would, if you could?''

''No, I'm not sure. The fact that you were ready to believe I could be pregnant by another man tells me you haven't changed. It's still easier to believe the worst of me than to deal with your own feelings.''

''I've said I'm sorry,'' he growled. She remembered an apology in there somewhere but was fairly sure it hadn't been for misjudging her. He raked long fingers through his dark hair. ''Hell of a way to find out you're a father. *Were* a father.''

It was her turn to say the words that had burned in her heart for so long. ''I'm sorry, too, about everything.'' She half turned toward the door, unable to concentrate on business any more than she was sure he would be able to now.

His grating words stopped her. ''Was the baby...did he...look like me?''

She turned slowly, feeling wetness fringe her lashes. Her thoughts spun back to that dark, rain-swept night only ten months ago. A hospital in chaos. Corridors clogged with accident victims on stretchers, too many to find beds for them all. Staff coping as best they could and extending their shifts far beyond the usual times, their replacements caught up in the traffic debacle outside the hospital. Despite being so harried, the midwife, a man named Ross, she remembered, had taken the time to place Tara's child in her arms and had sat with her while she wept out her goodbye to the son she had nurtured.

Many times she had replayed the scene in her mind, forever grateful that Ross had given her the chance to hold her baby. It had made her loss cruelly real and inescapable, but it had also provided a sense of closure.

Zeke would never have that chance and it was plain he resented her for it. She coughed to clear a clogged throat. There was one thing she could give him. "When I held him, he looked like a tiny, sleeping doll. He had a surprising amount of hair, though, and it was as dark as yours." It had been the only thing about the baby that reminded her of Zeke, she recalled, but didn't say so. She hated to hurt him any more than she had already, and it didn't change anything now.

"That's something, I suppose."

"Zeke, I really am sorry. I know it doesn't help and I should have told you, but at the time, I couldn't do it."

He lifted his head, the brightness in his eyes mirroring her own. "It's too soon for forgiveness, and that's what you really want from me, isn't it?"

"I don't want your forgiveness, Zeke," she flung back at him, fury sending spears of heat through her. "I don't want anything from you that isn't freely given. I never did."

He had always been light on his feet and now he shot out of the chair and across the room like an aimed bullet. Her hand had barely grazed the doorknob when he wrenched her around to face him. "I won't let you walk out of here as if nothing has happened."

"You can't stop me."

"Can't I?"

She tried to ignore the feel of his hand on her arm but a tingle raced along her veins, sending her heart rate into overdrive. Then he slid his free hand down her back and mice feet skittered along her spine. She gave a shiver, but whether with longing or fear, she wasn't sure.

He pressed her tightly against him as if he needed to hang on to something. His anchor, she thought again. How he must need one at this moment. She could only begin to guess at the distress his discovery had inflicted. She'd had ten months to mourn the baby he'd only just learned he had lost. Was it too much to lend him her support at such a time?

When his mouth found hers and she returned the pressure eagerly, she recognized the self-deception for what it was. She wasn't lending him support. She was taking what she had needed from him for a long time.

The sweetness of his hard mouth shaping hers stirred memories of kisses shared in the dead of night on a deserted beach, in a mountain chalet, almost anywhere sufficiently secluded. Their passion had run as hot as molten lava, she remembered, and Zeke had urged her to indulge it to the full. She'd been the prudish one then, fearful of being discovered.

"What if we are?" he'd said. "It's called freedom."

He may have called it freedom, but she had been a slave to ardor from the first. She felt the tug of it now as he pulled her against his hard body, making her tremble as a starveling might tremble at the promise of a feast.

No matter how great her hunger, this feast wasn't for her, she told herself as her head started to spin. "This isn't right," she said, her lips moving weakly against his mouth.

He lifted his head long enough to respond. "It feels more

right than anything I've done for months. I hate to think of what you went through alone, on my account.''

''It wasn't only on your account,'' she said hotly. She had accepted his embrace to help heal his pain, not once considering that he might be offering it out of pity for her. Rejection coursed through her and she tried to pull away.

At once his hold tightened. ''Considering I make a living out of words, they don't always work the way they're supposed to. I didn't mean to sound so condescending. I can't remember when my thoughts have been so tangled. This has come as a hell of a shock.''

''I know.'' She rested her head against his shoulder and felt his fingers thread through her hair. Her soft sigh whispered against the open neck of his shirt. ''In the heat of the moment, we all say things we don't mean.''

''I meant it when I said this feels right,'' he said, gravel in his voice. ''You can't deny it feels the same for you.''

''I should.''

''There are no shoulds,'' he said, quoting another Zeke aphorism.

She lifted her head slightly. ''Not even when it came to telling you about the baby?'' She almost wished he would go on berating her for keeping it from him. His compassion was far harder to endure than his censure would have been. She deserved his fury, she accepted, even while recognizing that he wasn't responsible for giving her either penance or absolution. They would have to come from within herself. Zeke was right. It was too soon for forgiveness, but too late for anger, as well.

''You did what you thought you had to do.''

In spite of her advice to herself, his generosity only served to heighten her anguish. Then she noticed the overbrightness in his gaze. Zeke had never subscribed to the belief that real men didn't cry, but she had never seen tears in his eyes before and the sheen in his gaze cut through her like a razor.

"All the same, it hurts, doesn't it?"

"More than I would have thought possible."

"Oh, Zeke, I wish…"

"Don't, please." He silenced her by the easiest means, clamping his mouth over hers. She returned the kiss in full measure, sensing that he needed an anchor now more than ever before. She needed it, too, and for a moment couldn't have said who was clinging to whom.

When the kiss changed from despair to desire, she wasn't sure. One moment he was kissing her as if she was his life-line, and the next he was plundering her mouth as if the world was about to end and there wasn't a moment to lose.

In an instant he became the Zeke she had both longed for and feared, because of the easy way he could make her lose control. Like a plane spinning out too close to the ground, she felt it happening all over again. Worse, she was going to let it happen. Resisting him once had cost them both so dearly that it wasn't in her power to risk it again, even had she wanted to.

She moaned as his lips traced a path across her forehead and down both closed eyelids. The feather-light touch was all it took to send waves of primitive need surging through her.

Instinctively she lifted herself to meet him but was stopped by the tightness of her miniskirt. He reached down and hitched it higher, letting his hand stray across her thigh until his fingers met the lacy edge of her panties. She gasped as he slid his fingers under the lace, caressing closer and closer to the center of her being. "You still wear these frivolous things?" he murmured.

Warmth pooled deep inside her as she arched closer to his questing fingers. "You never complained before."

"I'm not complaining now. I've missed you so much, Tara. You have no idea how much. Sometimes the need for you has been like a ravenous beast gnawing at my soul."

A specter rose up between them. "It didn't stop you turning to Lucy."

His teeth nipped the side of her neck and her moans redoubled, making the specter shiver into nothingness. "I was trying to quiet the beast. It didn't take me long to discover that only one person could do that."

Tara had endured her own beasts, tormenting her late at night from the cold, empty half of the bed. "The same for me," she whispered.

He let his hand fill her, making her arch her back so that only the hardness of the door behind her kept her from sliding bonelessly to the floor. She dragged air into her lungs in heaving gasps, wondering how much more of this sweet torment she could endure before she capitulated completely and begged him to make love to her properly. Now that he knew about the baby, she had no need to fear being betrayed by the changes in her body.

She opened her mouth to implore him to end this, when she became aware that he already had, but not in the way she craved. As he took his hand away and tugged her skirt down, she almost cried out in frustration until she saw that his face was set in an unreadable expression. "What is it? What's wrong?" she asked.

"You said you didn't want me using sex to control you, yet that's precisely what I was about to do."

He was so close she felt the caress of his breath against her cheek, but there may as well have been an ocean between them for all the warmth she felt from him now. "It was hardly one-sided," she pointed out, masking disappointment with a cold fury of her own.

He braced one hand against the door over her shoulder. "Why did you let me kiss you?"

Angry as she was, she couldn't bring herself to lie to him, not again. "You needed me."

He nodded as if she had confirmed a suspicion. "I sensed

it, but instead of taking what you offered in the spirit you were offering it, I wanted more.''

No more than she wanted, she all but cried out to him. ''It doesn't make it wrong, surely?''

''Perhaps not now, but what about afterward, when you realize you've betrayed your principles with a man you don't trust.''

''How can you think I don't trust you?'' she asked, horrified.

''I don't think it, I know it. If you had trusted me, you'd have told me about the baby.''

So this was to be her punishment, she thought as reality returned with a crash. He might understand her actions, he may even forgive her. But he couldn't overlook what it said about their relationship.

How could she argue with his logic? She should probably be glad he had the strength to call a halt before things got too far out of hand, but at some level she knew it was already too late. What she felt had nothing to do with gratitude. ''Do you expect me to thank you for saving me from myself?'' she asked, proud that her voice shook only a little.

He dropped his arm to his side and stepped back, making it obvious that the moment of abandonment was over. His voice was frigid as he said, ''I don't expect anything from you at all.'' He handed her the folder of notes the publisher had prepared and held the door open. ''We're done here.''

Anger whipped through her for allowing herself to be swept up in his kiss to the point of forgetting why she was angry with him. His comment reminded her. ''Not quite,'' she said acidly. ''I looked for you at the paper earlier.''

''Why do I think you didn't want to compliment me on my work?''

''Because I don't. What you wrote in today's column may have cost Model Children an important donor.''

He frowned. ''I didn't identify your charity specifically.''

''The donor read between the lines.''

''Then I'll have to choose my words more carefully in the future. I didn't intend you any harm.''

But harm was what he had done her, she thought as she closed the door between them, knowing she wasn't thinking only of the children's charity.

Chapter 5

''How does it feel, knowing you're a father but being denied the chance to raise your child?''

As he put the question to his interview subject and braced himself to hear the heart-wrenching answer, Zeke knew he was also asking it of himself. The answer was more complicated than he could have imagined. If he'd known that Tara was carrying his child, he knew he would have stayed in Australia. Not because she couldn't cope without him—hadn't she done just that? But he hated to think of her doing it.

For a moment he pictured her in the full flower of pregnancy, imagining how her delicate skin must have bloomed with color as her model figure slowly ripened to a different kind of beauty. He ached inside, knowing he would never see her like that, or splay his hand across her fecund belly and feel the ripple of movement as his child quickened inside her. He hadn't had to deal with the loss, either, but that was a deprivation of sorts, cheating him of his right to mourn, as well.

The man seated across the table from him screwed up his face as if he was fighting tears. Zeke knew how he felt. After confronting Tara, he had felt close to breaking point himself. It was no small effort to keep his emotions under control now.

It didn't change facts. He was a father.

His son, Brendan, had been born while he was thousands of miles away and he hadn't known a thing about it. He wasn't vain enough to think being with her would have changed the outcome, but at least he could have held his son as Tara had done. They could have cried together, healed together. How was he supposed to forgive her for denying him that chance?

Now he found himself wondering if his real father had known about his own birth? He had always believed that the man had walked away from his responsibilities, but what if Zeke's mother had never told him about his son? Never given him the chance to meet Zeke, denying them both the chance to know each other, as Tara had been prepared to do.

Pointless to agonize over what might have been, he told himself, but the thought burned inside him like a prank birthday candle that keeps relighting itself after it's blown out. Had his birth father been as much a victim of his mother's scheming as Zeke himself?

Had he known of his son's existence, would his natural father have made a home for him? It would have saved Zeke from being moved in and out of a string of foster homes, making attachments and being wrenched away until he was too gun-shy to trust anymore. Zeke knew the thought was impossibly idealistic. Things may well have turned out exactly the same. The hell of it was, he would never know.

His mother, the one person who could have filled in the gaps, had refused to discuss her relationship with his father, suggesting that Zeke was better off without him. Now she was gone and Zeke's efforts over the years had yielded no more information.

He would also never know how things would have worked out between him and Tara if he had been different. He had another vision of them together, holding hands across a baby's crib, a dark-haired infant kicking and squealing between them, and he felt an abyss open up inside him.

He had always sensed the darkness lurking within him, the shadowy places that had remained unfilled when he was a child, until he no longer trusted anyone but himself to fill them. With her generous nature and open heart, Tara had come closer than anyone to filling the emptiness. For a while she had made him hope that things could be different. Then she had pushed him away just like all the rest, her betrayal infinitely worse because he had allowed her to touch parts of his soul that he had shielded from all others.

He had come closer to loving Tara than any other human being. Perhaps without fully acknowledging it, especially not to himself, he *had* loved her. Part of him still hungered for the completion she represented. Why else would he have insisted on putting himself through that meeting with her? It had been a mistake to think he could stay uninvolved, and he had told Colin so when his new partner returned to the office. Colin had been disappointed, but had agreed to take over the contract negotiations with her. Zeke hated to think of Tara meeting with any other man, even on business, but it was safer than the alternative.

Remembering how he had nearly made love to her in Colin's office, he almost broke out in a cold sweat. Thank goodness he'd had the strength to pull back while he still could. It didn't stop his body responding automatically to the thought of her, the arousal strong enough to make him want to seek her out right now and finish what they'd started.

He was horrified at himself. He might hate what she'd done to him, but it didn't prevent primitive need from clawing at him, so hot and urgent that it threatened to stop him from doing his job. He had never allowed anything to do that, until now.

"How does anyone handle this?" He massaged his temples with stiff fingers, aware of an ache behind his eyes that refused to go away.

Across from him, his subject gave him a gratified look he didn't deserve. "That's it exactly. You do understand. My wife was afraid you wouldn't."

Zeke pulled himself back to the interview with a jolt, thankful that his miniature tape recorder whirred away between them, making up for his lapse in concentration. In his turbulent state of mind, he thought it safer not to trust his usually reliable memory. Now he found the man's admission intriguing. "What did your wife think I'd be like?"

The man looked down at the table. "She said you're too tough and streetwise to understand our feelings. Us and the other parents whose children were supposed to have died but were given to other people for money. As you said, how are we supposed to live with that?"

Zeke felt ashamed of being credited with more compassion than was his due, but an admission, while soothing his conscience, would only inflict further pain so he held it back. In truth, he hadn't really understood how the parents felt until Tara told him about Brendan. The resulting empathy had little to recommend it in his book, and he could do without having his gut twisted into knots as he worked on the story. Cool objectivity was far easier to handle, but it was denied him now.

"No one should have to suffer what you're going through," he said, not sure whether he was speaking for himself or the other man.

The man slammed a fist onto the table, rattling the coffee cups. "If you hadn't begun to investigate what really happened…"

"Strictly speaking, you should be thanking the father who came to me with his suspicions," Zeke interjected.

The man clenched his fists. "But you listened to him when nobody else would. The police and hospital authorities told him grief for his lost child was making him imagine things."

Zeke nodded. "I admit I had my own doubts when he told me how his wife had gone back to the hospital as an outpatient, and found herself sitting next to a woman with a new baby she swore was her child."

The man scrubbed his eyes. "It's easy to make yourself see what you want to see. After our little Clair died, I kept seeing her everywhere. I told myself I was imagining things. But it might not have been imagination."

Zeke inclined his head. "The other woman was so convinced she was right that she went home and forced herself to examine the photograph her husband had taken of their supposedly lost baby. Until then she hadn't been able to face it. This time she made herself study it more closely, and what she saw horrified her."

"It wasn't her baby in the photo, was it?" the man asked, sounding ragged.

Zeke couldn't blame him for his emotional state. The couples on Zeke's list must have been to hell and back a thousand times since Zeke started the investigation. "She says it isn't. She swears that the baby's hair color and eye shape were different from the child she gave birth to. Before the child could move or cry, the midwife whisked it away, ostensibly to begin resuscitation, although there had been no warning that the baby was in difficulty."

This was hard, when Zeke's imagination kept turning the baby into a boy called Brendan. He cleared his throat. "The mother was told that efforts to revive her baby hadn't worked. She was allowed to hold the child and say goodbye. She only saw her living child briefly, but she swears that the baby the midwife brought back to her was a different child.

It seems she tried to alert someone at the time, but it was dismissed as the hysteria of grief.''

He took a deep breath. ''I'm still digging, but it looks as if her baby was switched for one who died close to the time her baby was born.''

''Why didn't her baby cry, if it was healthy?'' the man asked.

Zeke had asked himself the same question, answering it during his research. ''Not all newborn babies do at first. Some have to be stimulated to take the first breath. The midwife could have pretended that the child wasn't breathing when, in reality, all it needed was a good smack on the behind. She could then rush it away, supposedly to care for it, but in reality to make the exchange.

''It seems likely there were variations on this scenario,'' he added. ''I interviewed one couple who say their child was fine for the first couple of days, then deteriorated overnight.'' The sleight of hand and the heartbreak involved made Zeke feel sick to his stomach, but he had seen enough in his line of work to know that some people were capable of anything if the price was right.

''You think their child was switched for an ailing baby that had been born to someone else, someone wealthy enough to pay for a healthy baby?''

''Allegedly ailing,'' Zeke corrected automatically. ''My informant at the hospital was secretly gathering DNA records to prove that at least two babies were switched at birth or soon afterward, and given to couples willing to pay the asking price. My informant is sure there were more, but the records have been conveniently mislaid or deleted. Until they're located, we won't know how many babies were involved, or where they ended up.''

The man's bright gaze bored into Zeke. ''How do you know it didn't happen the way we were told? Babies do die at birth, or get something wrong with them afterward.''

Zeke linked his hands under the table to stop them from shaking. It had happened to his own son. "I know, but the pattern is what bothers me here. I've uncovered at least four cases where parents either doubt the identity of a baby who died, or had a child who was healthy at first, then took a sudden turn for the worse. It's beyond coincidence, especially when the same group of people seem to be involved on each occasion."

He didn't add that his source inside the hospital was feeding him information scrap by scrap. His informant was a low-ranking employee whom no one suspected of having enough pieces of the puzzle to be able to put it together, but she had. She told Zeke she was too afraid to go to the authorities but when Zeke started nosing around, prompted by the father who had approached him, she had agreed to help Zeke, provided he kept her name out of the story altogether. He didn't blame her for being frightened. People who would barter children's lives for cash were presumably capable of anything.

As a result, she would only meet him for minutes at a time and kept her information frustratingly cryptic, wanting him to work things out for himself so nothing could be traced back to her. It made the going tough, but Zeke had never backed away from a challenge when a story was involved. If it held up, this one could well be the biggest of his career.

His interview subject reclaimed his attention by reaching a hand across the table to him. "You really think there's a chance our baby's still alive? We were told she died soon after birth, and my wife was too heartbroken to ask to see her. For her sake, I didn't insist. Now I wish I had."

"If we're right, it probably wouldn't have made any difference."

The man's features contorted. "These people have to be stopped."

"I think they've already stopped. According to figures I've

been shown, the infant mortality rate at that hospital took a dive a month after your baby was born, so either new security procedures were put in place, or the people involved decided to call it quits to avoid drawing any more suspicion.''

''Too late to help our baby and the others like her.'' The man's voice caught on tears. ''How can anyone sell an innocent life?''

Zeke leaned across the table. ''In my experience, anything's for sale if you have the money. For now, I want you to remember that whoever has your baby wanted her enough to risk a great deal for her. They aren't likely to harm her.''

It was small consolation, but the man pulled himself together with an obvious effort. ''I won't rest until I know what really happened and get my daughter back. Until you uncovered this scandal, we accepted that our baby was gone. The grieving was hard enough. Now, to think Clair might be living with some other family, not knowing she's our child, is beyond bearing. You're our only hope to put this thing right.''

Zeke met the man's troubled gaze with a direct one of his own. ''I'm no superhero, but if I possibly can, I will see justice done for you and the children.''

''Thank you.'' The man's voice cracked and he stood up. ''I'd better get back to my wife. The waiting is killing her.''

Zeke wished he could offer the man more hope, but he couldn't. He was doing everything in his power to find the answers that would give the man and his wife and the other parents like them peace of mind.

The man stopped and turned, his eyes shining. ''Find our baby, please.''

Zeke nodded in silence, knowing he had the masthead for his story. Find Our Baby, Please would tear at hearts around the country. It was tearing at his own, he acknowledged as he drained his cup of strong, black coffee.

After Tara's heartwrenching account of how she had cradled their child's lifeless body, he held no hope that his son was among those the ring of hospital employees had allegedly placed with new families in return for vast sums of money, so he wasn't doing this for himself. But Tara's revelation somehow made it more personal. It wouldn't bring his son back to life, but it might save other children from the hell he had endured, not knowing who they were or where they really belonged. Pocketing the tape recorder, he stood up. Time to start finding answers—and babies.

"Why do you keep all this stuff?" Tara asked her mother as she opened yet another carton filled with memorabilia from her childhood. It hurt to think that this was the last time she would help clean out this attic. Her mother had decided to sell the old family home and move to a smaller place. Her father was now living in an apartment near the beach, and had declined an invitation to participate, saying there was nothing he wanted from the attic.

Several cartons of toys that had belonged to Tara and her brother already stood to one side, along with clothes and other items to be donated to charity. A rocking horse and toy car would go to Tara's niece and nephew.

Lillian McNiven gave her daughter a faraway look. "Hanging on to this stuff is like hanging on to your babies, in a way. Giving it up means accepting that they aren't your babies any longer. When you have children of your own, you'll understand."

Tara sat back, fighting the urge to wrap her arms around herself and rock mindlessly. She had never told her parents she was pregnant, and her mother's words flooded her with desolation. Brendan should have inherited these things, she raged inwardly, not sure who or what her anger was directed at, but barely able to contain it.

"Don't look so sad. It isn't the end of the world," Lillian

said softly, touching a hand to her daughter's face. "They're only things. You still have your memories."

Tara nestled against her mother's hand. Her parents had separated during Tara's pregnancy, and Tara hadn't wanted to add to her mother's burden. Fortunately, her mother had gone away for a few months after the breakup, otherwise there was no way Tara could have kept the truth to herself.

"All the same, it's hard letting go of a baby," Tara said in a strangled whisper.

It was Lillian's turn to look puzzled. "That's an odd way to put it. What are you trying to say?"

A lump lodged in Tara's throat. "It wasn't you I was thinking about just now, it was myself."

"I still don't understand."

Tara knew that now was the time. "I was thinking of my own baby. I didn't tell you, because he was born at the time you and Dad were having so much difficulty. Then the baby died at birth, and there was no point saying anything."

"Oh, Tara, my poor child. I knew something was different about you, but I was so caught up in my own problems, it never occurred to me that you could be pregnant. Zeke was the father, wasn't he?"

Tara nodded. "There was no one else."

Lillian smiled wanly. "You were drawn to him like a magnet to metal from first meeting. Was the baby the reason you two broke up?"

"Good heavens, no. He never knew."

Lillian looked shocked. "You never told Zeke? Oh, Tara, you didn't have to go through the whole experience alone. I wish you had told me."

"Zeke had his dream job offer and you had so much to cope with already. It seemed unfair to burden you with my problem."

"Did it occur to you that a grandchild might have given me back something of what I was losing?"

In her desire to protect her mother from further hurt, Tara hadn't considered such a possibility. "I guess I wasn't thinking too straight, especially after I lost the baby."

Lillian's expression was so filled with compassion that Tara wanted to cry. But it was too late for tears. She felt something pressing against her breast and found that she was cradling a hard plastic doll as if it were a child. Her breath hitched on a sob and she put the doll gently to one side.

"Do you feel like talking about it?" her mother asked softly.

Kneeling among the debris of her childhood, Tara told her mother the whole story, ending with Zeke's return and his anger at being shut out of what he saw as the most important event of his life.

"The worst of it is, he's right," she concluded. "When I was pregnant, I didn't consider anyone else, not Zeke, not you." She rested a hand on her mother's knee. "Can you forgive me?"

"You're forgetting that nature programs us to shut out everything but the baby we're nurturing," her mother pointed out. "Even in the best-adjusted families, fathers can be made to feel they're more hindrance than help during pregnancy, because we become so inwardly focused. So there's nothing to forgive. I only wish that I'd been there for you instead of being so wrapped up in myself."

"Don't start blaming yourself," Tara said sternly. She recalled the words she'd said to Zeke. "It simply wasn't meant to be."

"What about you and Zeke?"

She had meant to close the discussion, but her mother's expression suggested she wasn't letting it go so easily this time. "What about him?" she hedged.

"Now he's home, will you get back together?"

Tara shook her head. "He hates me too much for shutting him out."

"He sounds a bit like your father."

Tara had barely spoken to her father since he'd walked out on her mother, not so much because he had ended the marriage, but because of his reasons for doing so. He had always put appearance before every other quality, manipulating Tara into following a modeling career regardless of her preferences, by arranging to have a friend in the business "discover" her at a shopping mall. By the time she found out what he'd done, she was under contract to an agency, being hailed as the new Elle McPherson and her career had developed a life of its own. Tara hadn't especially enjoyed the adulation, but neither had she tried to walk away.

Her mother had always been a beautiful woman and Tara's father had made no secret of his pride in the fact. As soon as her age began to show, he had paid for her to have a facelift, and had lavished huge sums on beauticians and dress designers to ensure she remained an ornament to him. Then she had discovered a melanoma on her cheek. While not malignant, it went deeper than first suspected and the resulting surgery had left a slight but visible mark.

To anyone else Lillian was still attractive, slim and youthful looking, Tara thought, looking at her mother now. Artful use of makeup concealed the damage. But Tara's father hadn't been able to accept the imperfection, not even in his wife of thirty-five years. First he had changed seats at table so he sat on what she called her "good" side. Then he had left altogether to think things through, or so he said.

Tara hated the idea that Zeke had anything in common with such an unfeeling man and said so.

"Your father has his good qualities," Lillian said mildly. "I simply meant they're both incredibly strong men who know what they want and go after it. They would never dream of accepting second best."

"You are not second best," Tara said hotly, unhappy to think her father could see her mother like that. Another thought struck her. "You don't mean that Zeke thinks of me that way?"

"No, but he's probably upset about what you took from him—the chance to be part of a real family."

What was her mother trying to say? Tara jumped to her feet. "I couldn't help what happened."

Lillian reached for her hand and tugged her down again. Tara resisted at first, then allowed herself to be guided onto an old tin trunk. "I never meant to suggest you could change what happened to the baby, only how you handled Zeke," her mother assured her. "He probably feels cheated of the nine months you could have shared. Remember, he never had a real family, as you and I knew it. Your father and I may have our differences now, but when you and Ben were children, we tried to give you a family home where you felt loved and secure."

"You succeeded," Tara said, squeezing her mother's hand as her vision blurred again. She blinked rapidly. "Maybe that's why I have such high expectations now."

"As long as you don't make them so high, no real man can measure up."

Tara was still weighing Lillian's words when she got home lugging a heavy bag of items and photographs her mother had wanted her to have as keepsakes. With no child of her own to pass them on to, Tara saw little point in keeping them but had bowed to her mother's wish.

Bracing the front door with a foot, she pushed the bag inside and pocketed her key before stepping inside and closing the door. Immediately some sixth sense told her she wasn't alone, and the small hairs rose on the back of her neck. Her hand froze on the doorknob. "Is someone here?"

Moving slowly, she reached for a club a golfing friend had left in the umbrella holder beside the door after an overnight stay. She felt comforted as her hand closed around the frayed leather grip. A large male shape loomed at one end of the hallway, backlit by the light from the living room. Her breath caught until she recognized who it was.

He came closer. "Tara, it's okay, it's only me."

Relief made her knees weaken. "So I see. One more step and I'd have brained you with this." She hefted the golf club to show him.

"Quite a weapon," he said sourly. "I'm glad you don't shoot first and ask questions later. I don't fancy a head with a hole in one."

"Very funny," she snapped, feeling tremors of reaction sweep through her. "What are you doing here? I thought you returned the key I gave you."

He tossed a key up and down in his palm. "I did. Then I remembered the spare you keep under the fake rock in the front garden. Wonderful security, by the way."

She made a mental note to find a new hiding place for the spare key. "It was fine until you got here." A lot of things had been fine until then, she was well aware. "Did you have to scare me half to death?"

"I'm sorry. I didn't mean to alarm you."

His stiff posture and cold tone finally registered with her. This wasn't a friendly visit, then. She accepted that his hostility was her own fault, but it didn't make it any easier to bear. "What are you doing here?" she repeated tiredly.

"Believe me, I don't want to drag this out any more than you do."

She wanted to go into the living room and sit down, but it meant moving past Zeke in the narrow hallway. She wasn't sure she could touch him without wanting to do more, so she stayed where she was. She made her tone light. "Then don't. There are such things as telephones. Heck, these days there's even fax and e-mail. I have all three, and the numbers haven't changed since you left."

"They work both ways."

She knew what he was saying. She could have contacted him in any number of ways after he went to America. She pushed the golf club back into the umbrella holder and braced herself against the front door. "I know. We could have done a lot of things differently. But it's too late now." She lifted a wide-eyed gaze to him. "You may not accept this, but I'll always regret not telling you I was pregnant. If there was any way to go back and change it, I probably would."

"Would you, Tara?" His cold tone rang with disbelief.

"Yes. So you didn't need to come over and lecture me."

"It isn't why I'm here."

For a split second her spirits spiraled upward although her common sense shied away from what he seemed to imply. Hardest to control was her body's primitive response to the thought of once more being loved by him as only Zeke knew how to love her. She told herself she was a fool, but the cravings refused to subside.

She needed to put some space between them. "Shall we go into the living room?"

Instead of stepping through the doorway behind him, as any sane person would have done, he flattened himself against the wall. "After you."

She almost groaned out loud. Hadn't he heard of women's lib? She took a tentative step toward him and her foot caught on the heavy bag of keepsakes from her mother. Zeke moved swiftly, catching her before she could sprawl all her length.

In her heart, she had sensed the risk in touching him, and now she knew it was more than justified. As his arms closed around her, flames tore through her until it was all she could do not to link her arms around his neck and pull him against her, locking her mouth with his until they both saw stars.

She saw her need reflected in his eyes as he set her carefully upright, his hands pulling away from her with obvious reluctance. As his palms skimmed her hips, her breath hitched and she pressed her hands over the tops of his, holding his in place. "Zeke."

"Tara, it's been so long." His fingers dug convulsively into her hips as if he was staking a claim.

"We shouldn't."

His gaze bore into her, dark as honey, urgent as a siren and every bit as impossible to ignore. "I notice you're not saying 'mustn't' or 'won't.'"

She gave it her best shot. "I mustn't. I won't."

But she knew she lied even to herself. The feel of Zeke's hands on her hips, urging her toward him, robbed her of the will to fight anymore. Not him, not her own desires. He must have felt her acquiescence but held her away from him, refusing to give in to the madness she saw in his gaze. "I need to know, Tara."

She threw her head back, her mouth open on as she fought for air. "Don't you know already?"

He nodded, his expression taut. This was as torturous for him as for her, she saw, and took a little satisfaction in the knowledge. "I still want to hear you say it so there's no misunderstanding."

At some level she knew he wanted to make sure she wouldn't regret this moment later. She probably would, but she would never accuse him of forcing himself on her, although she couldn't blame him for taking no chances. "All right, I'll say it. I want you, Zeke. If you leave without making love to me, I'll go crazy. Is that enough for you?"

"If it was enough, I'd go now." He sounded as starved as she felt. But she knew from the way he hauled her to him and ground his mouth against hers that he wasn't going anywhere for a long time.

Chapter 6

If Zeke knew nothing else, he knew how Tara liked to be loved. None of this lying back against crisp sheets in a bedroom scented with flickering candles. She preferred the adventure of different settings, unexpected places, the feeling of being taken just a little by surprise. He couldn't deny he liked the feeling of being in command—of the situation and of her. And unless she had changed more than he knew, so did she.

So he didn't sweep her off her feet and carry her to the bedroom. He started to make love to her right where they were, in the hallway, with a bag of old stuff strewn around their feet where she had fallen over it. Photos, junk and children's toys, he saw in some surprise. What on earth did Tara want with a dog-eared teddy bear?

Then he had no time to wonder about trivia. He was too busy doing what he had fantasized about for months, exploring every inch of her delectable mouth, throat and face with his lips.

His mouth surged over hers, taking every drop of sweetness she had to give. He drank her in like wine, his breathing quickening because this was only the first taste. The banquet was still to come, and he felt like a man who hadn't eaten in a long, long time. It made him cautious.

Her breathing was also ragged as she tore her mouth impatiently from his. "I haven't turned into fragile china since you left."

"But you have changed." He was only too aware of the ripeness of her breasts pressing against him, driving his excitement higher. What other changes awaited him?

"We both have. You're gentler, but more giving somehow."

He thrust his fingers through her hair, letting the silken strands fan away from his hand. A faint scent of some hair product she'd used recently teased his nostrils. "Do you mean I wasn't before?"

She dropped her head back, giving him access to the slender column of her neck. He dipped his mouth and accepted the offering with lapping kisses that made her close her eyes in ecstasy. "You weren't like this," she said on a husky note.

He frowned, trying to recall how it was before. He'd always been careful to make sure she was ready for him before he took his own pleasure. At least he thought he had. Maybe his judgement wasn't a hundred percent reliable. Since she seemed to like what he was doing now, he resolved to do more of it. The trouble was, he only had so much endurance.

Heck, that was probably it. Before, he had thought in terms of getting the first course out of the way so they could get to the main event. He had assumed it was what Tara wanted, too. But she seemed to be getting more out of the first course than he had realized. So be it. He only hoped he could last the distance without disappointing them both.

Giving her what she wanted wasn't exactly a hardship for him, he soon found. He trailed kisses down the shadowed cleft between her breasts, unbuttoning the first button of her blouse to give him better access. She took his head in both hands and pressed him closer until he registered the frantic beat of her heart through the lacy material.

He felt a surge of desire so powerful that he had to fight the urge to give in to it. Don't think, don't feel, he commanded himself, desperately calling up mental images of earthquakes, war fronts, solitary nights spent covering stories in far-flung places, anything to get his errant body back under control.

When he was sure he'd headed off disaster, he turned his attention to her bra, an item of female apparel that had always challenged him. This time it was a wisp of white nonsense that fortunately clasped in the front, so he was able to unclip it without too much fumbling. At last, at last, he could drink his fill of her amazing body.

Zeke's mouth felt hot against her sensitized nipples, and Tara dragged in air, feeling as if every drop of oxygen had been sucked out of the hallway. The wall felt cool against her back, but where his mouth touched, all was flame.

It threatened to devour her as he undid her blouse all the way to her waist. She responded by ripping the buttons open on his shirt, her shaking hands heedless of doing damage, wanting…needing…the touch of skin on skin. Under the hands she splayed across his chest, he felt smooth, tanned, hard as a rock. She explored frantically, muscles sliding under her fingers like Braille, the need to touch him driving her to the point of madness.

Her touch felt like fire on his skin. Didn't she know how hard she was making this, how hard she was making *him?* Much more of this and no amount of guiding his thoughts elsewhere would be enough.

He slid his arms around her, trapping her hands between them, stopping the maddening feathering of fingertips against his chest before it was too late. He had waited so long for this to happen that he wanted it to be good between them. Better than good, superlative.

That he might be staking a claim, alpha male to alpha female, he didn't like to consider. But there was a distant awareness of needing to brand her as his own, warn off all other contenders. If it made him a primitive, then all men were primitive, he decided, because he had yet to meet one who wasn't driven by the same need.

To perdition with analysis, he declared inwardly. This was a time to feel, not think. He kissed her fiercely, deeply, plunging his tongue into the moist cavern to seek out and twine with hers in a sinuous dance that ignited fires of response all the way to her core.

He wasn't gentle. He was finally getting the message that she didn't want him to be. Tara knew she wanted to be possessed by him in the truest, most elemental sense. Only then would she know that he had truly come home to her.

"We'll go into the living room," he said. When she nodded agreement, he towed her by the hand into the larger room. The curtains were half drawn against the hot afternoon sun, creating a narrow swathe of gold that burnished the carpet all the way to the plush, velvet-covered sofa.

Along this sunlit path he led her, her heart pounding with anticipation. When they reached the sofa, he let her go and stood back. "Now get undressed for me."

The order thrilled her with its unspoken promise that if she didn't obey, he would gladly do the honors for her. For a moment she was tempted to refuse, provoking him into stripping away her resistance along with the layers of clothing. But she didn't want to wait for him that long, so she meekly shed the unbuttoned blouse and bra, letting them drop to the floor so she was fully revealed to him from the waist up. "Is this what you want?"

His answering growl told her it wasn't nearly enough, but she knew a sudden moment of shyness as her hand went to the zipper of her pants. She hesitated, feeling like a bride on her wedding night, until she reminded herself that this was Zeke, for goodness' sake. Zeke, who had known every part of her more intimately than any man on earth, and who would again very soon.

The thought was enough to banish shyness, and she slid the zipper all the way down, stepping out of the designer pants and letting them join her other clothing on the floor. That left only a tiny band of lace around her hips.

Zeke's fingers went to it, tugging impatiently. "This, too."

She met his smoldering gaze with a challenging one of her own. "When I'm ready."

"Still don't know who's boss, do you?" he teased.

She loved this part of the game. It was the only time in her life that she willingly surrendered control to him because the fantasy was so enticing. She tossed her head back, letting her hair spin in a curtain around her bare shoulders. "I don't see any boss here, only you."

He crossed his arms over his bare chest, his shirt hanging loose around his shoulders. Her throat dried at the sight of his magnificent torso. He was a big man. In every way, she saw as he shifted restively, his trousers suddenly fitting very snugly indeed. "It seems you've unlearned everything I ever taught you while I was gone. I'm going to have to start the lessons from scratch."

She veiled her eyes with long lashes. "You and who's army?"

He didn't bother answering, but lifted her bodily and set her down against the sofa cushions. The velvet covering brushed her naked back, sending thousands of messages of desire like tiny arrows scattering through her. She gasped as he ripped the tiny scrap of lace from her hips, dropping the pieces on the floor. "Hey, they cost a fortune."

"I'll buy you more. Right now, they're in my way."

It was how she liked him best, running the show—well,

this show, anyway. She might be an independent woman, managing her own life in every other way, but she loved it when Zeke took control and loved her into submission. She began to melt inside at the thought of what was to come.

When he stilled above her, she looked at him in confusion. "What is it?"

"If we do this…"

If? She could no more stop now than she could fly. It alarmed her to think that he could. "What?"

"No regrets, no promises," he stated.

It was the grown-up way to do things, and he was reminding her that it was her choice as much as his. There was only one possible answer. "No regrets," she agreed, wondering if she was being entirely truthful with herself. It was evidently true for Zeke and she was astounded by how much it bothered her. But not enough to send him away, when every part of her begged for his touch.

In a flash, she accepted that her way hadn't worked. Why not try it his way, accepting only what he was willing to give on his own terms, without demanding forever? She only hoped she could live with the consequences.

For now it was almost impossible to think of the future when her entire concentration focused on the present and what he was doing to her. "Oh, Zeke, love me please, it's been so long."

His eyes flashed as he threw her own words back at her. "When I'm ready."

He *was* ready, she saw with a thrill of excitement as he discarded his remaining clothes and threw them onto a chair. But he wasn't about to put her out of her misery just yet. There was more, much more, sweet torment to be endured first. She saw the promise of it in his eyes as he lowered himself to the couch, and shivers of delicious anticipation gripped her.

The sofa was wide and deep and gave under his weight as

she shifted to make room for him alongside her. Kneeling on one knee and keeping one foot on the floor for balance, he began to caress her with slow, eddying strokes that sent liquid fire racing through every part of her. Instinctively she arched toward him and he slid his arms under her to lift her against him.

She linked her arms around his strong neck, feeling corded muscle under her fingers. His kisses rained over her face and neck, then he found her mouth and claimed it for his own.

''I've waited a long time for this,'' he whispered.

Her breathing came in short, almost painful gasps. If he didn't make love to her soon, she would explode. But she forced herself to match his pace, knowing the waiting would make the pleasure all the more rewarding, if she could only survive it. ''Is it worth the wait?''

''We'll soon see.''

He tugged a cushion under her head and slid another under her hips, then began the most torturous experience she had ever endured. Pleasure so extreme it verged on pain gripped her as he began to explore every inch of her. He wasn't content to look, but caressed every part of her, until she wanted to cry out with the volcanic needs he was building inside her.

She knew her breasts and hips were lusher and rounder than he would remember. Motherhood had left its own marks but she wasn't entirely unhappy with them. She knew the extra curves looked more voluptuous, but had never felt more of a woman as Zeke paid homage to her in the most primeval way.

When his attention shifted lower and lower, she felt tears bead her cheeks at the pure ecstasy of what he made her feel. She dug her fingers into the velvet as he traced lazy circles on the skin of her inner thighs, going deeper and deeper each time until he was a part of her. It was impossible to resist, not that she wanted to. Her muscles quivered and jerked until she felt a cry wrench from her and her back arch as she plunged into a raging river of sensation.

"Definitely an improvement," he murmured.

She fought her way back to reality with a supreme effort, conscious that her entire body ached with pleasure-pain. He sounded so in control of himself that she wondered if the sense of abandonment was all one-sided. Then she saw the dark torment in his hooded gaze and knew he was fighting a supreme battle with himself to give so much to her, without taking anything for himself yet.

This was a new side of Zeke and the discovery moved her beyond words. He touched a finger to the dew beading her lashes. "What's this? Am I hurting you?"

"Never," she said on a strangled breath. "They're only tears of joy."

"Then I'll brace myself for a flood because we've barely begun," he promised. He traced a line along her body. "You were always beautiful, but now..."

She regarded him in surprise. "It isn't often that words fail you."

"It doesn't matter. There are other senses besides speech."

"Like touch." He began to caress her and fresh waves of sensation radiated through her.

"And scent." He buried his face in her hair, breathing in the fragrant strands. Her own sharp intake of breath filled her with the musky male scent of him, mingled with sweat and a trace of something spicy he'd used earlier in the day. She hadn't realized that scent alone could be such a powerful aphrodisiac.

"And sight." He pulled back so he could drink in the sight of her lying beneath him. He didn't need to remind her that looking could be exciting. Watching desire infuse Zeke's expression, and knowing she had put it there, made her feel weak and powerful all at once.

"You're forgetting taste," she said on a sigh of delight.

Holding his face in her hands, she began to touch her tongue to his face, darting to his mouth and away before he could capture her in a kiss. He tasted of salt and skin and myriad man flavors that seared her taste buds. "Mmm, nice."

His gaze flashed an answering challenge. "If it's taste you want, I'm happy to accommodate you."

True to his word, he flattened his palm over her stomach and began to taste his fill. When his questing tongue encircled each nipple, she felt like molten lava and her head thrashed from side to side. Was it possible to die of pleasure?

"Now *this* is nice." Just when she thought he had completed his taste exploration of her body and it was safe to breathe again, he slid lower so he could drink from the essence of her femaleness. When she started to moan he said, "It's all right, just let me. Let me."

She didn't know how to do anything else. As of this moment he owned her body and it was his to do with as he chose. He seemed to know what she needed better than she did herself, so she gave herself up to the dizzying mindlessness of the moment, distantly recognizing that she was giving herself to him more truly now than she had ever done before.

Zeke sensed it, too, and marveled at the change. Knowing that she had given birth, he had expected physical changes in her, but not this other. Not the complete trust he sensed her placing in him now. It was as if she had let him make love to her before, but without really surrendering her essential self. The control thing had been a game between them. Whatever they pretended, she had never truly ceded control to him. But she did so now and it thrilled and humbled him to see it happen. It made him gentler, more aware of how easily he could hurt her when she was this open and vulnerable to him.

Straining to maintain his own control, he gave her everything in his power, rewarded by her moans of delight and little moves of resistance that weren't really resistance at all.

It was time, he felt as the thin cord of his control stretched to breaking point. "Hold on to me," he urged as he swung his leg across her quaking body and eased himself carefully into her. Her arms closed around him.

He didn't know what else he had expected to be different since the baby, but he hadn't expected to be sheathed as deliciously tightly or hotly as this. It took every ounce of remaining control not to plunge himself aggressively into her, in a sort of triumphal homecoming.

He felt the sweat bead his brow with the effort of holding himself back, but he forced himself to take it as slowly as he could, tantalizing her until her cries and whimpers told him she was ready. Only then did he give in to his own need for satiation, plunging into her with all his power, carrying her with him to higher and higher planes of sensation.

"I love you," Tara moaned through clenched teeth, her fingers digging into his back as she arched against him.

Even in the throes of passion, he felt himself tensing automatically as her words threatened to tangle him in a web of commitment and obligation he rejected instinctively. But it was too late to stop the tidal wave now as it rolled relentlessly onward, before finally crashing to the shore.

It was as if they had never been apart, Tara thought in astonishment. During the long year of waiting—and she faced facts, that's what it had been—she had often speculated on how it would be if he came back. Now he had, and it was better than she could have imagined.

In his dizzying exploration of the senses he had overlooked one. Hearing. She gloried in it now as she lay beside him, listening to the soft susurrus of his breathing, such a warm, reassuring sound against a backdrop of familiar city murmurings. She also heard, or felt, the drum of her own heartbeat, steadier when compared with the frantic beat Zeke had inspired. Just thinking of how wonderful it had been, the beat quickened again.

Careful not to disturb him, she eased onto her side and looked at him. He lay facing her with his eyes closed. Unable to resist, she ran a hand down his hard, muscular flank and felt a quiver of response.

His eyes opened. "Keep doing that and we'll be here all day."

"Does it matter?"

"I'm a working stiff," he reminded her, not sounding especially concerned.

She grinned. "So soon?"

He tried to look stern but his eyes danced. "I'm not so old that I need a decent interval to recover."

The need to make up for all the time they'd lost made her reckless. "Prove it."

"Minx." He kissed her face, her throat, her eyelids. "Do you have any idea what you do to me?"

If it was a fraction of what he did to her, pity help him. She shook her head. "You'll have to show me, I'm a slow learner."

"It didn't feel like it a little while ago."

"That was then, this is now."

She saw him fight with himself and tried to mask her disappointment when he shook his head. "I have to go."

"It's Saturday." When they were together—she forced herself not to think "the first time" although she felt it threatening to creep in—he had often worked on weekends. "You don't have to go to the paper right this second, do you?"

"I should." His elusive contact at the hospital had promised to call him between four and five. But he couldn't make himself stir. The call would be rerouted to his cell phone so there was no need to worry about missing it. But he didn't want Tara to overhear the call. Good news or bad, he wanted to break it to her in his own way. "What about you?"

"I'm attending a charity auction for Model Children tonight. You can come with me if you want to."

She said it casually, but felt her breath freeze as she waited for his reply. After a heartbeat, he said, "I may do that."

"It's black tie."

"I'll drag the tux out of mothballs just for you."

His words sent a thrill of response washing through her, even as she warned herself not to read too much into them. So he had a free evening, so what? It wasn't going to rekindle what they'd lost. Nothing could do that, not even sublime sex.

She remembered something else and levered herself onto one elbow so she could see his face. "Why did you come to see me today?"

He walked his fingers down her hip and she shivered. "For this."

She knew him well enough to recognize an evasion when she heard it. "No, really."

"Really." He kissed her eyelids closed and pulled her against him. His body felt cool and deliciously hard against her softness. She felt him harden even more as she snuggled against him. "If there was another reason, you drove it right out of my head."

He was doing the same to her, she thought dizzily. The sofa was wide but not wide enough for her to roll away from him and she didn't especially want to. There was a world of comfort in his arms. A world of delicious sensation, too. Arousal began to spiral through her all over again and she reached up, seeking his mouth.

He touched a finger to her lips. "You must know how much I want you," he insisted, "but I'm having a hard enough time convincing myself to get up from this couch as it is. You bewitch me, Tara."

"And you, me." She had been sure she would never let him make love to her again but it had taken so little to destroy her resolve. One touch, one kiss, and she was his again. In horror, she remembered murmuring something as he took her to the brink of ecstasy. Had she really said she loved him? It was the last thing Zeke would want to hear.

Maybe he hadn't. Or had dismissed it as the throes of passion talking. Why had she said such a stupid thing when she knew his background made him reject such declarations? "Zeke..." she began diffidently.

He pressed the finger to her lips again, silencing her. "No regrets, no promises," he reminded her. "Can't we simply enjoy what we have without complicating things?"

She knew what he meant by "complicating things" and had willingly agreed to his terms, so she had no one but herself to blame if she couldn't live with her bargain. "I know, but..."

He silenced her by covering her mouth with his, his kiss so deep and satisfying that she felt herself slipping over the edge again. He pulled back slowly, giving her time to recover. "Thank you," he said gruffly.

She felt puzzlement invade her expression. "For what?"

"For being you. For giving me so much. I don't deserve you, Tara."

"This isn't about who deserves what. It's about two people who have something to give each other. It's very, very mutual," she said.

"Exactly my point," he said on a small sigh.

She wanted to hit him. By playing devil's advocate, he had forced her to admit that she had gained as much from the experience as he had. Therefore there was no obligation on either side, and no commitment. It dawned on her that by "no promises" he had meant exactly what he said. She shouldn't be surprised. He had made no secret of preferring to live for the day. That much, at least, hadn't changed.

"Have I hurt you?" he asked. "It's the last thing I wanted to do."

"You haven't," she assured him. If anything, she had hurt herself, fantasizing about something that could never be. "Remember my friend Whitney Lee?"

He looked baffled at the apparent digression. "The psychologist up on the Gold Coast?"

She nodded. "Whitney has a sign in her office that says nobody can make you feel anything without your consent."

"It's true, of course."

Was it? She wasn't sure that the range of sensations Zeke had made her feel were truly consensual. She had agreed to let him make love to her, but his total mastery of her mind and body had taken her beyond simple permission into completely uncharted territory. Could she truly say he had made her feel so glorious? Or had she let herself be borne aloft on the strength of her own needs and desires?

She couldn't hold Zeke entirely responsible for sweeping her off her feet when she was such a willing accomplice. Yet she knew she wasn't in complete control of herself around him, either. Taking responsibility for one's own life was hell, she decided, banishing doubt into a far corner of her mind. Maybe he was right. Living for the moment was a lot simpler.

"Do you want to take the first shower?" he asked.

What she wanted was to stay right where she was, in the warm circle of his arms, but he was already levering himself off the couch. He stretched his full length, his fingers brushing the blades of the ceiling fan, and her heart almost stopped at the sight of his naked magnificence. "I think I'd better," she agreed, wondering if she should make it a cold one. No reason it shouldn't work as well for a woman as it supposedly did for a man.

He brushed her forehead with his lips. "This is just like old times."

Alarmingly so, she thought, suddenly fearful. She made an effort to scramble to her feet and pulled in a steadying breath. "I'll have that shower now."

"Do you still keep some champagne on hand?" he asked. "I didn't think to bring any with me."

"There's a bottle in the refrigerator," she said, relieved to hear that this had been as spontaneous for Zeke as for her.

"I'll pour it while you shower." Watching her head for the bathroom, gathering up clothes as she went, Zeke marveled at what they had just shared. He knew there was a risk that she would read more into it than there was, but he had done all he could to warn her. It didn't always help. Women were the worst creatures for mixing up lust and love. And he had no doubt this was simple, old-fashioned lust on both their parts. He wouldn't let it be anything else.

Without bothering to dress, he went to the kitchen and found the champagne in her refrigerator. Surveying the shelves, he was reminded of how organized she was. Crisp fruit and vegetables in their proper places, tubs of yoghurt. He lifted the lid. So that was what it looked like without a coating of green mold.

In his refrigerator, what passed for lettuce was usually limp and unappetizing and if you were smart, you sniffed the milk before using it. It was a vivid reminder of their differences. He took things as they came while Tara craved an orderly life that started with great sex but rapidly streaked ahead into marriage and family territory.

No chance. He set the champagne bottle down and rummaged in a drawer for an opener, pleased to see she still used the one he had given her after watching her trying to twist the cork off a bottle. She'd gotten there in the end but he hated to think of her lovely hands being so abused.

He could have opened the bottle the macho way, barehanded, but liked the feel of the metal grip in his palm, knowing she had held it last. Of course she may have given it to another man to use. It was a pretty high-handed assumption that there had been no one opening champagne with her since him. Zeke found he didn't much care for the idea.

The cork escaped with a satisfying pop but he stood still holding the bottle, wondering why the thought of her with another man bothered him so much. This was lust, not love, right? He hadn't been celibate since they'd parted and turn-about was fair play. It didn't make him feel any better.

She came into the kitchen as he was pouring the champagne into glasses. She had a bath sheet wound around her lithe body and was toweling her hair dry with another, and she looked if anything, more desirable than she had when she was naked.

Her gaze went to the countertop. "I think the glass is full."

"What?" In annoyance he saw that he had poured the champagne right over the rim of the glass. Cursing, he fetched a cloth and cleaned it up, then handed her a glass. "What shall we drink to?"

"Passion?" she suggested, knowing better than to suggest anything more meaningful or personal.

He gave a slow grin. "I'll drink to that."

The champagne slid down her throat like velvet. If it hadn't been for the certainty that Zeke took this afternoon at face value, she would have felt more content than she had in months. But wanting something more from him, knowing it was futile, robbed the champagne of its heady pleasure.

Losing the taste for it, she put the glass down. "I'd better not have too much or I'll be in no state for tonight's dinner."

"What's on auction?" he asked.

"All kinds of bizarre things, a walk-on part in an opera, the chance to fire the noonday cannon from Fort Denison, a romantic weekend away, fine art. Better bring your check-book."

"I don't see me in an opera, do you?"

She shook her head. Firing a cannon would be more his style. She refused to let herself think about a weekend away

with him. This afternoon had been risky enough. If she had
any sense at all, she wouldn't let it happen again.

She was working up the strength to tell him so when his
cell phone rang in the other room.

Chapter 7

It was a lucky accident that his phone was still in his pants' pocket in the living room, Zeke thought as he retrieved it. He had been wondering how to keep Tara from overhearing the conversation.

He looked toward the kitchen but she hadn't followed him. He flipped the phone open just before it switched through to the answering service. "Zeke Blaxland."

"Are you alone?"

The woman's voice was husky with fear. He wished he could reassure her that everything would be okay but he couldn't. Until the criminals were caught, she was vulnerable and they both knew it. He admired the courage it had taken for her to come him. As far as it was in his power to protect her identity, he would.

"I'm alone. Did you find out any more?"

"I'm sorry," she said in her liltingly accented English. "The baby boy was DNA tested soon after it was born. There's no possibility it could be your child."

Zeke hadn't known how much he was counting on a different answer until he felt the cold wind of despair howl through him. He felt drained, empty. Disappointed beyond belief. He had known the answer all along but had felt the need to double check, as much for his own peace of mind as for accuracy's sake. He was glad he hadn't shared his suspicion with Tara. No need for both of them to feel this shattered.

"Thank you," he managed to say. "What about the records of the other children? Did you—"

"Someone's coming, I have to go," she cut across him, her voice rising slightly. The phone went dead.

"Damn."

"What is it, Zeke?"

He looked up to find Tara watching him from the doorway. Her quizzical expression, coupled with the fact that her skin was still flushed from the shower, made her look sexy as sin. If ever there was an antidote for the disappointment he'd just endured, she was it. But she'd kill him if she found out he'd made love to her while waiting for such news.

For himself, it was no problem. Abstinence wouldn't have changed the result of the call one bit. But it was different for a woman. Had he told her what he was waiting for, she would have preferred to pace the floor and speculate endlessly although it wouldn't have changed anything, instead of losing herself in passion.

"Nothing," he said, hating himself for lying to her. "A lead I was following didn't pay off, that's all."

Something in his voice alerted her. "About the baby farming story?"

He nodded but couldn't meet her eyes. "My contact at the hospital was chasing some information for me. It didn't amount to anything."

She couldn't keep the tension out of her voice. "Did it have anything to do with our baby?"

"You know better than that."

She gripped the towel with both hands as if to hold herself together as much as to remain decently covered. She wasn't sure why she felt fearful suddenly, only knowing that she did. "Do I, Zeke?"

He gave a sigh, finally accepting that he wasn't about to get away with telling her any less than the truth.

Tara felt vindicated but more wary than ever, sure from his performance that whatever his news was, she wasn't going to like hearing it.

"Sit down," he said gently.

Like a cat walking on hot tiles, she crossed the room and perched on the edge of the sofa, trying to not look at the crushed places on the velvet cover. She made an effort to compose herself, made sure her breathing was steady, even managed a smile of encouragement.

It vanished the moment he said, "I've established beyond doubt that around the time you had your...our...baby, a group of hospital employees was switching sickly children for healthy ones, altering the records, and on at least one occasion, substituting a dead child for a live one." He passed a hand over his eyes, keeping it there as he said, "For a while I thought our baby might be one of the children taken."

Tara felt the walls of the room start to close in. She was grateful for the sofa beneath her as her legs turned to jelly. Could her baby have been switched for someone else's ailing child? The thought of a precious little life being bartered for cash made her sick to her stomach but if it meant her child was alive, she didn't care. She only wanted her baby. "Dear heaven, is it possible?"

"It turned out to be a false lead. I'm sorry," Zeke said quickly. "I didn't say anything before because I knew there was every chance it wouldn't be true, and I didn't want to raise your hopes before I heard from my contact."

Her eyes spat flames of fury at him. "So instead, you decided a little *distraction* was in order."

"I didn't plan on what happened. I only wanted to be somewhere nearby when I got the news, in case it turned out to be positive."

"When did you plan on sharing this with me?"

"I didn't," he said shortly. "I couldn't see the point."

"You couldn't see the point of telling me what you suspected, when my own baby was involved? Lord, Zeke, I know you have trouble handling your own emotions, but at least let me handle mine. How could you shut me out of the possibility of a miracle?"

Zeke's expression turned cold. "There is no miracle. It's true that another baby boy was born within minutes of yours, same black hair, similar medical profile. But hospital records show the mother had the baby DNA tested. It's her child beyond any shadow of doubt. Genetically, it can't be either yours or mine."

"Not it, he," she all but screamed at him. "To you, this may be a story, but those are living, breathing children, one of whom happened to be mine."

"I didn't tell you what I was doing because I was afraid you'd turn hysterical on me."

She dug her fingers into the velvet cushions, knowing she was only a hairbreadth from raking them down his handsome face. "I'm not hysterical. I'm as mad as hell. I can't believe you made love to me as if nothing else mattered, when all the time you were waiting to hear whether or not our baby could possibly be alive."

He raked stiff fingers through his hair. "I don't see how it would have helped to sit at opposite ends of the sofa chewing our fingernails."

"Maybe not, but I hate the thought that I was—" she almost choked on the words "—enjoying myself at such a time."

"Well, thank you, lady," he said on a heavily sarcastic note. "At least you're honest enough to acknowledge that you enjoyed it."

She felt hot color flush into her features. "That isn't the issue."

"Then what is?"

"The fact that you shut me out whenever emotions might be involved. It's what was wrong between us before, and nothing has changed."

"You mean I haven't changed," he said with a snarl. "You're probably right. Lucy said the same when she ended our relationship. Now you're also saying I'm an unfeeling bastard, so I guess I must be. If trying to protect you was wrong, then I'm guilty as charged."

She felt a familiar sense of frustration. "It wasn't wrong to protect me, only unnecessary."

"What should I have done? Tell me that."

"You should have told me what you suspected, as soon as you suspected it. My God, our child—alive? If I could have held on to that possibility just for a minute..."

"It was never possible," he said flatly. "It only seemed so because the circumstances were similar to the others. I knew it was a long shot from the start, but I had to check it out just in case."

An odd note in his tone alerted her. "You wanted it to be true, didn't you?"

"What do you think?"

"How can I know unless you're willing to open up and tell me?"

His brows slashed a dark line across his forehead. "This isn't going to work, Tara. Of course I wanted our baby to be alive. But spilling out my guts about what I've been going through for the last few hours won't make it so."

"I might have helped you to get through it."

Her softly spoken words arrowed through him straight to

the heart. "You did help me get through it," he confessed. "Holding you, feeling you so alive under me, no amount of discussing feelings could have done more."

"You say 'discussing feelings' as if it's a dirty habit. It isn't." She lifted her head. "And I don't appreciate being used as some sort of diversion therapy because you'd do almost anything rather than admit you have feelings."

"You were never a diversion, Tara. You must believe when we made love, it was the only thing on my mind."

"As I said."

He began to dress with jerky movements. "This isn't getting us anywhere. I came because I wanted to be near you when I got the news, good or bad. I didn't plan on making love to you, it just happened. You're probably right to suspect my motives. I'm not even sure I know what they are myself. But I do know this—I don't regret it as much as you evidently do."

She stared at him in amazement. "I don't regret it, Zeke. I only wish you had been more honest with me."

"Like you were with me?"

As his shot hit home she felt her stomach muscles clench. "Touché," she said in a voice barely above a whisper. "I guess I deserve that."

Fastening the buckle of his leather belt, he shook his head. "You deserve only the best, Tara, and I hope someone comes along who'll give it to you."

She fought to control a sudden flare of fear. "That sounds suspiciously like another goodbye."

Zeke finished buttoning his shirt. "It probably should be, but I said I'd escort you to that auction tonight and I will."

She could hardly bear to frame the question. "And then?"

"Then we'd better do the grown-up thing and try to part as friends."

How could she be friends with a man who meant as much

to her as Zeke? she wondered frantically. "I don't know if I can do that."

He nodded. "Me neither, so there's only one way to find out."

He finished dressing, slid his leather loafers onto his feet and came toward her. When he leaned over her, she flinched and he scowled. "Don't worry, I wasn't about to kiss you. I'm only reaching for my cell phone." He held it up as evidence.

He was probably right, they should part as friends now, while they still could. If they still could. The despair she felt suggested that it was already too late.

"I'll see myself out," he said as she started to rise. "I'll pick you up here at seven."

Moments later she heard the door close and the sound of his footsteps diminished down the path. She resisted the temptation to run to the window and pull the curtain aside to watch him leave.

She stayed where she was for a long time, her thoughts in chaos. Because her body ached from lovemaking, every move she made reminded her of him. She was furious with him for using sex as a distraction. But what did she expect? He had never pretended to believe in love, and she had never felt used before. But she did now, and couldn't fathom the reason for the life of her.

With all her heart she wished he had told her what he suspected. Even though it had proved to be a false hope, she could have shared it with him, shared the strain of waiting for news, hoping, believing in a miracle, at least for a little time.

Instead he had shouldered the burden alone, as he invariably did. When would he learn that loving someone meant sharing the good and the bad, for better or worse, as the ceremony said? There was good reason why couples agreed to share both. It created a unique bond between them.

She and Zeke had never known such a bond and probably never would. Was it why she had felt unable to tell him she was expecting his child? She had justified it by telling herself she didn't want to pressure him into staying with her when he didn't want to, but perhaps she was also guilty of shutting him out. She hated to think so, and would have liked to hold the hormones of pregnancy responsible, but knew in her heart that it wasn't the whole truth.

The truth was, they didn't have anything else but sex. A shiver rippled through her as she remembered just how good it was with him, but it wasn't enough. She hadn't told him about the baby because she had been afraid that if they took away the one thing they had together, there would be nothing left.

A sob burst from her throat. It was so simple and so dreadful. Why hadn't she seen it before? From her brother and sister-in-law, she knew the difference children made to a relationship. In one of their heart-to-heart talks, Carol had told Tara how difficult things had been after their first child was born. No matter how adorable the baby had been, she had come between Carol and Ben.

Carol's and Ben's love had helped them to weather the months of upheaval and sleep deprivation with their romance intact enough to have another child, proof that the experience was survivable. But what if great sex had been all they had? Would they still be together now? Or would they have fallen into one of those relationships where the passion dies but the couple goes on living in the burned-out shell?

Tara didn't want that so before telling him about the baby, she had waited for Zeke to show some sign that he loved her. In vain, as it turned out. He made love to her—pity help her, she still craved what only he could give her, even after all that had happened. But she recognized that the aching sensation deep inside her, making itself felt every time she moved, was more than physical.

"This isn't getting me anywhere," she said, snapping herself out of the reverie. She might be her mother's sentimental daughter but she was also her father's practical one, and there was work to be done. She had a speech to give at tonight's charity auction and it wouldn't prepare itself.

She had accused Zeke of distracting himself and now she was doing it. Trying to tell herself it was different didn't help. The only difference was that she meant to lose herself in work and Zeke had chosen to lose himself in her.

"I can't believe I bought an island," Tara said as they drove away from the black-tie dinner late that night.

"Only a part of one, the right to occupy it for a year," he corrected. "Not a bad buy for the price you paid."

"And it is on Phillip Island," she said dreamily. He knew that her grandparents had lived there and she had spent many childhood holidays with them. When the right to use the holiday home on the island for a year was auctioned, she hadn't hesitated. She could barely remember the details, only her determination not to be outbid for something she had wanted very badly.

She intended to spend every spare minute she could at the house. Maybe she could make an offer to buy it when the year was up. "It will be the perfect place to write my book," she mused. After their first, emotion-charged meeting, Zeke had decided to let Colin handle the rest of the negotiations, and she had signed the contract the previous week, so she was committed to the book now.

She was glad that Colin had accepted Zeke's excuse that he was too busy to be more than a silent partner in the publishing firm for the moment, because she wasn't sure she could have handled working with Zeke on a regular basis.

He shot her a speculative look. "Will you be happy shut away on an offshore island with only penguins and seals for company?"

"As somewhere to retreat to, yes, I will. In any case, Phillip Island is a modern community with a thriving population. It's far from lonely and bleak." She glanced into the back seat of his car. "At least I didn't get talked into buying a dog."

Hearing her tone soften, the puppy, a big-headed, clumsy-looking male with the distinctive blue-speckled coat of his breed, lifted his head and looked at her. "He's smiling at me," she said in astonishment.

"It's a trick of Blue Heelers," Zeke said. "They have the most expressive faces in the dog world."

"And this one's mother does heaps of television commercials, so he has personality built into his genes."

Because of its famous parentage, bidding for the puppy had been hotly contested. She remembered the intense expression on Zeke's face as he determinedly upped the ante every time another bidder got ahead of him, and glanced at him curiously. "I gather buying the dog wasn't a spur-of-the-moment decision?"

"It wasn't," he confirmed. "In one of the periods when my birth mother took me back to live with her, she bought me a dog."

"A Blue Heeler?"

He nodded. "A boy doesn't forget the first dog—the only dog—he ever owned. Meggs was my first real friend. He used to sleep beside my bed and follow me to school."

"Meggs?"

"After the Australian cartoon character, Ginger Meggs. The character is red-haired and my dog's coat was rusty-red-speckled."

"What happened to him?"

Such a long silence followed that she wondered if he was going to answer, then he said, "The same thing that happened to me. He was given away when my mother got tired of playing happy family with us."

Her hand went to his arm and she felt his muscles tense under the formal suit. "Oh, Zeke, that's terrible."

"At the time, I thought it was normal for a mother to get tired of having a kid around. But I did think she could have kept the dog."

"You must have missed him," She had condemned him this afternoon for being cut adrift from his feelings but how could he not be? He had learned from bitter experience that attachments didn't last. Eventually, he had stopped making them. She should know by now that she couldn't change his thinking.

"Why do you think I bid on Mungo?" he asked.

She felt her eyebrows lift. "Mungo? Is that going to be his name?"

He nodded. "It's Aboriginal for silent. The fuss of the charity auction must have bewildered a six-week-old puppy, but he didn't whimper or bark all evening."

She had thought he was extraordinarily well-behaved and said so.

"Blue Heelers are the most loyal, affectionate, hardworking animals in the world if you treat them right, aren't you, Mungo?" Zeke said.

As if to disprove his name, the puppy sat up and barked, an eager, high-pitched sound that made Tara laugh. "Won't he be a bit restricted in an apartment?" she asked.

"I'm looking around for a house with a garden."

He didn't add "where I can put down roots" because he wouldn't see it that way. But she did. *Too late, too late,* her heart cried. They had talked about buying a house when they were together, but he had shied away from the commitment.

She had understood his reluctance to set up house with her, when all his experience told him it wouldn't last, but it hurt to think he would do it for his dog. What did that say about their relationship?

They didn't have one, she reminded herself on a heavy

outrush of breath. All they'd had was good sex and a pleasant, if stilted, evening in each other's company. "Thank you for escorting me to the auction," she said formally.

He glanced sideways at her. "I'm sure you wouldn't have had to attend alone."

She'd had invitations, but nothing she was prepared to share with him, because they meant nothing to her. Affecting a shrug, she said, "Maybe, but your enthusiasm for the auction made it more enjoyable."

"I love auctions, the excitement, the challenge, the competitive atmosphere."

She laughed but felt uneasy because the appeals he listed didn't sit well with her own beliefs. "This was for charity, not life and death," she said lightly.

He turned serious. "I had another reason for wanting to be there. Mrs Beresford-Davis."

"I thought I saw you talking with her during the cocktails," Tara commented. "She was probably avoiding me because she felt guilty for letting Model Children down after saying she would support us."

"I think you'll find she's changed her opinion," he said, surprising her.

"How do you know?"

"Let's say I twisted her arm a little." After Tara had told him what happened when the woman read the column, he had been determined to fix things. He went on, "I wanted to set the record straight, so I assured her that I consider your charity above reproach."

"Oh, Zeke, thank you."

"No need, since I created the problem in the first place."

It was an extraordinary admission. "The column wasn't particularly kind to charities, but you only said what you believe."

"I still believe it. The world is full of do-gooders whose

main beneficiary is themselves. I don't resile from that, but I concede that your group isn't among them.''

She felt herself tense. ''Because it's my group?''

''Because I've investigated, and every cent your people raise goes directly to help the kids who need it. Not all organizations can say the same.''

It was a small victory but she rejoiced in it nonetheless. It wouldn't change his opinion about their relationship, but it was something.

''Zeke, turn left here,'' she said on a sudden impulse.

He looked at her with a mixture of confusion and annoyance. ''We're almost at your place.''

''I know, but I want to show you something.''

''You do know it's after midnight?''

She nodded, well aware of the time. She had a 9:00 a.m. appointment with a photographer to take publicity photos of her with a school group who were donating their pocket money to Model Children. It wouldn't do to turn up with shadows under her eyes, but the detour was worth it.

With a mutter that sounded suspiciously like ''women,'' he spun the wheel around. Soon they were cruising along a darkened avenue toward a small park with an arched entryway.

''Pull up beside the archway,'' she instructed.

Mercifully asking no more questions, Zeke complied. She glanced into the back seat, pleased to see that the puppy had gone to sleep.

When she got out of the car, Zeke followed and she led him under the arch. It was too narrow for two people to pass without touching, and her senses rocketed to alert as soon as his hard body brushed hers.

She had dressed for the charity auction and dinner in a flowing Aloys Gada gown of fuchsia silk that left her shoulders bare except for an amethyst pendant encircling her throat. The pendant had been a gift from Zeke and she had hesitated before putting it on. She needn't have worried. If he noticed or even remembered giving it to her on the first anniversary of their meeting, he hadn't commented.

He *was* aware of her touch, she noticed, because he snapped away from her as if burned. A tiny flame of satisfaction leaped inside her until she forcibly quelled it. This afternoon had given her ample proof of how much he still desired her. But as long as it was all they shared, it would never be enough.

"In New York, this is called taking your life in your hands," he said as she led the way through the darkened park, skirting beds of roses that perfumed the night air.

"It probably is in Sydney, too," she admitted, although when he was at her side, she couldn't feel afraid of anything. "We're almost there."

She stopped alongside a sandstone wall studded with plaques and small niches, some filled with flowers. The wall was surrounded by roses. She breathed deeply, as much to steady her chaotic emotions as to enjoy the perfume. Her fingers brushed one of the plaques. "This is for Brendan."

Zeke made a low, choking sound. "What is this place?"

"My brother told me it was established by a group of women whose babies had died either through miscarriage or at birth. They wanted society to recognize their children as having lived, so they raised the funds for this memorial garden."

She turned to him. "After I lost the baby, my brother wanted me to join their group. I argued, thinking I could handle it alone, but I couldn't."

She bowed her head, remembering how low her spirits had needed to sink before she'd accepted even her brother's help, although as an obstetrician, he understood what she was going through. Containing her grief deep within her, she had refused to believe that talking would help. Her baby had died.

There had been a service and a cremation. How could talking about it make a difference?

Then Ben had brought her to this beautiful, peaceful place to show her that she was far from alone. A dam had burst within her. She had finally shared her pain with him, and begun to heal. Placing Brendan's ashes here had given her the peace she'd needed.

She became aware of Zeke standing as still as a statue with his hands pressed against the wall. His shoulders were rigid. She knew better than anyone how he must feel. "It's all right," she said, knowing how inadequate it sounded. "It gets better."

He looked at her bleakly. "How did you stand it?"

"I didn't at first. Carol and Ben helped me. Ben told me about other patients who'd been through the same thing, and then he brought me here. But in the end, you get through it by yourself, one day at a time."

He grimaced. "When you told me, I wanted to kill you for keeping it from me. This makes it painfully real, somehow."

"That's the whole point," she explained. "The loss will always be painful, but this memorial proves that our child existed. One of the mothers in the support group Ben runs told him she hated people telling her how lucky she is to have two healthy children, as if they compensate for the one she lost to miscarriage. She loves her living children dearly, but she sees herself as a mother of three, not two."

"Is that how you see yourself, as a mother?"

"I was for a time," she said simply.

He bent and studied the plaque that read, simply, Brendan, and his birth year. When he straightened, his eyes glittered and his chest heaved with the effort of containing his emotions. For a heartbeat she wondered if he might share with her what he was feeling.

Then he released a long, shuddering sigh and she saw the

shutters come down again. Disappointment threaded through her. It wasn't going to happen.

What had she expected? she asked herself angrily. That visiting the memorial would allow him to truly connect with her? She may as well wish for the moon.

He surprised her by asking, "What do you think our son could have been? A doctor curing cancer? A rocket scientist?"

"A journalist like his dad?" she added, choking as her throat threatened to close. A glimmer of hope tried to shimmer through her but she rejected it. Zeke was what he was. No amount of wishful thinking was going to change reality.

He looked pensive. "His dad. That sounds so strange."

"It's not strange. You would have made a good dad."

"How do you know, when I don't?" The fierceness in his voice brought her head snapping up. "How could I be a father to anyone, when I never had a father of my own as a role model?"

"Zeke, I didn't mean..."

She reached for him but he shrugged off her hand. Bringing him here had affected him, she saw, but not in the way she had hoped. She saw sadness for the child he would never know, but also anger directed at himself. "It wasn't your fault your father wasn't there for you," she said.

"Before you tell me there was nothing I could have done, don't you think I've told myself so a million times? As a grown man, I know better than to think if I'd been a better child, my dad might have wanted me."

She heard what he didn't say, that inside him lived a little boy who would never be convinced. "I shouldn't have showed you this," she said regretfully.

He gestured in negation. "It's a fitting memorial for a brief life." His voice began to break. "I only wish I'd been here."

"Me, too." No amount of saying she was sorry was going

to give him back that opportunity. All they could do was go on.

Suddenly he bent over the memorial to retrieve something. "Do you come here very much?"

"I haven't for a couple of weeks. Why?"

He held up a single rose, its stem encased in a narrow tube, the kind florists used to keep individual blooms fresh. "Then you didn't leave this in the niche beside Brendan's plaque?"

"I don't usually bring flowers. Maybe it slipped from another plaque."

He shook his head. "It was too firmly lodged. It was placed there deliberately."

A chill traveled down her spine. "Placed by whom?"

"Someone who knows you?"

"Hardly anyone knows about the baby, except my brother and his wife and the medical staff. And my mother. I told her about the baby, but not about this place."

"Curiouser and curiouser," he quoted. "It's either a case of mistaken identity, someone leaving the flower at the wrong plaque, or we're not the only ones mourning our child."

"It has to be a mistake," she insisted. Anything else was too bizarre to contemplate. "What other explanation can there be?"

His fingers tightened around the rose's slender stem. "I don't know, but I intend to find out."

Chapter 8

As they headed back to the car, Zeke held the rose between thumb and forefinger as if protecting evidence, while Tara saw it for what it was, a flower left in the wrong place by mistake.

"Just let it go, please," she implored, hoarse with frustration. She held the tears back, refusing to break down in front of Zeke. She didn't know what she had expected from him, but it was a more emotional response than the one she was getting.

"You've just visited our child's memorial. Doesn't it mean any more to you than another piece of your precious puzzle?" she demanded.

"Not if there may be a connection," he said through clenched teeth.

"There isn't," she snapped as unshed tears burned the backs of her eyes. "I brought you here because I thought it would help give you some sort of closure, not to give you a new lead on your story."

In the park's dim lighting, his eyebrow canted upward, giving him a vaguely devilish look. "Closure? You've had months to mourn our child, yet you expect me to get over it just like that?"

"I didn't mean—"

"I think you did," he cut in dangerously. "You hate sharing this with me even now, don't you?"

She forced herself to meet his gaze. "That's crazy."

"Is it?" He made a sweeping gesture around them. "We shared something important, Tara. We made a baby together. I have to deal with that fact before I can begin to think of closure. You accused me of not sharing my emotions with you, and you're probably right. I haven't had much practice at it in my life. But this time you're the one who excluded me every step of the way."

Had she unconsciously tried to keep the baby to herself? She had told herself she was doing the right thing, but now she started to doubt. Had she kept silent because she didn't want to compel him to stay with her, or because she didn't want to share the experience? Not sure she could give him an honest answer, she said nothing.

"It's easier to accuse me of being cold and heartless than to accept that you didn't really want me sticking around at all," he said.

She was glad of the dim light to hide the coldness she felt invade her features. "It can't be true."

"Can't it? You told me you didn't have much of a relationship with your own father. You wouldn't have that problem if it was just you and the baby."

"I wanted my baby to have a father," she said in defence of herself.

"*Your* baby, Tara? It's an odd way to put it when I'm standing right here."

How well she knew it. Even in the face of the greatest mental turmoil she had experienced, she felt heat radiating from him into every part of her, making her ache for him. Telling herself she shouldn't want it didn't lessen the force of her desire.

She willed herself to calmness. "I never wanted to hurt you, Zeke."

"You didn't. What I feel since you told me is good, old-fashioned anger."

She couldn't blame him, although the intensity of it alarmed her. "You have the right, I suppose."

"You bet I do. After all we'd been to each other for over three years, I still don't understand how you could keep something as important as your pregnancy from me."

"Telling you felt as if I was trying to blackmail you into staying. Then afterward, I couldn't bring myself to admit how badly I'd failed."

A deep frown slashed across his forehead. "What do you mean, you failed?"

She lowered her lashes. "There had to be something I could have done differently."

His hands descended to her shoulders as if he wanted to shake her but was restraining himself. "That hardly sounds like a medical opinion."

"It isn't, it's my own."

"You must know it's crazy."

Her eyes flew open and she saw the hardness in his stance soften a fraction. "I do, but it doesn't stop the thoughts coming back. My father..."

Still frowning, Zeke turned her to look at him. "What does this have to do with your father?"

"If everything I did wasn't perfect...if I failed at something...." Her voice trailed off and she clenched her teeth to stop them chattering. It wasn't cold in the park but she felt a chill reach out to her from long ago.

"Go on."

Confusingly, she felt warmth and strength flow into her

from his touch. "He punished me to remind me that I could do better."

In the lamplight, she saw Zeke's face twist in dismay. "He beat you?"

She shook her head, emotions flooding through her, gripping her so that the park receded as memory took hold. "Nothing so straightforward. He would simply treat me as if I was invisible. He kept it up sometimes for days, until I promised never to disappoint him again, just to get him to acknowledge that I existed."

"How could a man treat his own child so cruelly?"

"He's a perfectionist."

"More like a bloody sadist. People like yours and mine shouldn't be allowed to have kids."

She shook her head in determined negation. "They're not all alike. My mother used to speak to me as soon as Dad was out of earshot. She refused to let me suffer."

"You did anyway," he said harshly. "Being treated as if you didn't exist would have hurt anyone, but especially an innocent child."

"It made me terrified of failing," she said, still finding it hard to admit.

Zeke shook his head. "What happened to our baby wasn't a failure on your part. There was nothing you could have done," he said fiercely, still holding her. She longed for him to crush her against him and let her feel the warmth of his arms around her.

At the same time, she knew why he didn't. He might deny that he held her accountable for the loss of their child, but how could he not? She knew he was entitled, and his reassurances didn't silence the nagging voice in her head.

She sensed that the little girl within her was still afraid of enduring the silent treatment. Afraid of being abandoned. The word resonated through her thoughts and she remembered how for weeks after Brendan's birth, she had felt an almost overwhelming urge to go back to the hospital for him, as if he was capable of feeling as lonely as she remembered feeling when her father behaved as if she didn't exist.

It had been all she could do not to revisit the ward where she had last held the baby. For a time, she had wondered if she was going mad. Her doctor had assured her that her feelings were normal, urging her not to fight them, but to own them. How did you do that? She still wasn't sure, but she had battled on until the urge to look for her child had lessened. Now she came to the park instead, finding peace in the leafy quiet.

The last thing she wanted was Zeke defiling this special place with his suspicions and his tough, journalistic rationalism. "The adult part of me knows it wasn't my fault," she said as evenly as she could. "But sometimes emotions take over, particularly when your hormones are all over the place to begin with. At least, that's what my doctor told me."

"He's right. So don't let me hear any more about this being a result of your failure. While I was researching the series, I discovered that miscarriages and natal deaths account for a surprisingly large percentage of all births."

"It doesn't help when your child is among the statistics."

"No, it doesn't," he agreed, and she heard the raw edge in his voice. It came to her that he wasn't as unmoved by seeing the memorial as he pretended. Her heart ached for him as she knew only too well what he was going through. Why couldn't he share it with her, instead of fighting the feelings and focusing on things that didn't matter, like a flower left by mistake?

For the same reason she couldn't entirely let go of her illogical sense of failure, she thought. They both had baggage from long ago that made it hard for them to deal with things in the present. It was probably why they were better off apart.

"I'm glad you brought me here," he said on a low note. She nodded, finally allowing herself to lean against his hard strength. "You don't know how much I wish I could go back and do things differently."

"It means a lot to hear you admit it." He seemed to become aware that she was resting her head against his chest and a groan rumbled deep in his throat. His mouth descended to the top of her head and he kissed her gently, while his hands slid up her neck and under her hair, to sift the strands through his fingers.

As his hands brushed her sensitive nape, she shivered. She became vibrantly aware of details like the rustle of the breeze in the wattle trees, the crunch of gravel under her feet and most of all, the warm, spicy man scent of Zeke.

She turned her head slightly so her cheek was pillowed against his chest. The steady pulse of his heart vibrated through her and she knew she was far from over him, no matter what she tried to tell herself. It didn't make them any more right for each other, but it was the simple truth. She told herself she should move out of his arms before things got more complicated than they already were, but her limbs were curiously unresponsive.

He made the effort she was unable to summon, and set her away from him. "We should get back. It's late."

"And the puppy..." she said at the same instant, to cover the acute disappointment raging through her.

But nothing could quell that feeling inside her.

A week later, Tara greeted her sister-in-law warmly as she slid into a seat opposite her in the coffee shop. "Sorry I'm late," Carol began, "I got to court to discover that my client flew to Europe last night. She didn't realize she was supposed to appear in person, and thought sending her secretary was good enough. It took all my powers of persuasion to get the case postponed until I can get her back here."

Tara had been too preoccupied to notice the time passing but she made a sympathetic noise. "Tough case?"

Carol nodded. "Rich woman ripped off by penniless lover. He absconds with jewelry worth a mint and says she gave it to him. She claims to only want the valuables back but I think she'd prefer him under house arrest at her mansion."

Tara laughed. "Quite a tangled web."

"If her family weren't long-standing clients, I wouldn't get involved. My guess is she plans to make him sweat as long as possible then drop the suit, hoping he'll come back to her out of gratitude."

"Do you think the boy will come back to her?"

Carol shrugged. "Anything's possible in a relationship."

Tara of all people, knew it was true. She had been a bigger fool over Zeke than she would have believed possible. She hid her face behind the menu and mumbled something about having the mushroom omelet and a small green salad.

"Make that two," Carol told the waiter when she came to take their order. Carol gestured toward Tara's black coffee. "One of those for me, too. I need the caffeine boost."

The waiter took their menus, leaving Tara with nothing to hide behind. She saw Carol make a swift assessment of her expression then groan softly. "Oh, Tara, don't tell me, you made it two out of two?"

Soon after Zeke returned, Tara had told Carol about driving him home and almost making love to him, adding that one out of two wasn't bad. Not more than a week later, she *had* allowed him to make love to her before accompanying her to the charity auction, and the ill-fated visit to the memorial. "How can you possibly tell?" she asked Carol uncomfortably.

"It was a lucky guess, but you just confirmed it."

Tara felt herself color. "Unfair tactic, counselor. I was beginning to worry that it showed."

Carol broke a bread stick in two and nibbled on it. "It does now I know what to look for. If I had to label it, I'd say you look more alive somehow."

The infuriating part was, she felt it, too. "Zeke has that effect on people."

Carol's eyebrow tilted. "On people?"

Tara felt her shoulders slump. "All right, on me."

She welcomed the arrival of their food as a distraction. "Physical attraction isn't enough to rebuild a relationship on," she said as much to herself as to Carol.

Carol grinned. "Repeat it often enough and you might start believing it."

Tara leaned across the table. "I have to believe it. I've moved on since Zeke. As well as my work with the foundation, I've got a book to write, and I've decided to go to Phillip Island to do work on it. Since I bought that crazy lease at the auction, I may as well put it to good use."

When she'd called to invite Carol to lunch, Tara had told her about signing the book contract, and buying the lease at the auction. Now Carol gestured with her bread stick. "It isn't crazy. If it makes you happy, what's wrong with it?"

Tara wasn't sure if what she felt amounted to happiness. A sense of something lacking nagged at her, but she told herself it was only the past, stirred up by Zeke's return. It didn't quell the arousal she felt at the thought of him, but it was a start. On the island, she might manage to erase him from her thoughts for good.

Carol forked salad on to her plate then gestured with the bowl. When Tara shook her head, her sister-in-law frowned. "A woman on a mission needs her sustenance."

In spite of herself, Tara smiled. "I'm going to write a book, not climb Everest."

"If you found writing as hard as I do, you'd think it was the same thing."

"Luckily I don't, so I'm looking forward to it."

Carol made a sooner-you-than-me face. "I'm thrilled for you, and I'll happily buy dozens of copies when your book comes out, but for myself, I'll stick to the law, thanks." She sobered abruptly. "On the phone, I got the impression that something else is bothering you. Want to talk about it?"

Tara drew patterns on the tablecloth with her finger. "You know me too well. Zeke found out about the baby. He found my name in the hospital records while researching the baby farming story."

Carol made a soft sound of sympathy. "I noticed that it was the same hospital so I'm not surprised that Zeke put two and two together. The timing puts you right in the middle of the story. How did Zeke take the news?"

Tara felt her eyes brim and blinked rapidly. "Hard. I knew it wouldn't be easy for him, but I didn't realize how much the idea of being a father appealed to him."

Carol looked surprised. "Isn't he against happy families?"

"He doesn't believe in them, and after his experience I can't blame him. That's why his reaction to fatherhood came as such a surprise. He reacted as if I'd taken something away from him, something he never believed he could have."

"You didn't, nature did," Carol reminded Tara when her voice began to shake. "He's going to need time to come to terms with it, just as you did. But I still have trouble picturing Zeke as a father."

Tara hated the tears that hovered so near the surface. She had believed she had her emotions under control at long last, but it seemed not. She pulled herself together with an effort. "You haven't seen him with his new puppy." She had also told Carol about Zeke buying the dog.

Carol helped herself to more salad. "Actually I have. I saw it on television yesterday, when he was interviewed about the baby farming story. Before the actual interview, they showed him in his office working on the computer, then outside playing with the dog in a park. Zeke looked the way Ben did when Cole and Katie were born, as if he never expected to feel so captivated by a helpless creature. Of course we're only talking about a dog, but from what I saw he has the right stuff to care for small, helpless creatures.''

Tara was gripped by a vivid image of Zeke on a blanket on the ground, playing with an infant. The room spun for a second until she got herself under control. It was a fantasy, nothing more. ''Did he look well?''

Carol's fork froze on the way to her mouth. ''Haven't you seen him since you told him about the baby?''

''Last week I took him to visit Brendan's memorial and...we had an argument.''

''Because you kept the truth from him?''

Tara nodded. ''Mostly, but there was something else, too. Someone had left a single rose in the flower holder on Brendan's plaque.''

Carol frowned. ''Do you know who it was?''

Tara had been hoping it was Carol, but her sister-in-law's reaction showed it wasn't. ''If it wasn't you or Ben, I can't think who else knows about the memorial but Zeke and me. It had to be a mistake. Someone probably left the flower in the wrong place.''

Carol's eyes narrowed. ''It seems unlikely, as all the plaques have the babies' first names on them. I gather Zeke doesn't agree with you.''

Tara leaned back in her chair. ''He's so caught up in his investigation that he's seeing conspiracies around every corner.''

Her companion's expression softened. ''Since the hospital involved is the same one you were in, and it all happened around the same time, is there any chance...''

''No chance,'' Tara cut in swiftly, on a knife thrust of pain. Since Zeke's story broke, she had seen some of the parents involved being interviewed on the evening news and in spite of herself she had felt consumed by jealousy. Their babies had been stolen from them and given to other families in exchange for large sums of money, but no matter how great their heartache, at least they had some hope of finding their children again.

On a radio interview she hadn't been quick enough to turn off, she had heard Zeke pledge to stick with the story until the babies were returned to their rightful families. The police were already following leads Zeke had turned up so it was only a matter of time before the people behind the whole thing were caught.

During the last few days she hadn't been able to turn on a talk show or a current affairs program without some mention being made of the crusade. It hadn't helped her peace of mind to have Zeke's face staring at her everywhere she turned.

The streets were papered with posters screaming Find My Baby, Please, the title of Zeke's series. Knowing him, she didn't doubt that he would find the stolen children and help the police bring the perpetrators to justice if anyone could.

For herself, Tara had no such hope. Zeke had checked out every possibility, including a baby born within hours of Tara's. If there was anything to be found, she knew he would have found it.

"There was one false lead," she told Carol, hearing her own voice catch. "But the parents had had the baby DNA tested and it was definitely their natural child. Zeke's contact at the hospital showed him a copy of the test results. There's no doubt."

Carol reached across the table, her hand covering Tara's. "I'm so sorry. I had hoped…"

"Me, too," Tara said. "That's why the single flower was so disturbing. Zeke seemed to feel it had to mean something. I haven't seen him since that night, except in the news when I can't avoid it," she told Carol.

Carol guessed what she'd left unsaid. "But you want to?"

"I suppose it makes me a complete idiot?"

Carol smiled. "No more than the usual human kind." She

looked at her watch. "I should get back to work, but if you want to talk some more, I'll call and postpone my next appointment. The nanny's with the children, so I can stay if you want."

As the host, Tara paid for their lunch, and shook her head. "Thanks for the offer but how does that song go? I will survive. I'll probably be stronger for it."

Carol regarded her warily. "In my line of work, I've seen people crack who should have held up under pressure. I've also seen people refuse to give in when doing it would ensure them the support they needed. Being strong isn't always a virtue."

"But it is sometimes a necessity." Tara stood up. "Thanks for letting me share this with you."

"Anytime. Goodness knows, you've been there for me often enough since I married your brother."

Tara smiled, thinking that Ben wouldn't appreciate being the subject of their sisterly discussions. But Carol knew she could rely on Tara's discretion, just as Tara relied on hers. She felt a small knot of tension dissolve. "Give the children my love."

"I will. They're still talking about the toys you brought when you came to dinner last week."

It had been the day before the charity auction, Tara remembered with a pang. As she hugged her sister-in-law, Tara tried not to feel jealous of Carol's happy family situation. She had work she loved, a husband who loved her, and two adorable children at home. But Tara had her own life, and it suited her. Mostly. "I will survive," Tara hummed determinedly as she headed back to her car.

She had driven for fifteen minutes before realizing where she was. She hadn't made a conscious decision to visit the memorial park, in fact she'd avoided it since the night she'd come with Zeke, but now she found herself outside the entrance without any clear idea how she got there.

She needed a few minutes of quiet contemplation, she told herself, and got out of the car. Moments later she was seated on her favorite bench close to the memorial wall. Afternoon sunlight glinted through the trees, creating small and oddly appropriate halos around the brass plaques. Contentment began to seep into her and she thanked the instinct that had guided her here.

A currawong's metallic two-note call echoed through the park, forcing her to smile. As a child, she'd been wary of the spindly legged black-and-white birds, refusing to go near them. Now she loved their peculiarly Australian sound. A kookaburra joined in the chorus, its raucous laughter further easing her tension.

She wasn't sure when her feeling of contentment began to erode, but she gradually sensed she was being watched. Uneasily she looked around. A man in dark coveralls was pruning a rosebush on the far side of the park. He looked up briefly then went back to his work. It was probably his presence she had registered.

But when she looked up again he had moved closer. He wasn't pruning the roses, he was merely fiddling with them to create that impression, she saw in a split-second assessment of his empty hands. Alarm coursed through her but she forced herself to stay calm. He could be checking them for bugs, anything.

He edged closer still and she decided enough was enough. As if it had been her intention all along, she rose and began to walk purposefully back to her car. He followed her and her steps quickened.

By the time she reached the park's arched entrance, she had the remote control in her hand and used it to unlock the car. By the time she slid into the front seat and engaged the central locking system, she was breathing like a marathon runner.

Her heart lurched as the stranger jogged up to the car and

pounded on the window. "Wait, I want to talk to you." She didn't hesitate, slamming the car into gear and roaring away, leaving him staring after her, his face a mask of frustration.

She didn't stop until she was safely home again. Telling herself the man got his kicks from accosting women in parks, but was probably harmless, didn't help. She began to wonder if Zeke was right and the mysterious flower did mean something, after all. Her hands shook as she picked up the phone and dialed Zeke's private number.

"Please be there," she murmured, her fingers drumming a tattoo on the tabletop as a recording announced that her call was being diverted to another number.

"Zeke Blaxland."

At the sound of his voice, she almost wept with relief. "Zeke, thank God."

"Tara, you sound terrible. What is it?"

"I feel terrible. I went to visit the park." She knew she didn't have to specify which one. "I was minding my own business, when a man followed me and tried to stop me driving off."

Instead of the reaction of shock she had expected, he let out a rush of breath. "What did the man look like?"

Didn't he care that she might have been attacked or worse? she wanted to scream at the phone. Instead he was ever the journalist, demanding facts. He was Zeke, she reminded herself, and took a steadying breath. "He was a head shorter than you, with sandy-colored, wavy hair almost to his collar," she said, dredging up details she hadn't been aware of absorbing. "His suntan looked fake, as if it came from a sunbed or a bottle." She shuddered, remembering.

"Bill Ellison," Zeke said down the phone.

"What? You know him?"

There was a slight hesitation then he said, "I should. I hired him."

She could hardly believe this. "You hired a pervert in a park?"

"He isn't a pervert. He's a private investigator and a good friend. He helps me dig up background information occasionally. After we found that flower, I asked him to keep an eye on things and report any suspicious activity."

"Why did he follow me and try to stop me from leaving?"

"I showed him your photo. He probably wanted to introduce himself." He paused for a moment, "Or else he had something to report."

Reaction began to set in and she pulled a stool toward her and slumped on to it. "What could he have to report? That the roses are in full bloom? There can't be anything else because there isn't anything. We have to accept it and go on." *He* had to accept it, she told herself.

He heard the rising note in her voice. "Are you all right?"

She almost laughed. "I'm perfectly fine. I was chased across a park by a strange man. It's every woman's idea of a good time."

"Are you at home?"

"Yes, but…" Sensing his intention, she started to say she was going out but he got in first.

"Stay there. I can be there in ten minutes."

"There's no need, I'm all right," she assured him but the phone went dead. He was on his way.

When the doorbell pealed, she thought of pretending she wasn't home, but he was quite capable of breaking the door down. She looked around frantically, then settled on mussing some cushions on the couch and opening a magazine to make it look as if she hadn't been pacing up and down, waiting for his arrival.

Not so long ago, she would have thrown herself into his embrace and they would have kissed deeply, she recalled, feeling her breath catch. It wouldn't have mattered if they'd seen each other hours or minutes before. Every reunion was like the first time. Now she fought the urge to go to him, instead fiddling with the pages of the magazine. "You didn't have to rush over here. I'm not in a Victorian swoon."

He dropped into a chair across from her, as elegant as a prowling cat, a very large, pantherish cat, she thought. He looked tired, as if the demands of his work had him approaching some sort of limit. That it might not only be his work, she wouldn't let herself consider.

"You sounded upset," he said.

Had it taken so little to bring him to her side? She made herself remember that this was all in a day's work to Zeke. He had hired the investigator in case the flower was tied in with his current story.

She shook her head, not sure what she was denying. "I was upset, but I'm getting over it. If your friend in the park had touched me, he'd probably be out cold on the grass by now."

His expression was amused but she saw concern darken his eyes and it gave her a completely unwarranted boost. "I'd forgotten you took those self-defense classes a couple of years ago, but I should caution you, Bill has a few moves of his own."

So did Zeke, she recalled, driving the thought away. This wasn't the time or the place. "It's surprising what you can do when you're cornered."

"I'm sorry you felt that way. I only asked Bill to investigate because I wanted answers."

She began to roll a corner of the magazine between thumb and forefinger. "You always want answers, Zeke, but they don't always exist."

He leaned forward, resting his bent arms on his knees. "A lot of people wanted me to think so when I started digging into the baby farming story. If it hadn't been for one employee with a conscience, I wouldn't have gotten past first base."

"Is she the anonymous contact you mentioned on the radio?"

His eyes narrowed. "How do you know whether my contact is male or female? I carefully avoided giving any clue to their identity."

Tara had spoken without thinking. "I don't know. I assumed it's the sort of situation that would trouble a woman more than a man."

He straightened and glowered at her. "Where on earth did you get that idea?"

"I don't know, I only thought…"

"That a man can't feel about a baby the way a woman feels? The way you feel?" he demanded, looking as if he was about to leap out of the chair and take her by the throat. He sounded as if he was talking about more than the story.

"Of course not." She thought of Carol's comment about the way he had treated the puppy, and had to suppress another image of him interacting with a small child. "Men and women regard attachments differently. You hear of more men walking out on their families than women deserting their children."

"True. The men are the ones driven to suicide or violence after being denied access to their children."

"There are no winners in these situations," she said, thinking of herself and Zeke. Fairness made her ask, "Is your informant a man?"

He shook his head, but looked gratified. "No admissions, even to you, sorry."

"I understand. Given the kind of people who would sell babies, your informant probably put themselves at great risk by coming to you."

He nodded. "More than you know."

She was relieved to have the discussion back on neutral ground. "What about the culprits?"

"The people we can identify are all small fish. The biggest

fish, the doctor who organized the whole baby swapping scheme, has gone underground, last heard of heading for South America. There's a former midwife at the hospital I'd like to talk to about records that were altered. So would the police, for that matter. But he's disappeared, too.''

She could see how the admission outraged Zeke's strong sense of justice. ''What about the babies?''

His expression cleared. ''We've had more success there. One of the children is due to be reunited with her real parents today. The story will be on the news tonight if you care to watch.''

Tara sensed his elation and rejoiced for him. ''I wouldn't miss it. What will happen to the people who handed over money in exchange for a baby?''

''One couple was arrested this morning. They carry the gene for cystic fibrosis and were too old to adopt, so decided to help themselves to someone else's child.''

''It must be terrible to be that desperate.''

Zeke frowned at her. ''Don't feel sorry for them. Their attorney has already started playing the sympathy card for all it's worth. Remember they allowed another couple to believe their baby died. They don't deserve an ounce of your pity.''

''You're right.'' She saw him flip open his cell phone. ''Who are you calling?''

''Bill Ellison, the private investigator.''

Tara swallowed hard. While they talked she had almost forgotten the man who had followed her. Now she wondered what he had been so anxious to tell her.

Chapter 9

Zeke listened for a few seconds then he closed the phone with a snap of annoyance. "Recorded message. He's turned his blasted phone off."

Relief flooded through her. The investigator's news couldn't be too urgent or he would have made an effort to locate Zeke. "Maybe he's gone home for the day," she said.

"Good thought," he agreed. He keyed in another number and waited, swearing again as he encountered what she gathered was another recording. He dropped the cell phone into his top pocket. "No luck there, either."

"Maybe he didn't have much to report, after all," she said. "You could be right, he was only trying to say hello."

Zeke's scowl deepened. "I don't have time to chase after him. When you called, I was on my way to the television studio to take part in a panel discussion." He consulted his watch. "Luckily the program is taped but the producer is probably pacing the floor, wondering where I am."

"I didn't intend to hold you up," she said.

"It was my choice. I wanted to be sure you were all right," he said. He rubbed his hands over his jaw. "After the week I've had, one more television interview more or less won't make any difference."

"You've become a real celebrity." She couldn't keep the pride out of her voice.

He heard it, too, and looked at her in surprise. Hadn't he expected her to care? They shared too much history for her not to feel proud of his achievements, especially this time, when his work had done so much public good. She said so.

A half smile ghosted across his face. "I doubt if the people who sold the babies will agree with you. After ten months, they probably thought they were home free."

She nodded. But for Zeke's efforts, those children might never have been reunited with their real families, she thought, feeling her blood chill. "The babies that were taken were too young to know they'd ever had any other parents."

"They will now." He stood up with an obvious effort. "The only downside of being a so-called celebrity is being accosted in the street by people who think they know you after seeing you on the news. Even doing the daily editorial for the morning show didn't attract this kind of attention."

Aware of the danger of straying into areas of intimacy again, she tried to sound light. "Poor baby. Do you have hordes of teenage women chasing you down the street demanding your autograph and trying to tear your clothes off?"

His shadow fell across her. "It's no joke. Yesterday I was in the men's room when a man stood alongside me and wanted to talk about the story."

He really did resent the attention, she understood. A lesser man would have reveled in it, but all Zeke wanted was to write his story and know he'd made a difference in people's lives. It was all he had ever wanted. "It will die down," she said, knowing he knew it as well as she did. They had both shared the limelight often enough to understand how it worked. "In the meantime, focus on the good you're doing."

His eyes flashed gratitude at her understanding. "I only wish there was more of it, but I got onto the story too late. The trail was already getting cold." He grimaced then said, "I'd better go." But he seemed reluctant to leave. "Can I see you tomorrow? I'd come after I finish the taping, but it's liable to go on until all hours."

His offer tempted her more than he knew. It would be so easy to welcome him back into her life with open arms, the way she had already welcomed him into her bed. But that way lay heartache on a scale she wasn't prepared to put herself through again. "I don't think so. I'm going away tomorrow."

"Going away where?"

It pleased her to see that he didn't welcome the news. It wouldn't change anything but she was woman enough to be glad he didn't want her to leave.

"I'm flying to Melbourne, renting a car and driving to Phillip Island to check out the cottage. If I like it, I'll stay for a few days. Then later, I'll arrange a longer stay and make a start on the book."

She felt his resistance to the idea of the trip as he frowned. "I'd rather you didn't leave Sydney until I speak with Bill Ellison."

Her temper flared. "And find out what? That I was right all along and some poor grieving relative left a flower in the wrong place. Leave it alone, can't you? This concerns our child, not your story, and having you poke and pry at it brings it all back. It hurts too much."

She hadn't intended to break down, but suddenly her breath came in great gulps and her eyes burned. She turned away, her knuckles whitening on the edge of the table as she fought for self-control.

"Don't, please, Tara. I don't want to distress you."

She kept her back turned. "Well, you're succeeding brilliantly. I wish I'd never taken you to the park in the first place."

"You're forgetting one thing. This involves me, too," he said quietly.

She swung around, feeling her eyes blaze. The censure froze on her lips at the undisguised suffering she saw on his chiseled features. He must be dead tired to let her see it, she thought, and steeled herself not to weaken, although she longed to offer him the comfort of her arms. "I see. You're getting even with me for shutting you out."

She recognized the moment when the shutters came down on the transparent feelings and he became Zeke Blaxland, Reporter of Steel, again. While it made him easier to deal with, she yearned for the other Zeke who had emotions she could reach out and touch. She'd had enough fleeting glimpses to know that *that* Zeke would be far easier to love, and far harder to leave. She should probably be thankful he didn't appear often.

"That's nonsense and you know it," he said tautly.

She swallowed the sympathy welling up inside her. His dismissal of her concern was so typical that she wondered if she had imagined the thoughtfulness of a moment before. "Call it nonsense if you like, but you can't grieve as long as you insist on clutching at straws. It only lengthens the process." She ought to know. She had fought against her loss with everything in her, only to discover that denial was as normal a part of grieving as eventual acceptance.

He nodded coolly. "Perhaps you're right, but I have to do this my way."

She almost laughed. "You always did."

He stepped closer. "Don't go to Phillip Island yet. Wait a few more days."

If she did, she would probably not go at all. "My flight is booked."

''At least tell me where I can reach you.''

She wished she had the courage to tell him she didn't want him to contact her, but the words refused to come and they wouldn't be true, anyway. ''There's a phone at the cottage. I don't know the number yet, but my cell phone number is still the same.''

Why did she tell him that? she wondered. She had practically invited him to get in touch. Why couldn't she make up her mind what she wanted?

As she berated herself, he went to the table and studied a map showing the location of the cottage, and the photographs that had been given to her as the successful bidder at the auction. She'd been looking at them before going to lunch with Carol. ''Is this the place?''

She nodded, wishing she'd had the foresight to put them away. ''It's not far from Cowes, where my grandparents lived after retiring from farming.''

He picked up a photo showing the cottage set against a vibrant seascape with seals swimming in the background. ''It looks beautiful. Peaceful and relaxing.''

She heard what he didn't say. Peace was at a premium in his life at present. She bit back the invitation trying to force its way past her lips. ''I think so. I haven't been back since my grandmother's funeral so I hope it hasn't changed too much.''

''Probably gotten busier like the rest of us,'' he said.

The slump of his shoulders and the wistful note she heard in his voice was her undoing. ''You could use some time in a place like that.''

Speculation lit the gaze he turned on her. ''Is that an invitation?''

She didn't know what it was. She only knew she could hardly stand seeing him like this. ''I only meant you look tired.''

''Concern for me, Tara?''

"I always was concerned about you. Not that you took much notice."

He glanced at the photographs. "Maybe I will, this time. How many bedrooms does this cottage of yours have?"

She felt tension grip her again. She had brought the question on herself by opening the way to this discussion, and it was too late to take it back. "Are you thinking of coming to the island?" she asked carefully.

"Do you want me to?"

Why did it always have to be up to her? He never deferred to her on anything else, except where their relationship was involved. Resentment bristled through her at being forced to take all the responsibility yet again. "You don't usually base your actions on my wishes. Why start now?"

"Why not?" He prowled restlessly around the room, picking up some of the small Capodimonte figurines she had collected over the years, inspecting then replacing them. He must have seen them before, but his actions suggested he was really seeing them for the first time. Was something similar happening to the way he saw her? she wondered. She dismissed the thought as fanciful. However much she wished it, Zeke wasn't going to change.

"After the taping and tonight's reunion, I could take a couple of days off and spend them on the island," he said.

She shook her head. "The amount of space isn't the issue. The cottage belongs to a wealthy Melbourne family so I'm sure there's plenty of room."

His eyebrows drew together. "Then what is the issue?"

"You're asking me if I want you to come but what do *you* want?"

"This isn't the right time..."

"Exactly my point. You have time to dig every last detail out of a story, even if you have to go without food and sleep to do it. I'm not saying it's wrong, especially when as much good comes of it as it has this time. But when it comes to us, you still expect me to make all the running.''

It was so clear now, so obvious that it was a wonder it hadn't dawned on her before. ''When you decided to go to America, you never said you *wanted* me to come with you. You talked about the fantastic career opportunities, the fun we could have seeing the sights, but you didn't come out and say you needed me with you.''

''I didn't want to pressure you. It had to be your decision.''

She shook her head furiously. ''It should have been *our* decision, by mutual agreement. Instead, you set it up so the whole burden fell on me. My choice to go or to stay, to keep the relationship alive or to finish it. If you had admitted you needed me, just once...'' She couldn't go on, and busied herself tidying the photos on the table.

His hand claimed hers, stilling the jerky movements. ''I may not have said I needed you, but you must have known it.''

She lifted shining eyes to him. ''I told myself you did, but then you left the country and next thing I heard, you were involved with someone else.''

He gave a rueful half smile. ''I see what you mean. There's a Zulu quote that says, 'I cannot hear what you say for the thunder of what you are.' ''

''Actions speak louder than words,'' she interpreted.

''And mine weren't saying what you needed to hear.'' His fingers tightened around hers. ''You didn't come running to me when you found you were pregnant.''

She withdrew her hand. ''That's different.''

''Is it, Tara? Frankly, I can't see how. You say you wanted me to need you but when did you ever lean on me?''

As her stomach began to tie itself into knots, she slid the photos into their folder along with the lease she'd purchased at the auction. ''I guess neither of us felt up to making the first move.'' She swung around, linking her hands in front of her. "It only goes to show that we did the right thing in ending it."

He regarded her thoughtfully. "I'm not so sure it is ended." He took a deep breath. "You still haven't told me how many bedrooms that cottage has."

"And I don't intend to. We've been over this, Zeke. Maybe we didn't end it by design, but the universe ended it for us." It always would, she suspected. "I think it's sensible to let it stay that way."

Zeke slammed one fist into another, the explosive sound making her jump. "I don't know what it is, but being around you makes me anything but sensible."

"See," she said as if he had just proved a point. "We're not doing each other any favors by dragging this out."

"You could be right." He didn't sound as if he was giving in and she regarded him suspiciously. But he rolled back his cuff to look at his watch. "Damn this TV show."

She told herself it was for the best but part of her wanted him to stay so much that she almost blurted it out loud. She hadn't, she realized, as he shrugged on his jacket.

Phone in hand, he turned. "Will I see you when you get back?"

"I don't know when that will be," she prevaricated. "If I like the cottage, I may stay there and start on the book right away."

She had taken him unawares, she saw as his eyebrows flickered upward. "I didn't have you pegged as a country girl."

"I am on my mother's side. Dad preferred living in the city but my mother would have moved away like a shot. Now she's talking about living somewhere like Phillip Island herself."

"What about your charity commitments?"

"The island is only a couple hours' drive out of Melbourne. It isn't the moon. I can come back when I'm needed.

And with faxes and e-mails, it's easy to stay in touch.'' Harder to drop out if you wanted to, she thought. Even if she hadn't given Zeke her number, he would find a way to contact her if he wanted to, so she probably hadn't done herself any harm.

''I have to go,'' he repeated, reluctance still evident. His phone rang and he gave a grimace of apology as he turned aside to answer it. From his end of the conversation, she gathered it was the television producer. Zeke flipped the phone shut. ''The taping is running an hour or so behind schedule, so they haven't missed me yet. Can I call you when you get to the island, and tell you what Bill Ellison has to say?''

Hadn't he heard a word she'd said? She didn't care what the private detective thought or said. She just wanted to let things lie. But she didn't possess the energy to fight Zeke on this anymore. ''Do whatever you want,'' she said tiredly, knowing he would, anyway. ''You know where I'll be.''

Knowing where she was and being with her were two different things, Zeke thought as he drove to the studio. He found he wanted the latter more than he probably should, and he cursed the physical reaction that followed the thought.

That's all it is, physical, he told himself. He'd had plenty of relationships based on nothing more, and they were satisfying enough in the short term. Since he didn't believe in the long haul, it was as good as he was going to get.

Tara was the first woman to make him want more, to expect more, he amended inwardly. It bothered him to feel more attracted to her than ever. In the heat of their lovemaking, she had blurted out that she loved him and he still felt the force of his rejection of this idea. He didn't want her to love him, any more than he wanted to love another human being. Be with them, glory in what they could be to each other, but never bind themselves to each other with ties that were all too easily broken.

Love didn't last. It was as simple as that. If he needed more evidence than he had gained in his early years, there was Tara's concealment of her pregnancy and her refusal to accompany him to America. Pregnant women traveled all the time. Why couldn't she have had the baby there? Plainly she hadn't wanted to, and had used the assignment and the baby as excuses to end the relationship.

Then there was Lucy's roller-coaster-ride idea of romance. One minute vowing undying devotion to him. The next, agreeing with indecent haste when he suggested she'd be better off without him. He hadn't really believed in the devotion, or the crocodile tears she shed at their parting. She hadn't been too heartbroken to find someone else within weeks of them splitting up, he remembered.

Oddly enough Tara's resistance to him bothered him far more than the breakup with Lucy. Did it make him the unfeeling bastard Lucy had accused him of being? Or did it simply mean that Tara had engaged more of his emotions all along? He had a strong suspicion which it was and didn't much care for the conclusion.

The light ahead of him changed to red. He tapped his fingers against the steering wheel. This thinking wasn't getting him anything except a headache. Between researching and writing the story and promoting it, he was tired to the bone.

Thinking of Tara on her island, a sense of longing swept over him. He dismissed it. When he suggested joining her, she had done everything but bar the door to him. Couldn't he take a hint?

No, dammit, he couldn't, he thought angrily. Since when did he let a little resistance decide his actions? He wanted her, maybe not in the happy-ever-after sense, but in every other way a man could want a woman. He knew she felt the same, and his blood heated as he recalled how much. It wasn't in him to force himself on a woman. But she hadn't said no, not when he wanted to make love to her, and not when he brought up the notion of joining her on Phillip Island. What did it mean?

He sighed. It meant he had another mystery to add to the one Bill Ellison was investigating. And since he wasn't going to get answers to either one right now, he'd better focus on the panel discussion ahead. He almost groaned out loud as he thought of the hours of sitting under bright lights, waiting while shots were set up and angles determined, all the while trying to behave like the life of the party when it was the last thing he felt like doing. How did he get himself into these things?

Matthew Brock was waiting at the studio when he got there. In Zeke's opinion, the photographer hadn't received enough credit for the baby farming story. His pictures had done a lot to tug the nation's heartstrings and lead to justice being done. Now he pulled out a folder of proof photographs for Zeke's okay.

"I had to bring these here because we don't see much of you in the office lately," he said a little breathlessly.

Zeke glanced over his shoulder but the producer of the panel discussion was nowhere in sight and the set was still empty. "It looks as if I have a few minutes yet."

"A few hours, more like it. I gather there's a power supply problem."

At least they hadn't missed him, Zeke thought. He bent over the proof sheets. They showed a mother, father and child playing, apparently happily together in a backyard swimming pool. Only he, Matthew, and the police knew that the innocent-looking parents had bought the baby in a dirty deal from the hospital moments after he was born. He whistled softly. "How did you get these?"

Matthew looked pleased. "Long lens, stepladder, helpful neighbor, the usual."

"I'd better warn Hollywood. We'll make a paparazzo of you yet."

Matthew pouted. "No need to get insulting."

"Seriously, these are brilliant." He stabbed a finger at one of the postage-stamp-size shots. "Blow this one up for the front page. Run the rest in a strip alongside the article, with the faces obscured of course."

"Innocent until proven guilty," Matthew agreed, accustomed to the protocol.

Zeke scowled. "The only innocent is that beautiful little boy."

Matthew looked surprised. "Getting clucky in your old age?"

"None of your business."

Matthew spread his hands. "Okay, no need to bite my head off."

Zeke stabbed his temples with his index fingers. "Sorry, just tired, that's all. This has been a long campaign." He jerked a thumb toward the now-lighted set. "This stuff doesn't help, either."

Matthew nodded in sympathy. "Too much waiting around for a few minutes of activity, but it's worth it. Once the police move in on this pair tomorrow, that's the last of the parents who bought babies."

"Apart from the major players the international police will have to nail, we've done the best we can." Zeke clamped a friendly hand on Matthew's shoulder. "You deserve a Walkley Award for this job."

Matthew reddened but he looked pleased. "If there are any awards being handed out, they're yours. With the new security measures in place at the hospital as a result of this story, it will be a long time before anything like it happens again."

Zeke nodded, gratified. None of the personal publicity or TV stardom compared with the satisfaction of knowing he had done his job. Out of the corner of his eye he saw the other members of the panel being herded onto the set. "Looks like something's happening."

As the producer started toward him, Zeke's cell phone rang. He nodded dismissal at Matthew, mouthed, "one minute," at the producer who tapped his foot impatiently, despite causing the holdup thus far. Zeke ignored him and flipped the phone open. "Blaxland."

The producer pointed ominously at his watch. Zeke nodded. In his ear he heard the voice of Bill Ellison, the private investigator. "I've been trying to reach you," Zeke said.

"I turned the phone off. I was following someone and didn't want to tip them off. Looks like I've got a lead for you."

Zeke's heart double-timed and he debated whether to abandon the panel show and follow up whatever the investigator had uncovered. But he was too much the professional, the producer's frantic body language a vivid reminder that he had given his word. He sighed into the phone. "Good news, Bill. But right now I'm stuck with something that can't wait. Where can I reach you when I'm free to talk?"

"At home, watching the cricket," the man assured him.

Zeke felt a wry grin start. "Half your luck." He warned that it could be late before he called again, and got the investigator's assurance that he'd be awake. The call left Zeke feeling unsatisfied, his journalistic instincts on red. But he wouldn't let the producer down at this late stage. With a sigh, he closed the phone, switched it off, and headed toward the lighted set.

Chapter 10

Tara felt a sense of homecoming as she drove across the suspension bridge linking the fishing port of San Remo with Phillip Island. The island was only about twenty-three kilometers long and ten wide, with beautiful coastal scenery and an enviable location at the entrance to Westernport Bay. On impulse, she had rented a silver Branxton cabriolet at the airport, and with the top down, her hair streamed like a banner in the sea breeze. The salt-laden air tasted of her childhood.

As she drove toward the main town of Cowes, for a moment she was a teenager again, visiting her grandparents. It was hard to think they wouldn't be there to greet her, having died within weeks of each other after more than forty years of marriage, when Tara was twenty-two.

Her mother had inherited the old house. Tara's father had persuaded her to pull down what he called "that ancient eyesore." Tara was sure her mother regretted letting him have his way. She certainly did. Despite the lack of modern conveniences, she wished she was going there now. Her grandfather would hug her so tightly she would feel his bones through the hand-knitted cardigan he wore year 'round. Her grandmother would have lemon tea and homemade coconut cake waiting and they would talk long into the evening. Her eyes started to mist as memories crowded in.

Where their house had been was now a tourist hotel, she saw as she drove past it. Her grandparents had farmed chicory on the island before retiring to the cottage near the town. Tara's grandfather had told her of how he used to harvest the turniplike plants used as an additive in all kinds of foods, especially coffee. He had shown her the kilns where the chicory root had been sliced and dried, ready for sale. The tumbledown buildings, disused now, were still found all over the island.

Maybe there was a story for Zeke in the forgotten industry, she speculated, wondering why it hadn't occurred to her before. She might write it herself. Zeke would probably find her attempt amusing, but he would encourage her efforts. He always had.

For a moment she missed him with an intensity that rocked her. She almost wished—no, she clamped down on the thought. Inviting him to accompany her would have been a recipe for disaster. Hadn't she learned that it was better to leave well enough alone? They had parted on good terms, if not exactly as friends, and she had the memory of one afternoon of ecstasy in his arms as a parting gift. It was more than she had expected. He had said he would call but she didn't intend to wait by the phone. When he did—if he did—she amended inwardly, she would keep things strictly business.

As she drove past Cowes beach she wondered how Zeke would react if he knew that a century before, the pier had been described as a meeting place "sure to be fatal to any susceptible bachelor." He was a bachelor, she thought, but she had been the susceptible one, for all the good it had done either of them.

When she'd last seen him he had looked drained, as if the baby farming story had exacted a heavy toll. She hated to think their reunion had contributed to his condition, until she reminded herself that *he* had sought her out. That it might be because he hadn't given her time to contact him, she didn't like to think.

How must it feel to not have at least some happy childhood memories, she wondered, seeing his life through his eyes. Her father had been demanding and unfeeling but her mother's and grandparents' unconditional love had made up. Zeke's memories were of abandonment and rejection, and her heart ached for him.

Why had he come looking for her? He hadn't known about the baby then. She didn't believe it was only in pursuit of a story. That was more likely an excuse. And he was an intensely attractive man. He wouldn't have to look far for female companionship, if that's what he needed. A thrust of something like jealousy accompanied the thought. Make up your mind which you want, she ordered herself. Well, she had come to the right place to do it.

A car horn sounded behind her and she started, looking in the mirror to see a man leaning on his horn. It couldn't be. She smiled broadly, recognizing the driver as he had evidently done her. She pulled off to the side of the road and waited while he pulled in behind her. She got out as the driver hurried up to her.

"Tara McNiven, I thought it was you."

"Ryan Marshal," she said on a delighted note. "How did you know it was me?"

"Once seen, never forgotten," he said. "I'm glad you're not too famous to say hello."

She laughed, feeling a weight of care lift from her shoulders. "Never. You're practically family." His parents managed a tourist shop at Summerland Beach where a colony of fairy penguins paraded up the beach to their nests each evening, drawing hordes of sight-seers from all over the world.

Tiring of the crowds, Ryan had spent more of his school holiday hours at her grandparents' place than at his own home. She felt a pang of regret at not making more of an effort to keep in touch with him after her grandparents died.

He didn't seem to hold it against her. "Your grandparents were great people. I still miss them."

"And my gran's apple and cinnamon muffins," she said, remembering how many of them Ryan had been able to put away. It hadn't done him any harm, she noticed, admiring the wide set of his shoulders and his athletic build. She remembered him as a lanky youth. In the years since they'd last seen each other, he'd filled out. "Unless I've shrunk, you've actually grown," she said.

He made a cheeky assessment of her from head to toe. "Nothing I can see has *shrunk*. You're still breathtakingly beautiful."

"Flatterer," she said, but smiled. A little ego boost wouldn't hurt as long as she didn't let it go to her head. "Do you still live on the island?"

"Not far from here," he explained. "The family business grew until it employed me, too."

She grinned. "As a boy, you thought it was boring."

"We all change," he said. "As I recall, you were going to be a marine biologist and work with the penguins."

She remembered that dream. She had been fascinated by the small creatures waddling up the beach at the same time every night, carrying in their own stomachs the food they would pass on to their chicks. The chicks themselves bounded up and down on the beach, waiting impatiently for their parents' return.

"Yes, well, I didn't have much of a head for science," she confessed.

"I doubt your *head* is what appeals to the magazine buyers," he teased.

She pretended to be insulted. "Modeling takes brains, as well, you know."

"Yeah, right."

It felt like old times, sparring contentedly with someone who had been as much a brother to her as her real brother. Except that Ben had hated the island, using every pretext to avoid accompanying her. She hadn't minded, regarding it as her private preserve and Ryan as her exclusive companion.

He held out his arms and she went into them, the hug setting the seal on her sense of homecoming. She pulled back a little. "What's been happening with you?"

Pride beamed from him. "I'm married, with a little boy."

Another pang shot through her although she told herself how illogical it was. As a child she had told Ryan she would marry him herself as soon as they were old enough, but it had never been more than a game. "Who's the lucky woman?" she asked.

"Jeanette Bury from Melbourne, and she *is* a marine biologist," he said.

"You always did find science sexy."

"No, only scientists," he amended with a laugh. "Jeanette came to the island to study the penguins, and never left."

"It sounds like a marriage made in heaven," she said, pleased to see the happiness fairly radiating from him.

Disengaging from her, he pulled out his wallet and extracted a photo. "This is our son, Jonathon. He's two."

She admired the photo, saddened to think that she would never be able to pull out a photo of Brendan and show it off.

"Are you still married to your career?" Ryan asked, as if zeroing in on her change of mood.

She affected a shrug, reluctant to talk about herself. "You know what it's like in the big city."

"Not really. I never wanted to live anywhere but here."

"Wise man." She patted his arm. "Your son is gorgeous, just like his father."

His color heightened and he fumbled the photo back into his wallet. "What brings you to Phillip Island?" When she explained about leasing the cottage, he said, "I know it. Pretty flash place but the family who built it hardly seem to use it."

"That's probably why they donated the lease to the auction."

"When you've settled in, how about joining Jeanette and me for dinner?"

She nodded agreement. "That would be lovely."

"Tomorrow night, then?"

She nodded. "It's a date. Now can you direct me to my new abode?"

"I'll take you there myself. It isn't far."

She glanced back at his vehicle. "What about your car?"

"I'll come back for it later. I'm not passing up the chance to drive this beauty."

Tara pulled a face at him. "So the appeal isn't me, it's the convertible."

He shrugged. "A man has to have priorities."

She punched his arm lightly. "I've missed you, Ryan."

He sobered. "And I, you, Taz," he replied, using her childhood nickname. Once they were settled in her rental car with Ryan at the wheel, he asked, "Do you have a husband or boyfriend joining you later?"

"None of the above. I'm still footloose and fancy free." Strange how hard it was to admit, feeling more like a confession than a declaration of independence.

"I hope you won't be lonely at Manna Cottage—that's its name," he said. "It's perched on a headland with great views, but no real neighbors."

She soon saw what he meant. The timber cottage was set high up to catch the sea views. Small windows fronted the road, and the weathered timber finishes and red corrugated iron roof blended with a grove of the soaring Manna gums that she guessed gave the cottage its name. They were the preferred food of koalas, she recalled, hoping that some of the cuddly-looking marsupials lived in the trees.

Inside, she was delighted to find that almost every room had an ocean view. Sunshine spilled through large expanses of glass at the rear and there were vertical blinds she could close if the heat became oppressive.

The open-plan living areas were painted in a pale green with chairs covered in soft grey leather, echoing the colors of the surrounding bush. She was pleased to see a covered verandah opening off the modern timber kitchen. The deck was furnished with built-in seating, and pots of impatiens added splashes of color.

"I can sit out there and read when the sea breezes aren't too cool," she said, opening doors onto it and taking the tangy air into her lungs. "I'm about to start writing a book, so the view will inspire me."

"You don't need a view for inspiration. It's inside you, and always was. Remember the poems you wrote when we were kids?"

She pulled a face. "Don't remind me, they were hideous."

"They weren't. I still have some of them."

"It's a nice compliment but misplaced," she told him. "I may be able to manage nonfiction but I doubt if my poetry will ever be collectible."

He seemed to pull himself back from his memories. "They are to me. We had some good times, didn't we, Taz?"

She nodded then asked on impulse, "Are you happy, Ryan?"

To her relief, he nodded. "Everything I want is here on the island—a beautiful woman who loves me more than I deserve, a gorgeous child, my work. You?"

She hesitated. By Ryan's standard, she was missing two

out of the three ingredients for happiness. "I'm doing okay," she said lightly, hoping to convince one of them. A change of subject was called for. "You'd better tell me your address if I'm coming to dinner tomorrow."

"Right." He scribbled the details on the back of a supermarket docket and handed it to her. "Do you need a hand with your unpacking?"

She gave him a playful shove toward the door. "I've kept you from your family long enough. You still have to walk back to your car."

Ryan's grin was rueful. "Still Miss Bossy-Boots, I see." When she made a mock-threatening move toward him, he held up his hands. "I'm going, I'm going. With you and Jeanette both ordering me around, I can see I'm totally outgunned."

She was still laughing when he pulled the door shut, rammed his hands into his pockets and strode up to the road, whistling cheerfully. Meeting her childhood friend again was a good omen, she told herself, turning to the task of unloading the car. She only wished he hadn't reminded her so forcibly of the contrast between their lives.

Would it have made a difference if Zeke had accompanied her? She doubted it, finding it difficult to picture him being content for long in the island setting. Ryan had never wanted anything else, she recalled. She had teased him about it when they were children, but part of her had secretly envied his contentment.

Now wasn't the time for introspection, she told herself briskly. After a thorough check of her options, she chose a spacious bedroom that was simply furnished, with a huge picture window so she would wake up to the sight of the ocean. Timber shutters could be folded across the window at night, presumably to keep the weather out since they were hardly needed for privacy, she concluded.

The bed was large and the mattress new, still in its wrapper, requiring some wrestling to liberate it before she could make it up with the crisp bed linen she found in a cupboard off the hall. In the same cupboard she found piles of fluffy blankets, although she doubted she'd need more than one at this time of year. She looked longingly at the capacious corner spa bath in the en suite bathroom, deciding to reward herself with a dip in it after she'd finished settling in.

She was checking the kitchen cupboards to see what supplies she'd need to buy in Cowes when she was startled by the first notes of "Jingle Bells."

With a resigned sigh she reached for the phone, hoping that some work problem wasn't about to spoil her tranquillity. It might also be Zeke, she thought, feeling her heart start to race. It was.

"I wanted to see how you're getting on," he said.

She was glad he couldn't see the shock on her face. Zeke *never* made purely social calls. "I'm fine," she assured him, pleased that her voice shook only a little. "The cottage is lovely. It's quite luxurious."

She heard Mungo yelp in the background and Zeke quieted the puppy in a low voice before he asked, "How about the neighbors?"

"There aren't any. Manna Cottage is perched on its own headland, about a fifteen-minute walk or short drive away from town."

"It sounds a bit isolated. Are you sure you're okay on your own there?"

She suppressed the urge to laugh, finding his concern novel enough to be flattering. "This isn't the city, Zeke. On the island people still leave their cars unlocked and their windows open."

"I trust you'll do no such thing. Some of the worst murders I've covered in my career were committed in idyllic rural surroundings."

"Thanks for the reassurance. I wasn't scared before."

"I didn't mean to frighten you. I only—hell, Tara, just take care, will you?"

Something in his tone nagged at her until she remembered. "You were going to talk to your private detective. Did he find out anything interesting?" Was Zeke's sudden concern for her security based on something he'd learned?

There was a short, tense silence, broken only by Mungo's soft whine of disapproval at being ignored. Then Zeke said, "I spoke to him. You're right, the flower probably was a mistake."

You don't really believe it, she thought, but didn't say it out loud. What else had the private detective uncovered? Zeke waited until he was sure he had his facts right before he revealed anything. Wise journalistic habit, she supposed, but it left her feeling uncomfortable. If he had a suspicion that something was wrong, surely he should share it with her? Even if it turned out to be a false alarm, at least she was forewarned.

"Is there something you're not telling me?" she demanded.

His hesitation fueled her suspicion. "You're imagining things. I'm sorry I mentioned security now. I guess I was thinking of the city after all. There's no danger where you are."

But there was danger elsewhere, she read between the lines. Her heart began to hammer and she gripped the phone so tightly that her knuckles whitened. Why won't you tell me the rest? she wanted to scream at him, knowing that persuading Zeke to say any more until he was ready was as difficult as pulling teeth.

She decided to try another tack. "How did the panel show go?" Keeping him talking, although it was the last thing her nerves needed, might encourage him to let something slip.

"It was a circus, but we finally got the show in the can by midnight," he said, the weariness in his voice alarming enough to undermine her wish to stay uninvolved. Could she ever do that with Zeke? She was beginning to doubt it. "The program airs tomorrow night if you want to see it," he added.

His reticence tested her patience to the limit, but she couldn't prevent the regret that washed over her from straying into her voice. "Tomorrow? Oh, I'll be out. I ran into an old friend, Ryan Marshal. He invited me to dinner tomorrow night and I haven't had time to master the cottage's video recorder yet. Can you tape the program for me, so I can see it when I get back?" It would give her an excuse to see him again, the thought intruded, making her wonder at her own motives.

A chill wind whistled down the phone in the form of his sharp breath. "It isn't important. You've heard it all in other interviews I've given. I'd better go. Mungo wants feeding before he demolishes my shoes instead. Take care of yourself."

The coldness in his voice and the suddenness with which he rang off left her feeling bemused, until she replayed her end of the conversation in her mind. She had mentioned dining with Ryan Marshal, but without adding that the party included his wife and child, she realized.

Zeke cared. The thought made the blood sing in her veins until she forced herself to think more clearly. He was a possessive man. He had regarded her as his possession until he went away. He wouldn't take kindly to another man muscling in on what he probably still thought of as his territory. It was no more than alpha male to beta male, vying for supremacy, she told herself. It didn't mean he wanted her for herself, or that there was any hope for them.

All the same, as she wrote out a list of supplies she would need to pick up from town, she felt lighter of heart than she had for days.

Chapter 11

For several minutes after he cut the connection, Zeke stared at the phone, ignoring the puppy worrying at his shoelaces. He knew his anger was a waste of energy. It was none of his business if Tara wanted to go out with some man she knew on Phillip Island. An old friend, she'd said. How old and how friendly?

"Did you tell her?"

Zeke snapped himself out of the reverie and shook his head at Bill Ellison, private investigator and friend since they were at university together. "I didn't see any point. She's safe where she is."

"It wouldn't hurt to let her know what we've uncovered."

"What *have* we uncovered?" Zeke demanded. He began to tick off points on his fingers. "A woman called Jenny Fine had a baby at the Roses hospital at a time when her sister was the senior midwife and quite possibly up to her neck in the baby-swapping scheme. The midwife delivered her sister Jenny's baby. It's against hospital rules, but it's hardly criminal. My source has promised me copies of the ward records altered by the midwife, enabling at least two babies to be switched with those who died or were ailing. But until I get the proof, our case against the midwife adds up to zilch.''

''Then you don't think...''

Zeke made an impatient noise. ''I've already been down the road you think you're on, and it leads nowhere. Jenny Fine had her baby DNA tested. I've seen the original record myself and the test was conclusive. It's her child. No mystery there.''

Bill Ellison rubbed his chin thoughtfully. ''Why would she do a thing like that?''

''Like what?''

''Have her own child tested?''

''Maybe she suspected her sister was involved in something underhanded, and started to worry about whether the baby was really hers.''

''If she had doubts, it would explain the test,'' Bill mused.

''Doubts we've well and truly laid to rest. Whatever other involvement the family had in the crime, it was their own baby the Fines took home.''

''If you say so.'' Bill didn't look convinced.

Zeke told himself it was his friend's job to be suspicious. ''I'm more interested in why you saw Jenny Fine leave another flower in the park.'' He hadn't wanted to worry Tara by telling her this, preferring to let her go on thinking it was a mistake for now. But it wasn't. According to Bill, the woman had deliberately placed the flower in the niche beside his son's memorial.

With an impatient sigh, Zeke disengaged Mungo from his shoelace and carried the puppy to the kitchen, setting it down on the floor. As soon as Zeke brought out a can of puppy food, Mungo began to paw the air excitedly. ''Down, boy,'' he said absently. An almost-forgotten technique came back to him from boyhood, and he held a small piece of food above the puppy's head, forcing Mungo to sit nicely to accept it. He rubbed the pup between the ears. "That's it, sit, Mungo. Good dog."

Bill lounged against the kitchen door frame, looking fascinated. "Hey, that's a good trick. I always wanted a dog, but in my job I never know when I'll get home to feed and walk it. Can I borrow yours sometime when I'm not on a case?"

"You serious? It would be great to have somebody to mind him when I'm away."

Bill looked pleased. "Delighted, pal. I'll be his godfather."

Zeke shot him a wry look. "I don't think it works for dogs, but you're welcome to share him. Here, Mungo, meet your godfather." The puppy had his head buried in a dish almost as big as he was, and didn't look up.

Bill didn't seem put out. "Once he gets to know me, he'll come to love me."

"He's a dog, not a saint."

The investigator grinned. "He lives with you, doesn't he?"

Zeke thought immediately of Tara and growled. "It probably takes a saint." He led the way back to the living room, leaving Mungo to his meal. "I'd like you to keep an eye on the Fines," he said to Bill, picking up their discussion where he'd left off. "Now that we know the midwife spent time in a psychiatric unit, I don't like to think of her getting anywhere near me and mine."

Zeke hadn't told Bill that Tara had also given birth on the same night at the same hospital, or that the Brendan on the plaque was the son he never got the chance to know. Bill wouldn't like being kept in the dark, but Zeke couldn't bring himself to talk about the baby yet, not even to his old friend. He didn't think it would shed any more light on the story.

He was fairly sure he had worked out why Jenny Fine

brought the flowers. From what Zeke had read and heard about the birth experience, although admittedly not a lot, he gathered that women were in labor a long time. Tara and Jenny probably got to know each other over several hours. Then after Tara lost the baby, the woman probably brought the flowers to show her support. It didn't completely satisfy Zeke, but with nothing else to go on, it had to do.

"You still haven't explained why you're so interested in who visits that memorial," Bill said with deceptive casualness.

Zeke wondered how far the other man had gone in working it out. "And I don't intend to," he said shortly.

The investigator shrugged. "Suit yourself. But I work better if I have all the facts. I take it if I turn up anything that— ah, relates to you, I'm to keep it to myself?"

"Share it with me verbally and I'll tell you if you're on the right track," Zeke said. "I'm sorry, Bill, this time I'm not the only one involved, okay?"

"I'll remind you of that next time you're on someone else's trail," Bill said good-naturedly.

In spite of his mood, Zeke felt a grin lift the corners of his mouth, doubtless what his friend had intended. He made a rude gesture. "Get out of here and let me get some work done."

When the other man left, Zeke opened his notebook computer but didn't switch it on. He couldn't write while his thoughts were fixed on Tara and what she was or wasn't doing with this Ryan character. Zeke knew he was jealous although the strength of the feeling alarmed him. Judging from the testosterone surging through him, if Ryan Marshal popped up right now, Zeke would probably slug him one.

Odd that he hadn't felt this way about the man Lucy paired off with after she left. The society pages had been full of it and Zeke had wished her well. But the man Tara had mentioned so casually nagged at him like a sore tooth. When you had as many relationships torn asunder in your life as I have, you learned to fight for what's yours, he told himself to justify his reaction.

So why in heaven's name was he sitting back, letting another man move in on Tara? Action was what he needed. He slammed the notebook shut and headed outside, managing to catch Bill before he drove off. "Sure, I'll mind the little feller for you," he agreed, and waited while Zeke fetched the puppy and his things.

Back inside, he reached for the phone. The airline reservation number was recorded in the machine's memory, so he was through in seconds. It didn't short-circuit the recorded voice telling him how important his call was, and how soon they'd get to him, but for once, he found the delay helpful. It enabled him to plan.

Tara was on her hands and knees in the cottage garden, trying to rescue some spring bulbs that were in danger of being smothered by beds of impatiens. The owners of the cottage employed a gardener to keep the weeds down and the lawn mowed, but the small jobs were evidently ignored. She had already cleared a space around some young gladioli shoots. In another few weeks they would be spectacular.

She should probably be doing something more practical such as stocking the pantry, but had decided to postpone the shopping while she tidied the garden beds. Now it was past lunchtime. Breakfast had consisted of coffee and some fruit and cheese she'd bought on the way to the island. With the fresh sea air sharpening her appetite she was getting hungry, but it was such a glorious day that she felt more like being close to nature.

Gloves might help, too, she thought, making a mental note to buy some. She sat back on her heels, splaying her fingers and frowning at her hands. Usually perfectly manicured, today they were ingrained with dirt and there was a small scratch on her wrist from a rosebush. She'd been careful not to break a nail, but if she kept this up it was only a matter of time. Vanity wasn't the issue. Appearance was her livelihood.

"I didn't have you figured for a gardener," an all-too-familiar voice stated.

Her heart did a quick backflip and she stumbled to her feet, almost trampling the flower bed she'd so carefully tended. "Zeke, what are you doing here?"

She had a feeling she knew the answer before he said, "You invited me."

Funny, she didn't remember that part. "I remember discussing the number of bedrooms available," she said, willing herself to not color too obviously.

He shrugged. "Same thing. Besides, in my experience, we only ever needed one."

She spun the trowel down so it lodged in the dirt like a thrown knife. "One was fine when we shared it." She made her tone remind him that things were different now.

He looked at the cottage perched on its isolated headland. "A place this size ought to have at least two bedrooms. A spectacular view, too."

"From almost every room." She welcomed the change in subject. Seeing him in what she already considered her private retreat was disturbing enough without discussing bedrooms.

Right away, she knew she was going to let him stay if he wanted to. Not used to seeing him anything but self-possessed and bursting with energy, she was disturbed by how exhausted he looked. This story had taken a lot out of him, she saw, and wondered if it was the reason she couldn't bring herself to send him away, or if there was another one she wasn't sharing with herself.

She pushed a lock of hair out of her eyes, suspecting she left a trail of dirt. From the way Zeke's gaze locked on to her, she couldn't look too unattractive. She felt warm inside suddenly and couldn't quite convince herself it was from exertion. "You may as well come in and see the rest of the house."

Tension gripped her as she watched him stride to the rental car and heft an overnight bag out of the back seat. So it was to be as simple—and complicated—as that. Only when they were inside the open-plan living room, and Zeke was admiring the view, did it occur to her that he might have another reason for arriving unannounced.

Recalling his phone call, she felt a frown start. "Did your private investigator dig up something to make you worry about my safety?"

He gave a not-too-convincing shake of his head. "He turned up some worrying facts, but we don't have the whole picture yet. One of the hospital staff allegedly involved in the baby farming racket turns out to have a history of psychiatric problems. There's more. Bill found out that the person leaving the flowers on our baby's memorial is a woman who gave birth on the same night you did."

She felt the small hairs lift on the back of her neck. "Do I know her?"

"Her name is Jenny Fine."

The room spun crazily until Tara gripped the back of a chair. "I remember her. Dear heaven, what's going on here?" She couldn't bring herself to put into words the hope tearing through her against all common sense. What if...

"We don't know what it means. Probably nothing." His words throttled off the hope before it bloomed too wildly. "Until we turn up enough evidence to hold up in court, I don't want to take any chances."

She masked her disappointment with anger. "So you decided to baby-sit me. Thanks, but I can take care of myself."

"I know you can, against most things. But we're dealing

with someone who senses they're under suspicion, and who has a history of mental instability.''

''Why would Jenny take flowers to the park? Her baby was perfectly healthy.''

He pushed aside the sheer fabric curtaining the French doors, and filled his lungs with bracing air, speaking over his shoulder, ''That's what I want Bill Ellison to find out. It could be that she remembers you and wants to show she cares about your loss.''

''We weren't that close. I had too many things on my mind.'' Such as the agonizing awareness that she was having Zeke's child and he wasn't there to share it with her. Afterward she had been moved to a private room on another floor, away from the distressing sight of the mothers and babies in the maternity ward. As far as she knew, she hadn't seen or spoken to Jenny Fine again.

''But you did make her acquaintance?''

Tara put a hand to her head, sifting through memories that were mercifully foggy. ''I—yes, I did. It was a terrible night because there was a huge traffic accident that brought the city almost to a standstill. Many of the staff couldn't get to the hospital so everyone was working double shifts. When Jenny Fine and I checked in we discovered that both our doctors had been delayed. We talked about how lucky we were to have reached the hospital safely, without getting caught up in the accident, although we were both nervous about having to manage with just the midwives.'' She frowned. ''She tried to reassure me by telling me she was related to one of the midwives working an extra shift that night.''

Her sister, thought Zeke, linking the comment to what he already knew. ''I got that from Bill,'' he confirmed. ''He was the one who dug up the psychiatric record.''

''I'm surprised they'd let someone like that work at a hospital.''

Zeke's shoulders lifted. "The hospital might not have known, if it was covered up or the job application falsified."

She shuddered. "Do you think it means anything?"

"Possibly not, but Bill's on top of it. He'll tell us if there's anything to worry about."

"You must think there might be, or you wouldn't be here."

He debated whether to tell her that his motivation was nothing more laudable than good old-fashioned jealousy and decided she might throw him out on his ear, so he said instead, "You made the island sound inviting so when Bill offered to mind Mungo, I decided to see the place for myself. If you really don't want me here, I can go to a hotel." He was gambling a lot on the remnants of their relationship, he knew. Uncertainty gripped him as she took longer to consider his offer than he liked.

"I should let you," she said after an uncomfortably long interval. "This isn't likely to be good for either of us."

"Can't two friends share a house without it getting complicated?"

She couldn't share anything with Zeke without it getting complicated, Tara thought unhappily. It would serve him right if she let him go to a hotel. But the tense set of his shoulders and the strain she saw around his eyes undermined her resolve.

He hadn't talked much about the story lately, but it wasn't hard to imagine the strain of dealing with stolen babies, desperate parents, and even more desperate people trying to hang on to children they had acquired by criminal means. So much emotional baggage would overload anyone's resources, even a man as resilient as Zeke. Then there was the loss of their own child. His current assignment would be a constant reminder of what might have been. She couldn't find it in her heart to send him away. "Forget the hotel. I'll make up another room."

He followed her along the hallway. "I can do it, if you show me where things are."

"I'm only just finding everything myself." She half wished he would return to the living room but he dogged her footsteps as she retrieved another set of bed linen from the well-stocked shelves. He took them from her and she added a blanket and pillow until only his eyes were visible above the pile. The expression in them unnerved her. The scene was so cozily domestic that she had to remind herself that it didn't mean anything.

"That's my room," she said as he fumbled open a door around the pile of bed linen in his arms.

The look in his eyes asked why they were making up another bed, but she pulled the door resolutely closed and continued to the next bedroom. Belatedly she recalled that it shared a bathroom with her room, and started to close the door on that one, too.

He blocked the opening with a foot. "What's wrong with this one?"

Since he didn't know about the bathroom, the room could only interest him because it was next to hers, she thought on a surge of anxiety. What on earth made her think they could share a house on any sort of platonic basis?

She imagined lying awake listening to the small sounds he made getting ready for bed, knowing every move he made as well as she knew her own. Did he still sort his loose change into neat stacks? she wondered. She had pointed out that he only jumbled it all together again in his pocket in the morning, but he insisted it was part of his bedtime ritual.

"The room at the end of the hall is larger, with its own bathroom," she said, hearing panic clog her voice.

His slight smile suggested she'd been read like a book. "This will do fine. I won't be spending a lot of time in here."

Her hand froze on the doorknob and her gaze flew to his face, but his eyes gave nothing away. "You'll be spending the night in here,'' she said under her breath. It was the only logical solution. She only wished it felt less disquieting.

To his credit he let the subject drop but didn't remove his foot. She had little choice but to lead the way into the room and start the bed-making ritual. He moved to the far side of the bed and helped her as if he'd done this with her hundreds of times.

As he helped her, Zeke tried to make his inquiry casual, ''When are you meeting this old friend of yours, Marshal Ryan?''

''Ryan Marshal, and I'm having dinner at his house tonight,'' she corrected. She saw the sudden narrowing in his gaze and wondered at the source of it. ''His parents live on the island. We've known one another since we were children. When my grandparents died, he was away at university so I haven't seen him in years.''

He watched her toss the blanket over the bed. It landed evenly spaced on all sides, with the satin bound top edge just touching the padded headboard. How did women do that? She bent to tuck the sides in and he felt a sheen of perspiration start at the glimpse the movement afforded him of the deep cleft between her breasts. She wore a low-cut white top that fit like a second skin, tucked into olive-green cargo shorts and he thought she looked as beautiful as he had ever seen her.

Her movements made the mundane chore look so fluid and graceful that he ached with wanting her. Her skin glowed from her outdoor activities and she had dark patches on her knees where she'd been kneeling on the ground. He couldn't remember when she'd looked more gorgeous. It didn't please him to remember that she had other priorities. ''He didn't waste much time inviting you to dinner,'' he said gruffly.

''Along with his wife and child,'' she said with heavy emphasis. ''It's a friendly invitation, not a romantic assignation. Ryan was more like a brother to me than anything else.''

News of a wife and child changed things somewhat. He could already feel some of his tension ebbing and decided he might like this Ryan Marshal, after all. ''I didn't think it was romantic,'' he said with less-than-total conviction, because he *had* thought so. ''What you do is your own affair, Tara.''

She straightened and pushed a lock of hair off her forehead, revealing a smudge of dirt. He wanted to kiss it away but made himself keep the width of the bed between them, not sure he'd be able to stop at a kiss.

''I'm glad we agree on something.'' With a pillow halfway into a case, she paused. Her voice dropped to a husky register that made a hard fist close around his heart. ''Why did you come?''

He debated continuing his white-knight impersonation then thought, to hell with it. ''I am concerned about what Bill might discover. I didn't make that up. But it wasn't enough to get me on a plane. I'm sure you're perfectly safe here.'' He took a deep breath. ''I came because I couldn't stay away.''

It was what she both wanted and feared. ''You still haven't said why.''

His look turned savage but she suspected it was directed at himself. ''Do you need it spelled out?'' At her nod, he spread his hands, palms upward. ''Very well, I want you, Tara. Knowing you were here, I couldn't think, couldn't write.''

''Because of Ryan Marshal?''

''I didn't like to think of you spending time with another man,'' he admitted.

''I told you he's an old friend.''

''And carefully left out the part about a wife and child,'' he observed. ''Why would you do that?''

She didn't like to think it was to bring him running, but perhaps it had been an unconscious decision. "It wasn't deliberate," she said in her own defense.

"But you did want me to come?"

She fiddled with the corners of the pillow, smoothing an already-smooth cover, not able to meet his eyes. "All right, I hoped you would."

"I'm here. Now what?"

Did she have to say it? Very well, she would. "I've tried to tell myself we're better off apart but it isn't working for me, either." She had never felt more miserable.

She saw him read the fact in her expression and nod as if at a truth he recognized in himself. "Do you want to try again?"

"I want..." She let the pillow slide to the bed and raked her fingers through her hair. "I have no idea what I want."

"Perhaps I can clarify things a little." Unable to hold back a moment longer, he came around to her side of the bed and took her into his arms.

Still she wasn't sure it was the right thing to do, no matter how right it felt. "I'm all dirty," she protested.

He took a grimy hand and lifted it to his lips, his eyes sparking a challenge at her as he kissed each finger in turn. "Mmm, tastes earthy. I like it." He turned her hand over and frowned at the scratch from the rose. A shiver took her as he ran his tongue along the injury. "I see I got here just in time to tend your wounds."

"It's nothing," she said, but every nerve in her body argued the opposite as she suspected that the wounds he meant to tend were not physical. Anticipation rocked through her and her knees buckled.

He shook his head. "I disagree. Lie down while I make sure you have no other injuries."

"I don't," she said on a nervous laugh, but she let him

ease her down on the bed, afraid she would fall down otherwise.

Slipping her shoes off, he started at the ankle then slid a hand along her bare leg in the manner of a doctor checking for fractures, making a tut-tutting noise as he came to a slight graze on one knee. She hadn't grazed her knees since she was a child. She felt anything but childlike as his hand skimmed higher up her legs. He sat on the edge of the bed and gathered her into his arms.

There was nothing tender about his kiss. It spoke of hunger, of need, of desperation, and she answered out of her own need, fastening her mouth to his and catching his inside lip between her teeth.

He groaned softly and used his tongue to edge her lips apart, exploring, touching, twining in a dance so sensuous that eddies of pure pleasure whipped through her. The need for him throbbed along every vein and desire flooded every part of her body, even the small injuries and the grime. How could she not love it when he loved it all, with his demanding mouth and his tantalizing touch?

She knew her mention of dinner with Ryan Marshal had triggered this, but couldn't make herself care. Whoever said all was fair in love knew what they were talking about. Maybe she had wanted to make Zeke jealous enough to follow her. But now he was here, there was no room in her thoughts for anyone or anything else.

How quickly everything came back to her. The small movements he made when she touched him, the noises he made when those same touches pushed him to the brink of reason. The power of her desire, and all the clever ways he knew to satisfy her.

She felt weak and powerful all at the same time. Hot and cold. Wanting and needing, yet delaying the moment of satisfaction, because the wanting was itself so wonderful.

Somewhere between his playfully clinical checkup and this

magical moment, Zeke had undressed her and shed his own clothes. She wasn't sure when or how, being barely aware of anything except her joy at being in his arms again. *Loving* her. She was almost afraid to think it but it stole into her mind, threatening to dull the edge of her pleasure. She pushed it away but the doubts persisted.

He wasn't promising her forever. He had only agreed to help her discover what she wanted. Could this truly be enough? He retrieved a small packet from his wallet, opening it with his teeth. She felt gratified that he cared enough to protect her, but couldn't suppress a pang that there wouldn't be a baby, probably never again. Then he moved over her and eased himself carefully into her, and that was the end of conscious thought. His movements piled need upon need, sensation upon sensation. She felt the moment when his control reached its limit. Hers wasn't far behind and she reared up to meet him, her thoughts swallowed in a whirling vortex of passion that had her edging toward madness.

As she surrendered to the mind-shattering peak at last, silver flashes of light danced across her vision and ripples of sensation gripped her like the aftershocks of an earthquake. A second or two later, Zeke's body also went rigid as the earthquake caught him, too. His fingers dug into her shoulders, then he shuddered and was still. "Dear, Tara. Every time. Every single time," he said in a rasping voice.

She knew what he meant. Their lovemaking had a magic she had never known with anyone else. It thrilled her to hear him admit it was the same for him. He wasn't the only one capable of feeling jealous. Since he'd left, there had been times when she had wanted to transport herself to America and scratch his Lucy's eyes out. Telling herself it was illogical didn't help.

Love wasn't logical.

And it *was* love. She could not call it anything else. She had never stopping loving Zeke, even when he'd gone away and found someone else. Knowing it hadn't worked out helped a little, but it didn't matter, anyway. She loved him through thick and thin, right and wrong. "For better or for worse." The words intruded into her thoughts, forcing her to face the literal truth of them. No matter how Zeke felt or what he did, she could no more change her feelings than she could fly.

Zeke braced himself on his arms and smiled down at her. "I must be a dead weight on top of you."

She linked her arms around his neck and pulled him back down. "You feel just right."

"Believe it or not, this wasn't meant to happen."

"So why did you come? To admire the scenery?"

He dropped butterfly kisses onto her nose and eyebrows. "From my viewpoint, it has a lot to recommend it."

"Even though I'm a mess from gardening?"

"You're a beautiful mess. I've never seen you like this before."

She felt a blush start. "This is hardly our first time." The certainty with which he had pleasured her gave the lie to any such notion.

He grinned, evidently sharing the thought. "I meant, so natural. Not a shred of makeup, skinned knees, black nails."

She held a hand up, inspecting her fingernails over his shoulder. "They are not black."

"Grimy, then. And you have a huge smudge of dirt on your forehead and weeds in your hair."

Now she knew he was teasing her. "I do not have weeds in my hair."

He pulled a tiny piece of grass out of her hair to show her, then kissed the offending mark. "Weed, singular then. And you do have a smudge."

She squirmed beneath him, feeling an achy sense of pleasure-pain that threatened to spiral into something more if she didn't move soon. He looked as if he wouldn't mind, and she knew he was more than capable of it, but a sense of self-preservation kicked in, belatedly she knew, but there all the same. "That does it, I'm going to take a shower."

His eyes sparkled wickedly. "Alone?"

"Certainly alone."

"Over my body."

That was moot since his was over hers at that precise moment, but she bit back a murmur of protest when he shifted. "The shower isn't big enough for two," she insisted.

"We'll stand very, very close together."

He was as good as his word. The shower wasn't large, as she had warned him, and he did, indeed, stand close to her. So close that he was forced to make love to her again, making her laugh as he snagged a condom from her toiletries bag and struggled to put it on under the streaming cascade. It was a novel experience. In all the time they were together, they had never made love in a shower before. When she said so, he smiled lazily. "I can't think why not."

Neither could she, now she had tried it. Being pressed against the cool tiled surface by the weight of Zeke's body, feeling warm water stream over them while he eased himself into her, was one of the most extraordinary experiences of her life.

Afterward he kissed droplets of water off her nose. "Have I told you how beautiful you are?"

She shook her head. "I must look like a drowned rat."

"A water nymph," he amended. He turned off the water and kept an arm around her as they stepped out of the shower in tandem.

She shivered slightly as he wrapped a bath sheet around her and began to towel her dry with slow, eddying strokes that stoked new fires of desire deep within her. "I never dreamed that having a shower could be such an experience," she said.

"So sexy, you mean?" He dabbed water off her face and

kissed her again. "Haven't you heard the saying, 'variety is the spice of life'?"

She fluttered her lashes at him. "Life with you is definitely spicy."

"Keep that up and we'll never get out of this bathroom."

The thought didn't particularly bother her, she found. She had never felt more womanly, more gloriously alive, than she did right now. She sent a prayer of thanks to the woman from the hospital whose odd behavior had driven Zeke to come to the island. And to her old friend, Ryan, for making Zeke jealous enough to bring them back together.

If they *were* together, came the disturbing thought. However wonderful this interlude might be, and it was already proving to be pretty amazing, she wasn't sure what it meant for the future.

She decided not to worry about it now. For this time, however short, Zeke was hers again, and she was most definitely his. She wondered how she could feel so exhausted and exhilarated all at once.

"Hungry?" he asked as he finished toweling himself off.

"Yes, but we'll have to go out. There's no food in the house and I...haven't had time to shop."

"It's all right, I brought groceries."

A pang shot through her. Had he been so sure of her? Then he added, "I wasn't counting on anything, if that's what you're thinking. I thought if you wanted me to go to a hotel, I'd leave the supplies for you. You mentioned on the phone that the cottage was isolated."

It was something, she supposed, not sure she believed him. She hated to think this had been coldly premeditated when, for her, it had been as unexpected as rain out of a blue sky. It was probably easier to think of it as an aberration, than that she couldn't live without him, she acknowledged to herself. But it wasn't true. If he hadn't flown to the island, she would have found some excuse to go back, she knew.

She reached for a hair dryer hanging on the wall, but paused before switching it on. "What would you have done if I'd turned up on your doorstep in America?"

His hungry look was almost an answer. "Were you planning the trip?"

"I was thinking about it." Only the thought that he was involved had kept her away.

She saw him read the thought and he took the dryer from her hand, letting it dangle by its cord as he enfolded her in his arms. "God, Tara, why did we waste so much time?"

"Oh, Zeke, I love you."

She hadn't meant to say the words, and knew from the shock in his eyes that he didn't want to hear them, but she couldn't take them back. She touched a finger to his lips. "I don't need you to say you love me. It's enough that you're here."

He freed his mouth. "It wasn't enough before."

"It was, only I didn't know it." She nestled closer against him. "I was influenced by my father, I think, wanting perfection, thinking I needed the gown, the altar, the piece of paper."

His expression became bleak. "Lord knows, any woman is entitled."

She shook her head. "They don't mean half as much as I thought they did, and not a fraction as much as what I have here right now."

He gave her a wondering look. "You'd settle for so little?"

"How can it be so little, when it's everything you have to give?"

His hold on her tightened and her heart melted as she felt him tremble with the force of being so completely understood. "I don't deserve you," he rasped. He drowned out her reply in a kiss so scorching that she felt control slipping away again. "Perfect," he muttered.

When he released her she felt dizzy, but fear made her say, "I don't want to be perfect." She never again wanted to live up to her father's impossible standards, or expect anyone else to live up to them for her.

"You can't help it, you already are, for me."

Understanding what he meant, she felt relief sweep through her. Unlike her father, in Zeke's eyes, perfection wasn't something she had to aspire to, it was bestowed on her through the power of his feelings. If he didn't want to call it love, she could live with it, she told herself. As long as he never stopped looking at her the way he was doing now.

"We'd better get some food," he said, stepping back and returning the hair dryer to her.

She understood that, too, and felt desire sweep through her again. He was telling her she was going to need the fuel.

Chapter 12

"When she was little, I told Tara that the penguins were windup toys put out on the beach by the rangers every evening for the tourists, and she believed me," Ryan said with a laugh. They had reached the coffee stage of an excellent meal and Tara was impressed to find that his wife, Jeanette, was a great homemaker as well as a skilled scientist. Liking her immediately, Tara rejoiced that her childhood friend had so obviously found his soul mate. She and Ryan had been happy to include Zeke in the dinner invitation. Now Tara wondered if seeing them together would influence Zeke.

Did he ever yearn for what they had? Tara wondered, feeling a soul-deep longing grip her. Earlier in the evening she had watched him read to their gorgeous two-year-old son, Jonathon, and he'd been so good at it that a lump rose in her throat. At the child's insistence, Zeke had carried the little boy to bed on his shoulder.

She knew family life fell a long way outside his personal experience but everyone could change. Her father's perfectionism had dominated much of her young life, but she had made a conscious decision to be different.

It wasn't easy. There were still times when her best efforts seemed inadequate and she was tempted to demand too much of herself and others. Instead, she reminded herself that her father's way wasn't the only way and made herself enjoy the journey as well as the destination.

But first people had to want to change. Did Zeke really want things to be different between them? The question nagged at her. As things were, he had everything, including her, without sacrificing his precious independence or committing himself to anything beyond the moment. She hoped it was going to be enough for her.

She made herself pay attention as Jeanette gave her husband a playful shove. "Tara was only—what?—five years old? You could have told her anything."

He nodded. "I probably did."

Zeke rested his chin on one hand. "I'm having a hard time picturing Tara at five."

Glad to redirect her errant thoughts, she shook her head furiously. "I was awful. Skinny as a rake and always too tall for my age."

"She was full of beans, into everything and wanting to know everything," Ryan remembered. "She kept asking me how the penguins found their way back to the same beachhead every evening."

"You told me they put signs up in Penguin," she said accusingly.

"It was better than telling you I hadn't a clue."

Jeanette gave her husband a fond look before leaning forward. "As you know, Tara, a man would rather make up something than admit he doesn't know the answer, even if he's only eight years old."

Ryan contrived to look affronted. "Are we going to stand for this slander, Zeke?"

Jeanette laughed. "You could storm off to the kitchen and fetch more coffee."

Ryan gave a sigh of being put-upon but started to get up, taking the hint good-naturedly. Before he could leave the table, Zeke stood and motioned for their hosts to remain seated. "I'll get it. My turn."

Tara rose, too. "I'll help Zeke. You and Ryan have done enough this evening."

She followed Zeke into the kitchen and found him staring around the kitchen, a look of confusion on his face. "Why do women always hide things? I can't see any coffee here."

Grinning because he was unwittingly proving Jeanette's point, Tara indicated a coffee percolator on a stand almost under Zeke's nose. "Do you think this could be it?" Checking to see that it was filled, she switched it on and rested her back against a cupboard while she waited for it to boil.

He gave her a long-suffering look. "You're enjoying ganging up on Ryan and me, aren't you?"

She touched his nose playfully, wondering if the wine Jeanette had served with dinner had gone to her head. A little, she decided, but it was more likely the afternoon she'd spent with Zeke, both before and after they'd finally managed to eat. It was just as well he'd brought supplies because they never did make it to the shops.

"You must admit, it's better than what you thought I'd be doing with Ryan."

He folded his arms and contrived a bland look. "I didn't think anything."

"Yes, you did. You were jealous."

"Was not."

"Were, too. Stop arguing and come here," she said, pulling him into her arms and kissing him. She wondered if he could taste Jeanette's beef burgundy on her mouth, as she did on his. She felt him stirring again. But it felt so good to have her arms around him and his lips on hers that she couldn't make herself move away.

"Bold tonight, aren't you?" he said, his mouth moving sensuously against hers.

"Blame it on the red meat."

One eyebrow canted upward, giving him a wicked expression. "If I'd known that's all it would take, I'd have brought steak with the groceries."

Laughter bubbled inside her. "We did okay on canned oysters and asparagus."

"Both well-known aphrodisiacs," he pointed out seriously.

"Do they still count if they're canned?"

His fingers threaded through her hair. "They did for us. But then, we never needed aphrodisiacs, did we?"

She could hardly summon her voice. "No." All they had ever needed was each other.

"How soon do you think we can escape back to the cottage?" he asked, reading her mind and the desire she was afraid showed in her eyes. "It isn't that I don't like our hosts' company. I do, but..." He didn't need to say any more.

"I know. I feel the same way."

"Then what are we doing here?"

His hand wasn't quite steady as he picked up the now-bubbling coffeepot. She replenished the cream and sugar and followed him back to the dining room, feeling as if she had a neon sign around her neck: Property of Zeke Blaxland.

"One more cup then we'll call it a night," he said on a slightly husky note. "It's been an exhausting day."

Tara almost choked, thinking of how he came by his exhaustion. He hadn't looked tired a moment ago when they were in the kitchen. In fact he looked far more vibrant than he had when he arrived this morning, she would swear. It was as if an afternoon of passion had given him a new lease on life. Or perhaps it was the prospect of the night still to come. Picturing it, she felt her pulse quicken.

"This baby farming story must have taken a lot out of you," Jeanette commiserated, making her own assumption. "Ryan and I talked about it and we think you deserve an award for the work you've done."

"Seeing those babies reunited with their real families will be award enough," Zeke insisted. "In any case, much of the detective work was done by my informant at the hospital, allowing me to tie it all together much faster than I could have done otherwise."

"Is that the end of it now?"

Zeke shook his head. "The whole thing will be in court for years while the police and the lawyers fight their legal battles." How could he sound so calm and self-possessed when she was churning inside? Tara wondered. She knew he felt the same way. In the kitchen, the stirring of his need for her had been unmistakable. If not for the presence of their hosts, she suspected he would have taken her there and then, and she would have been more than willing.

But he went on as if nothing was amiss. "I'm checking out a couple of remaining angles. You'll read about them when I have enough to go public. Then I'll feel I've done my job as a journalist."

"You must be proud of what you've achieved."

"I'll be happy when the last of the guilty parties is brought to justice, although that could take years."

Tara put a hand over Zeke's. "I'm proud of him. So are the parents whose babies he traced." The informant may have provided the information, but Zeke had put it all together and forced the authorities to take notice, she thought with satisfaction.

Jeanette stirred sugar into her coffee and looked thoughtful. "What must it be like for those poor children, coming to know one set of people as parents, then being handed over to other people who are strangers to them?''

"It's pretty traumatic stuff," Zeke agreed, thinking of one of the heart-wrenching scenes he had witnessed firsthand. Millions of others had shared the first of the reunions when it was broadcast on the national news. "The paper is arranging for professional counseling for the families, to help them adjust. It will take time."

Jeanette passed around a plate of handmade chocolates. When they reached her, Tara shook her head. "I've already overindulged in your wonderful cooking." She might not be modeling anymore, but she was still the public face of Model Children. Zeke was a bad influence on her, she decided. He made her reckless and self-indulgent, but when he was around, she couldn't seem to hold back.

"I'm glad you enjoyed the meal. It's not often we have celebrities to dinner."

Zeke waved away the description. "Tara might qualify, but I'm only a working journalist. Sometimes the publicity is an inescapable part of the job but I'm glad most of it seems to be dying down now."

"There's no chance of the babies remaining with the wrong families, is there?" Ryan asked.

In the act of reaching for the cream, Tara paused, glancing at Zeke. He shook his head. "Of course not. Those criminals don't deserve to have children."

"But if they were innocent, as one of them claims to be, what then?" Tara said. "In your article, one of the women who received a stolen baby was quoted as saying she didn't know what her partner had done. She was devastated to discover that she'd given birth to a sickly child and it had been exchanged for someone else's healthy baby."

Zeke looked dubious. "I can't believe she's as innocent as she says. Surely a mother knows her own child?"

"She might have suspected something was wrong, but new

babies can look very similar. That's why hospitals put identity tags on them as soon as they're born," Tara said, thinking of the newborns she had seen before she was moved out of the maternity ward. They had all worn wrist and ankle tags.

Zeke frowned. "If the price is high enough, tags can be switched and records altered. That's what happened with the four infants who were given to new families in exchange for payment before the organizers shut the operation down. They didn't give up because they feared being caught, but because they had made enough money to head for safe havens overseas."

Ryan stirred his coffee thoughtfully. "Then you weren't able to trace the key figures?"

"The ringleaders have left the country, but the law will catch up with them eventually. In my final piece, I hope to name one more staff member who was involved, as soon as I have access to the hospital records. Then the rest is up to the police."

"It's exciting stuff," Ryan said. "No wonder Tara has stars in her eyes whenever she looks your way."

Tara lowered her eyes but Jeanette placed a hand on her arm. "Don't let that husband of mine bother you. He has a big mouth."

"And Tara McNiven has the most expressive face I've ever known," Ryan said with a laugh. "She never could hide anything from me. Remember the Anzac biscuits your grandmother made?"

"Unfair," she protested, relieved to have him change the subject, even if it was to a more embarrassing one. Ryan was right, he did know her far too well. He was quite capable of seeing that she loved Zeke completely, whether or not it was what Zeke wanted to hear.

Zeke leaned forward, his eyes agleam. "What happened?"

"You'd never know it from how she looks, but little Tara had the biggest appetite for miles."

"She still does," Zeke interjected with a dark-eyed look that left Tara in no doubt what he meant. She looked away, feeling suddenly feverish and restless, glad that Ryan hadn't seen her reaction.

He went on, "Her grandmother left a plate of freshly baked cookies cooling on a windowsill and Tara ate all but one. I was accused of eating them. I denied it, but her grandmother didn't believe me. Then she got one look at Tara's face and knew who the real culprit was. It wasn't the crumbs on her clothes that gave her away. It was that transparent expression she gets when she's up to something. If I didn't know better, I'd swear she has it now."

So he had noticed. "You're imagining things," Tara said, flustered at being read so easily. She called on all her model training to keep her expression calm and aloof, although it was far from how she felt inside.

But Ryan was relentless. "Too late. What gives with you two? Is there anything permanent on the cards?"

Jeanette came to her rescue. "Enough, already. If Tara has something to share with us, she'll do it in her own good time, won't you, Tara?"

"There's nothing to share," she denied. Her friend had always been perceptive but she doubted whether he knew her as well as he claimed. She had probably given herself away in other ways when they were children, but he had preferred to let her think he could read her every thought.

She had confessed to loving Zeke and had agreed to accept whatever he was prepared to give, even though it would never be as much as she yearned for. Tonight, watching Ryan and Jeanette together, so easy in each other's company, and so obviously perfect for each other, she had seen exactly what she had agreed to give up. But she loved Zeke and she intended to honor her agreement, no matter what it cost her.

Zeke pushed his chair away from the table as if he sensed her growing discomfort, although she hoped he hadn't guessed the real reason. "We must go. Thanks for a wonderful evening."

"The meal was delicious," Tara added.

"I hope you aren't letting Ryan get to you," Jeanette said, sounding concerned.

"Hardly. He's like another brother to me."

"You mean, equally trying?"

Hearing the affection that softened Jeanette's words, Tara shook her head. "Seriously, it's good to see you again, Ryan. We'll catch up again while I'm here. Lovely to meet you, too, Jeanette," she told his wife.

Ryan kissed her lightly then shook hands with Zeke. "Shall I drive you back to Manna Cottage?"

"Thanks but there's no need," Zeke said. "Stay and finish your coffee. It's such a lovely night, we'll walk back."

"Thanks for rescuing me," Tara told him when they were out of earshot of the house. The path was painted silver by a lustrous moon, but she welcomed Zeke's arm to guide her over the rough patches. "Ryan still thinks of me as a kid he can tease."

Zeke's eyes flashed a denial. "Then it's time he got his eyes tested."

"He's well aware that I've grown up, but old habits die hard."

"Yes, they do."

Something in his tone alerted her. He stopped midway along the path and turned her to face him, tilting her chin so her mouth was within reach. When he kissed her, a shiver ran through her although his words made her uneasy. Was she simply a habit with him? She had accepted his explanation that lasting commitments were not his style, but was it the whole story?

He sensed a change in her and he lifted his mouth from hers, his gaze questioning. "Is something the matter?"

"No, everything's fine. Why?"

"Because Ryan's right. You do wear your heart in your expression. I can't believe I never noticed it before."

She strove for lightness but missed by a mile. "You shouldn't listen to him. He also said I believe in signposts written in Penguin."

"He's right about this."

What was her expression telling him now? Nothing he wanted to know, she feared. She summoned a smile and tried to avoid meeting his look. "Then you should be getting the message that I'm tired and ready for bed," she said lightly.

"I'm ready for bed, too, but not because I'm tired, and I don't think you are, either."

She wasn't. Every nerve ending sang a siren song of need that she knew would keep her wide-awake if she tried to sleep now. "I don't think I like being so transparent," she complained. Useless to deny what he could see for himself.

"Only to people who know you well."

She lifted her chin, determined to brazen this out. "Then what am I thinking now?"

In the moonlight, he studied her intently and a lazy smile spilled across his features. "The same thing I'm thinking. Why wait until we get back to the cottage?"

"Zeke, we can't," she squealed, horrified because it *was* in her mind. But he caught her hand and tugged her off the path toward the beach. At this late hour it was deserted, the hordes of tourists who came to see the penguin parade rarely venturing to this part of the island. It didn't mean a local fisherman wouldn't come along.

"Live dangerously," Zeke urged when she hesitated.

"Life with you is always dangerous," she said, knowing she didn't mean his life as an investigative journalist. That kind of danger at least made sense. This threat was to her deeper self, urging her to compromise her ideals to keep him in her life. How far could she go and still face herself in a mirror? As far as it took, she accepted on a silent exhalation. With Zeke she had few boundaries, fewer limits, and almost nothing she wouldn't do for him and with him. What kind of fool did that make her?

He led her through the undergrowth to a secluded cove ringed by bushes sculpted by the sea breezes into strange shapes that looked eerily alive in the moonlight. Removing his jacket, he spread it out on the sandy soil, then pulled her down on top of it. Tonight, Tara had worn a short pewter-colored shift. Now the tweedy texture of his jacket chafed her bare knees and her dress rode higher on her hips. When she tried to tug it down, he cupped his hands around her hips and pulled her against him.

With a sigh, she linked her arms around his neck. When had she ever won a battle with Zeke? Or with herself when he was around?

"I've wanted to do this all evening," he said when he tore his mouth away from hers at last. "I've wanted you all evening."

"Me, too," she agreed. She didn't add that much of her suffering came from seeing Ryan and Jeanette together and knowing she could never have what they had.

Stop feeling sorry for yourself, she ordered herself angrily. With Zeke she had more than many women ever dreamed of. Wanting more was pure greed and she wasn't usually greedy. It was only around him that it surfaced, she acknowledged. It was time she started counting her blessings.

He grazed a finger across her forehead, smoothing the crease her thought had put there. "A frown, Tara? Was it something I said?"

She shook her head. "You aren't responsible for the whole universe, you know."

He nibbled at her ear. "Just this corner of it."

She closed her eyes, almost purring as he trailed kisses along the slender column of her throat and down to the cleft between her breasts. When she felt him slide the zipper of her dress down, she didn't protest. Nor did she demur when he pushed the garment off her shoulders and let it pool around her waist. She was too busy trying to deal with the sensations rioting through her.

She felt hot and cold by turns, none of it having to do with the weather. The evening was balmy and the sea breeze whispered gently across her skin. So Zeke's mouth had to be responsible for the liquid fire raging through her even as she shivered with delight.

Her hands shook as she undid the buttons of his shirt and pushed it off his shoulders. At last. She splayed her hands across his ribs, tracing the outline of them with her fingertips before she pushed further down, past the waistband of his trousers, then lower still until her touch made his breath escape in heaving gasps. Two could play this game.

He opened passion-filled eyes. "Tara."

Her name seemed to be dragged out of him as if speaking cost him. She knew how he felt. There were no words for the turmoil inside her, so she didn't even try. Instead she pulled him down with her, heedless of the sand rasping her back. He paused long enough to tug at his jacket so she was cushioned by it.

She wanted to scream at him to forget comfort, forget being civilized. She wanted him crazy with need for her, beyond reason, beyond thought. Certainly beyond words. He had chosen this place. He could hardly blame her if she regressed to match the surroundings.

So had he, she saw as she met his gaze. He looked primitive, dangerous. She had no time to wonder what she had unleashed before his mouth crushed hers.

Still, she sensed that a word of objection would have pulled him back from the brink. But she had no objections to offer. She pulled his head down, feeling her world explode in flames.

His hands usually so gentle, became demanding as they explored, drove into, skimmed across her until she arched her back in ecstasy. His passion was relentless, but she matched it easily, desire carrying her along as if on a tide.

She felt as if she had touched off a volcano.

Zeke felt the volcano build and knew there was no way to stop it now. He could be risking everything by giving free rein to the driving need he could no longer restrain. But he couldn't seem to get enough of her in his hands or his mouth.

As her increasingly uninhibited responses unleashed the beast in him, he felt heat and hunger grip him until they were almost unendurable. He fed his need by suckling her glorious breasts in turn, taking as much pleasure from her gasps and mindless murmurs of encouragement as from satisfying his own cravings.

Skin touched skin, nerve seared nerve. Still he wanted more. He wanted everything she had to give. He wanted to give her everything.

He pulled the dress all the way off her, tolerating no barriers between them, not even the flimsy thing she was wearing. He had to stand up to shed his own clothes but he did it fast, not caring what fastenings he tore or where things landed. Then he knelt between her beautiful long limbs, worshipping her with his touch, the flames leaping through him all but consuming him.

He had already discovered that her body had changed, but wondrously so, he recalled through the haze fringing his vision. He marveled anew at how soft and round she was, with the faintest silver tracery of marks around her hips. How come he hadn't noticed them before? They must be the stretch marks women made such a fuss about. To him they were a web of beauty and intrigue, hinting at mysteries no man could hope to penetrate. He ran a finger over the marks and she bucked beneath him.

Surely they weren't sensitive? he thought in confusion. Then he understood that Tara herself was sensitized to his slightest caress, not only on the faint marks but everywhere he touched her. He experimented, glorying in her responses as he drove her higher and higher.

"Now, now," she gasped, lifting herself to meet him. "I can't stand any more, Zeke."

He fumbled for his wallet in his discarded pants. His hands shook as he found what he needed, the shaking intensifying as he put protection on. He wanted Tara so much that he felt like throwing caution to the wind, but he was rational enough to want to protect her, although just barely.

When he entered her she enveloped him like molten silk until he felt as if he was dying, but he clung to sanity long enough to make himself move slowly. No need to drive into her like a barbarian, even if he had never felt more like one.

"Please."

Was he hurting her in spite of his care? The fingernails raking his back made it hard to believe and when he looked into her eyes, they were wild and her head was thrown back, her breaths coming in great gulps. He almost stopped until his fogged brain decoded the message in her protest. She didn't want this slow and easy any more than he did. So be it.

As he gave her what she wanted and more, his name became a sob on her lips, then a demand, then a cry that lost itself in a searing, mindless moment when time stood still, before he plunged headlong back to earth, shaken and soaking with perspiration.

She was the same, he saw when his vision cleared. Her whole body trembled with little aftershocks and there was a tiny bruise on her upper lip where his teeth had nipped her in a too passionate kiss. He hadn't been aware of inflicting it and he felt badly at the thought that he had damaged her in the slightest.

He pushed a tendril of hair out of his eyes, and took his weight on his elbows, wondering how to apologize for being such a brute. She was the only woman who could drive him to such excess. Why didn't she open her eyes and tell him she hated him? He deserved it. He deserved a firing squad, he thought when he saw a tear trickle out from her closed lids.

"I'm sorry," he said, his insides twisting into knots. "I didn't mean to be so barbarous."

She did look at him then and her eyes shone wetly, but she was smiling. "You weren't. It was wonderful. You were wonderful."

He stared at her in consternation. "You mean I don't have to shoot myself for behaving like a love-starved teenager?"

She shook her head. "Please don't. I'd hate to think this was the last time."

Not if he had anything to do with it. Still, he couldn't believe she was letting him off so lightly. "But I acted like a caveman."

"And I was your cave woman." She pulled his face down, kissing him lightly. "Aren't you the one who believes in living for the moment?"

"I certainly did this time."

"We did," she reminded him. "I had some say in it, too, you know?"

If he had given her a choice, he couldn't remember it, but evidently she did. He offered a prayer of thanks to the gods who protected men in the throes of passion and allowed some shred of decency to prevail. "Then I'll stop groveling, but not until you assure me I didn't hurt you."

"You didn't," she said, knowing he could only hurt her if she expected more from him than he was able to give. And surely that was up to her?

He eased away from her and wrapped his arms around his bended knees. "As a boy, I got so used to taking what I needed that I sometimes forget things are different now."

The pain in his voice shook her. "You don't have to take anything from me and you didn't tonight. We gave to each other."

"You may think so, but I know how I felt."

Sitting up, she traced the hard ridge of his backbone with a finger, seeing him shudder. "You don't need to worry about being abandoned anymore," she said softly, sensing the cause of his distress. "I'm not going anywhere."

"Even though I haven't offered you forever?"

"You don't have to. What we have is enough." As she said it, she knew it was true. Seductive as it was, she could learn to live without the domestic vision she'd seen played out between Ryan and Jeanette tonight as long as she had Zeke.

"But I left you," he reminded her hoarsely. "I was involved with another woman." Why did he feel as if he had to rub it in? To remind her that nothing lasted, not even the miracle they had just shared.

She forced aside the hurt that threatened to well up, recognizing what was going on at long last. "Nothing you can do will make me reject you ever again. I'll always be here for you."

Zeke stared at her. Could it possibly be true? Everything in him distrusted the notion, although he had enough evidence by now that she meant what she said. "You didn't come with me to America," he reminded her, wondering again why he was stubbornly clinging to his old beliefs. Insurance against pain, he decided. Would the need for it ever go away?

Tara felt her expression turn bleak. "It wouldn't have worked. As soon as you found out about the baby, you would have offered to marry me and ended up hating me for it."

"I could never hate you."

"But you would have resented the pressure. Perhaps even the baby in time."

He shook his head. "I had too much experience of being an unwanted child myself, to do that to anyone else."

"You wouldn't have meant to," she accepted. "But you would have hated being forced into something you didn't want." Still don't want, she added silently.

"So you played the good little woman, waiting at home?"

"Not intentionally. I had no way of knowing you would ever come back."

"Did you hope I would?"

She had never stopped hoping, she saw now, although she had managed to hide it from herself. She nodded.

Zeke pillowed his head against her breast, feeling as if he could hardly breathe. "You're a gift to me, Tara. I..." He stopped, aware of almost crossing a boundary he had never considered crossing before. Three words, that's all they were, but saying them would change everything and he wasn't ready for that.

"Gifts are meant to be unwrapped," she said at his hesitation.

He wondered if she heard that laughter held as much relief as arousal. "There isn't much wrapping left."

"But there are still surprises."

This time she made him lie back, taking her own gratification from discovering the heights to which she could drive him with her touch and her kisses. Seeing him shuddering with needs she had called up, she felt powerful, sensuous and giddy with love. When a small voice of demurral raised itself in some far corner of her mind, she managed to override it. If this was all she and Zeke ever had, she was determined to make it sensational.

Chapter 13

Tara was accustomed to waking up and finding Zeke's side of the bed empty, so when she opened her eyes and saw the bedclothes thrown back, she smiled lazily. He was probably writing down some idea that had occurred to him during the night.

Then everything came back to her. They were in the cottage on Phillip Island, having managed to get to bed—to sleep, anyway—as the first fingers of dawn stained the sky. It was after eight now, she saw from the bedside clock.

Useless to feel slighted by his absence, she told herself. Zeke was Zeke. Work had always been his priority. The aches in her body when she stretched luxuriously reminded her, if she needed it, that she had occupied more of his attention yesterday than anything else, even eating and sleeping.

Still, a cup of coffee would be nice, she thought, glancing at the bedroom door as if he might come through it carrying a tray. When he didn't, she bounded out of bed. She was perfectly capable of getting her own coffee instead of swooning against the pillows like a love-starved maiden.

She grimaced at herself in the mirror. She definitely wasn't love-starved and there was sand in her hair. Wrapping a robe around herself she padded barefoot through to the kitchen. "Zeke?"

No answer. Through the window she saw that his rental car was gone. Dismay stabbed through her. What was going on? She had agreed not to demand forever, but that didn't mean she would tolerate being abandoned next morning without so much as a goodbye kiss.

Then she saw the note propped against the door of the microwave. A phone call had alerted him to a new development in the baby farming story, she read. She frowned, annoyed that she hadn't heard the call. She wasn't to worry, he added in the note, but he was catching the twelve-thirty flight to Sydney and thought she would be safer staying where she was. He would call her later.

Safer? A frisson of anxiety rippled through her as she remembered the man Zeke had been concerned about, Jenny's husband, who was a midwife at the hospital. According to Zeke's research, he had turned out to have a history of mental instability. Did he know that Zeke was on to him? What did Zeke fear he might do?

Anger eclipsed Tara's fear. So he would call, would he? What was she supposed to do in the meantime? Sit by the phone until Zeke remembered her existence? He should have told her what was going on and given her the choice of staying or going with him. Typical, she fumed. He wasn't prepared to commit to her, but he was more than ready to take charge of her life. She felt her eyes widen. Was his behavior a commitment of sorts, perhaps speaking louder than words?

In a flash she recalled what he'd said last night. "You're a gift to me, Tara. I…" I—what? Love you? Her heart picked up speed. He hadn't said it and he wasn't going to, so why torment herself? But what if he had shown it in other ways and she had missed the signs?

She was back in the bedroom and throwing clothes on before the decision reached her conscious mind. It was still early. He had the same long drive back to Melbourne that she did, and she knew the road better. If she didn't waste time, and bent a few road rules along the way, she might manage to catch up with Zeke before he flew back to Sydney.

His flight was boarding by the time she tore along the walkway at Tullamarine Airport, the last passenger to make the flight that had been delayed by a further stroke of good luck. Having a well-known face had its advantages, and she had shamelessly used her celebrity status to talk her way, not only onto the flight but into a seat across the aisle from Zeke.

He was scanning the pages of the *Melbourne Age* and didn't see her take her seat. She refused the flight attendant's offer of a drink, and fastened her seat belt, her heart thumping as she waited for Zeke to notice her.

When he folded the paper and looked around, his expression turned thunderous. ''What in blazes are you doing here?''

''Coming back to Sydney with you,'' she said demurely. ''After last night I couldn't bear to stay on the island without you.''

She had deliberately lifted her voice and heads turned their way. Zeke looked embarrassed and furious by turns. Some of the other passengers looked envious. ''You have no idea what you've done,'' he growled.

''Oh, I have a good idea. I ache in places I didn't know I had muscles.''

''You know I didn't mean that.'' The envy turned to smiles but Zeke's angry gaze swept the cabin. The faces swiftly disappeared behind newspapers and in-flight magazines.

"My contact at the hospital stumbled over some misfiled documents that will help me nail the midwife."

"Shouldn't you let the police handle it?" While he stayed with her, she added silently, finding that his priorities hurt more than they had any business doing.

"My contact won't talk to anyone else. And with the midwife's history, I want to pin her down quickly. In her mental state, she could be capable of anything."

Tara felt her heart leap into her throat and touched his hand across the aisle, ignoring the heat that infused her touch. This was no time to let herself get sidetracked. "Wait a minute, the midwife you're looking for is a *woman?*"

He nodded. "Jenny Fine's sister-in-law, Rosemary. She was on duty at the hospital the night you were there. She was flouting medical ethics by delivering her sister-in-law's baby, but according to my source, she made a habit of bending the rules to suit herself. No one knew about her past history until Bill turned up R. Fine's psychiatric record."

Across the narrow aisle, Tara's fingers tightened around his arm. "Zeke, you could be looking for the wrong person. R. Fine could also be Jenny's husband, Ross. He's a midwife, too."

He recoiled visibly. "What? There's no record of a Ross Fine working at the Roses."

"Jenny said he used a different name because the hospital wouldn't allow two family members to work in the same ward. She said they needed his job because she'd had to give up hers to have the baby. She only confided in me because I was so scared when my doctor was delayed. She assured me her husband would look after me."

Zeke leaned closer, keeping his words between them. "If he's the one I think he is, he called himself Ross Crichton."

Recognition pulsated through her. "I'm sure that was his name."

"Some of the altered ward records carried his signature.

He was only a small part of the operation, but he might lead us to the main players. His trail disappeared after he left the hospital, and I assumed he'd gone overseas."

"Then he could still be in Sydney."

He nodded. "Possibly working in another hospital under his real name."

"If he is the one with the psychiatric record, and he finds out you're on to him…"

"There's no telling what he might do."

Fear gripped Tara along with horror as she remembered the midwife who had delivered her baby. At the time, she had thought him distant but kind, apologizing for the absence of her doctor and assuring her she was in good hands. He had shown no sign that he was mentally unstable, or that he was involved in anything untoward.

When her baby hadn't cried at birth, Ross had reacted swiftly, hurrying the baby into an adjacent resuscitation room. On the verge of panic, Tara had never suspected the midwife's true nature. Or that if her son had been healthy instead of stillborn, he could have been among those stolen. It was hard to take in.

The businesswoman sitting next to Tara broke into her thoughts by leaning across her. "Would you and your friend like to sit together?"

Zeke didn't hesitate. He was out of his seat and beside Tara before the other woman had settled in his vacated seat. Tara moved to the window so he could have the aisle seat. As he took it and their thighs touched, her senses went into red alert. It had been easier to talk rationally with the width of the aisle between them.

"I don't think…" she began nervously.

His hand settled on her arm. "There's something else you should know."

The urgency in his voice was alarming enough but the

pressure of his fingers set her nerves jangling. "Do you think Ross Fine might follow us?"

"I don't know where he'll turn up or even if he will," he repeated. "This is more personal. As of now we're married."

She stared at him. "Have you lost your mind? How can we be married?"

"We ran away to do the deed," he repeated firmly. "You're now Mrs. Tara Blaxland."

He had lost his mind. "Maybe a few more days off will help."

He rubbed his chin. He hadn't taken the time to shave before leaving the island, she noted. He looked fierce, piratical, capable of almost anything except marriage. Her pulse accelerated at the very idea. He gave a crooked half smile. "I know it sounds crazy. But Bill Ellison also told me my competitors have discovered that you had a baby at the Roses hospital at the time of the scandal. They're baying for blood."

"I suppose they're asking why you didn't mention me in your series?"

He nodded. "Thinking I'm covering up a personal angle on the story has made them dig deeper. They found out about the baby." He took a breath that shuddered slightly. "The timing of the delivery has convinced a couple of my colleagues that there's more to it than we're letting on."

Her fingers whitened around the seat arm. "They think you're looking for our baby." Without waiting for his response, she said, "You didn't want me with you because you expect them to be waiting for you at Mascot, don't you?"

"I'm afraid so. I'm sorry it's come to this."

"How will pretending we're married help?" Even saying the word in connection with Zeke felt peculiar but, she admitted to herself, it was dangerously attractive.

"It's the best diversion I can think of at short notice."

A bitter taste filled her mouth and she wished she had

accepted the attendant's offer of orange juice. But she had also refused the meal tray, as had Zeke. She ran her tongue over her lips. Of all the ways she had ever imagined Zeke proposing to her, this wasn't one of them.

"The hounds will be watching the incoming flights, ready to besiege us with questions. They'll want to know if you knew anything about the scandal before I broke the story, that kind of thing," he went on. "Brace yourself for one of them to ask if you think our baby could be alive and if so, where you think he might be."

She felt the color leave her face. "Oh, Zeke, no."

"I'm afraid so." He gave her a rueful look. "It's what I'd do in the same situation."

She shook her head in denial, having seen him at work. He was never deliberately hurtful if it could be avoided. "Do you think telling them we're married is enough of a diversion?"

"They're not expecting it. The surprise might buy us enough time to get out of the airport and come up with a better idea. If you agree?"

What choice did she have? She couldn't face discussing her lost child with a group of strangers thrusting microphones and cameras into her face. "I agree."

He removed a fine band of gold from the little finger of his right hand. It had belonged to his mother, she remembered, and was the only memento he had of the woman who had borne him. She may not have been the best of mothers, but he honored her memory, Tara knew. A tremor gripped her as he took her left hand and placed the ring on her wedding finger. "Looks pretty good, Mrs. Blaxland."

She felt her eyes brim, knowing she would give a lot to have this be real. It wasn't, she reminded herself over and over. It was convenient, that was all. She looked at the ring on her finger through a veil of moisture. "It fits well."

"My mother was about your size," he said distantly. "Did I tell you she was beautiful?"

"No, you never did." He had said very little about his mother, other than to tell Tara how she had surrendered him to foster care and claimed him back several times when he was little. "What was she like?"

"She never had any money so she bought clothes at charity places, but she made them look like a million dollars. I remember being proud of the way heads turned when we walked down the street and she was holding my hand. She said she was proud of me, too, but it only lasted until the novelty wore off."

She touched his arm. "Don't, Zeke. She loved you in her own way. She just wasn't a very good parent."

He nodded. "I always vowed I'd be different if I had children."

Her heart turned over. "I'm sure you would."

He half turned in his seat, shielding her from the other passengers with his body. "If we're married, shouldn't I kiss the bride?"

"Here?" She knew her alarm was more for herself than the people around them. With his ring on her finger, the gold still warm from his hand, she felt raw and vulnerable.

His warm gaze slid over her like honey dropped from a spoon. "You've obviously never heard of the Mile High Club."

She swallowed hard, showing that she had. He read her reaction as an invitation and wrapped an arm around her. Then his mouth found hers, hot, demanding, and so very sensuous that she felt the kiss all the way to her toes.

When he lifted his head, his eyes danced. "I can't wait for the honeymoon."

She tried to match his light tone. "I thought we had that yesterday."

His eyes darkened. "Honeymoon, wedding, proposal. Do you think we'll ever get the order right?"

Could he hear himself? She had never expected Zeke to use words such as wedding and honeymoon so casually, at least not where she was concerned. She couldn't bring herself to answer.

It was just as well. The plane began to make the approach to Sydney airport, and Zeke released her to fasten his seat belt. "We got married in Melbourne yesterday," he whispered. "Quiet ceremony, no fanfare."

"What church?" she asked frantically, wondering what she had agreed to. The other journalists were bound to check the facts and would soon find out they didn't hold up.

"If we don't mention one, it will take them longer to check," he said, anticipating her thought. "We can truthfully say we spent our wedding night on Phillip Island."

"Not quite what I had in mind," she said almost to herself. A bride wouldn't haven awoken to find the bed empty and the groom on his way back to Melbourne.

He gripped her hand. "I realize it's a rough deal. I'll make it up to you, I promise."

What part? she wanted to ask, but the plane jolted to a halt on the tarmac. A few minutes later they joined the other passengers streaming from the plane.

The carpeted walkway was clear ahead, but a crowd of people pressed against the doorway they would soon have to pass through. Flashbulbs popped as they approached and Tara instinctively huddled against Zeke. When he put a protective arm around her, the bulbs popped even more frantically. As soon as they stepped into the terminal, the questions began.

They were as uncompromising as Zeke had warned her, but she couldn't help flinching when she was asked about the baby. She made herself remain outwardly calm, needing all of her model's training to maintain a poised appearance while she was crying inside. Then a journalist asked her about the possibility that her baby was still alive, and her defenses threatened to crumble.

"Wait a minute, I have a scoop for you," Zeke said before she could answer. Looking at him, Tara wouldn't have guessed that any of this bothered him, until she saw a faint tightening around his eyes. She recalled how depleted he had looked when he arrived on the island and sensed that he held exhaustion at bay by sheer willpower. A day away from all this had helped, but she suspected the improvement was only surface-deep. He couldn't keep going indefinitely.

This must be as difficult for him as for her, but he said evenly, "Let me introduce my bride as of yesterday."

To Tara's astonishment his announcement had the desired effect, turning the questions in much safer directions and causing the journalists to scribble furiously or to check their recorders to make sure they captured every detail. Most of the photographers had melted away after the first few minutes, presumably to process the pictures they'd taken.

Zeke hadn't stopped moving, she was aware, forcing his colleagues to follow him like a swarm of bees. They had to spread out to fit on the escalators and by the time they reached the bottom, Bill Ellison was waiting for them. Zeke whispered that he had called from Melbourne and given Bill his flight number. Bill looked surprised to see her, too, but took it in stride.

"Luckily you only have carry-on baggage. We'd better hurry, I'm parked in the limo bay," Bill said, taking her arm and hustling her through sliding-glass doors.

By the time the journalists had recovered enough to realize they weren't heading for the baggage carousels, Bill was easing his car out into the traffic. Tara slumped in the back seat and gave Zeke a look of relief. His arm came around her.

He leaned forward. "Thanks for getting us out of there so fast, Bill."

The investigator's gaze was warm in the mirror. "Anytime, pal. What did you do to throw them off the scent?"

"I told them we were married."

"Nice touch." A beat. "You aren't, are you?"

"I'm not that fast a worker. And the topic is not open for discussion," he said, forestalling whatever Bill was about to say.

Zeke turned his attention to Tara. "Are you all right?"

She nodded. "A bit shaken. The questions were rather blunt."

"'In-depth' is the industry term, but they were rough even by my reckoning. You did well."

His praise lifted her spirits. "So did you, coming up with the marriage ruse."

"It worked for now, but we'll have to keep up the deception for a few days until the fuss dies down. Will it be a problem for you?"

For herself, she could keep it up forever, but since that word wasn't in his vocabulary, there was no point fantasizing. "I don't mind," she said, more frankly than he knew.

"If we don't want to tip them off that it's a sham, you'd better stay at my place."

"Or you could come to mine." She knew she'd feel a lot more comfortable on her home ground. Moving into Zeke's place was too reminiscent of their old relationship.

He shook his head. "I have the dog to consider."

Bill glanced at them in the mirror, following the discussion with obvious interest. "I could—"

"You could stay out of this," Zeke cut him off. She saw Bill give a suit-yourself shrug and wondered what that interchange was all about.

"Then you probably don't want to hear about the TV crew camped outside your place," Bill said with another lift of his shoulders.

Zeke groaned. "If I go near the hospital with that lot on my tail, my contact will run a mile."

"Speaking of running, Rosemary Fine has already done it. She was seen boarding a flight to Europe the day before yesterday."

Zeke swore quietly, plainly aggrieved that she had escaped justice for now. "We'll just have to hope the overseas authorities catch up with her," he said. "But she may not be the one we want." Quickly he told Bill what Tara had told him about Ross Fine.

It was the investigator's turn to swear. "Shows what comes of making assumptions. I stopped looking for any other R. Fine after we fingered Rosemary. At least now I know who I'm looking for, I should be able to connect Ross Crichton with the R. Fine in the psychiatric records."

"My source at the hospital can probably help, but I don't dare go near the place until things cool down."

Bill nodded agreement. "Maybe you should lie low for a few days."

"I don't have a choice." Zeke rubbed at his forehead. "I can't even go home without facing another barrage."

"What about a hotel?"

His expression cleared. "I have a better idea. Turn left at the next lights, Bill."

"Why not? I'm only the chauffeur."

Zeke tapped his friend's shoulder. "Put it on my account."

"If I did that every time you needed a favor, you'd be flat broke."

Tara felt a flash of envy as she listened to their easy banter. They were obviously long-standing friends and for a moment she wished—no, she wasn't going to start dreaming again. The kind of friendship they had wouldn't suit her with Zeke, but she was afraid it was all she was ever going to get.

They pulled up outside a rundown Federation cottage and

Bill shot Zeke a look of confusion. "Hey, this is my place. I don't have room for guests."

"We're not staying." Zeke got out and opened the driver's door. "You are."

"This is also my car."

"And you'll get it back tomorrow in pristine condition. I'll even have it washed for you."

Still grumbling, Bill relinquished the driver's seat to Zeke then helped Tara into the front passenger side. "Make sure he takes care of this baby," he instructed her.

"I'll do my best, but you know Zeke." This was another example of how he went his own way.

"Sure do." He leaned into Zeke's window. "I need it back tomorrow. I have a job to do in the afternoon."

"Guaranteed." Zeke started the engine.

She heard Bill say, "I take it you plan to leave the dog here for a few more days?"

"He's minding the puppy?" she guessed as Zeke gave his friend a wave of thanks and drove off.

"He loves every minute of it. Do him good to have somewhere to put all that affection he stores up."

"He isn't in a relationship?"

"He was, but she left. His working hours aren't exactly compatible with a happy home life."

It didn't take irregular working hours to destroy a relationship, she was tempted to point out. An excess of independence and a reluctance to trust could do it equally well. "Where are we going?" she asked.

"A secret hideaway not even Bill knows about."

Thoroughly intrigued, she watched the streets as he drove steadily northward until they were on the outskirts of the city where the houses were more imposing and the gardens larger. The wide streets were lined with mature trees, giving the area a country feel. "Peaceful," she murmured.

He looked pleased. "Exactly why I bought it."

She blinked in surprise. Zeke didn't believe in permanence, in tying himself to bricks and mortar. He'd always said he preferred to own property as investments rather than homes. When he bought the puppy, he had told her he planned to buy a house, but she hadn't believed he meant it. "You've bought a house here?"

"This one. Welcome home, Mrs. Blaxland."

The torrent of emotions unleashed by his choice of words almost made her miss her first sight of the house. It was lovely, she saw when her vision cleared enough to focus on it. "It reminds me of an English country cottage," she said.

"Exactly why I bought it. It has a history, a past."

The very things Zeke himself felt he lacked, she knew. "I love the dressed stone foundations, and the mellow color of the bricks."

"The seller was born in the house and only sold it because he's moving into a retirement home. He told me the bricks are from an inner-city church that was demolished last century. The kauri floorboards and pine doors are from an old city council office. There's also a marble fireplace from the same building."

Her throat threatened to close as she walked up the flagstone path, noting the ancient wisteria twined around the verandah, which was shaded by a bull-nosed iron roof. She ran a hand appreciatively over the carved wooden balustrade edging the verandah. If Zeke wanted permanence, he had found it in this place. It had already stood for more than a century and looked set for a couple more.

He glanced at her hand. "Is that bothering you?"

She realized she had been twisting the ring Zeke had placed on her finger and she stopped abruptly. "Not really." She was glad he hadn't asked about the house because it *was* bothering her. This was a place to shelter generations of one family. She could almost hear the shouts of children as they raced around the cottage garden. She could see a swing hanging from the Moreton Bay fig tree.

She turned away, not wanting Zeke to see how troubled she was by dreams that were out of her reach. She wished he had never shown her the house. How she was supposed to stay here, she had no idea.

He rested his hands on her shoulders and spoke close to her ear. "Something is bothering you. Was it the scene at the airport?"

She took refuge in the distraction. "It wasn't pleasant."

"Put it out of your mind. No one knows I own this place yet and the title deeds are registered in the name of a trust, so we won't be traced easily." He frowned. "The only problem is, I haven't had time to furnish it yet. A few period pieces came with the house, but that's all."

The lack of furniture troubled her less than the lack of a firm foundation for her and Zeke. She had told herself she could handle it, but here in his house, she was no longer so confident. Having his ring on her finger, however spuriously, didn't help. "Maybe we should go to a hotel after all."

He bounded up the front steps, key in hand. "Too risky. Besides, I want to show you the house."

She held back as he pushed open the front door. In a surprise move, he swung her into his arms. "What are you doing? Put me down."

"Carrying my bride over the threshold," he said with a laugh. "It's traditional, isn't it?"

Cradled against his chest with her arms linked around his neck, she struggled to speak. "I think we have the order wrong again."

"It's becoming a habit with us." He set her down inside the door. A heartbeat passed while he looked at her against the backdrop of his new home, then he pulled her into his arms and kissed her. "Welcome home."

It wasn't her home and never would be, but in his arms

she felt more at home than any place on earth, and she surrendered to his kiss with a sigh. She had promised herself
she would accept only as much as he wanted to give. She
might as well start now.

When he lifted his head, his eyes were full of questions.
"Seeing you here makes me wish this was our home," he
said, his voice barely above a whisper. "You make me wish
a lot of things."

She shook her head. "Don't say them, please. Let's be
content with what we have."

"Are you content with it?"

What choice did she have? "Of course," she lied. "We'd
better get our bags inside."

"I'll get them. You look around. There's champagne in
the kitchen." Intercepting her quizzical look, he explained,
"I planned to open it on my first night here, but we need it
more now. There's no food, but we can send out for pizza."

The kitchen was one of the few rooms that looked ready
for occupation, she soon found. A magnificent cedar slab
table and chairs dominated the generous floor space. It wasn't
hard to imagine how lovely the room would look with
kitchen knickknacks and floral-print fabrics adding to the
country atmosphere.

She had to hunt for the refrigerator, finding it was paneled
in the same beech timber as the cupboards. In it she found a
bottle of French champagne sitting in solitary splendor on
the top shelf.

She was wrestling with the wire fastening when he came
in. "I've put our things in the bedroom."

"Bedroom?"

He took the bottle from her and opened it efficiently.
"There are four, but only one is furnished. After yesterday,
I didn't think you'd mind."

She stopped herself from blushing but it was close. He

was right, she didn't mind. "We don't seem to have any glasses."

He opened a door on a walk-in pantry. There should be jars of home-made preserves on the shelves, she thought, but there was only an unopened pack of disposable glasses. "They should be crystal for such an important moment, but these will have to do."

It was a day for compromises, the ring on her finger weighing so heavily that she wondered if it was the greatest compromise of all. She had made the choice, she reminded herself, and knew that it was no real contest. She wasn't giving up anything. She was gaining a love beyond anything most people ever imagined.

She remembered what she'd told herself on the island. Was it only this morning? It seemed like half a lifetime ago. She had realized that Zeke, who didn't believe in forever, was planning a future with her, whether he knew it or not. He might regard the ring as a convenience, but it was a huge step for someone so resistant to committing himself. Now he had brought her to the first real home he had bought in his life. She had to start seeing things through his eyes. He was making the only commitment he knew how.

She raised the plastic glass of champagne he gave her and felt joy flooding through her. It was easy to say, "To us." Whatever was missing from their relationship, they had one another. She wouldn't allow anything else to matter.

His gaze was warm as he touched his glass to hers. "To us."

The bed was a magnificent four-poster, too cumbersome to be moved out of the room, Tara guessed, so Zeke had bought it with the house. A light-as-air duvet and two feather pillows had evidently been made to fit the huge bed. They would have to make do without sheets.

She was again assailed by a vision of children bouncing on the bed between her and Zeke. Stop it, she ordered herself.

What was it about this house that made her imagine such things?

She was already showered and in bed by the time Zeke came upstairs. "I just got a call from Bill," he said.

"Has he located Ross Fine yet?"

"A man answering his description was seen near the family home late this afternoon, but when Bill called the house, Jenny Fine denied knowing where her husband was."

She cupped her hands behind her head. "Do you believe her?"

"Bill said she sounded strained, but that could be due to her husband taking off." He shrugged out of his shirt a little too carefully, as if a great weight settled on his shoulders. It was confirmed when he said, "Right now, I'm too tired to think about it."

When he got into bed, there was a huge gap between them and he made no move to close it. She was tired, too, she told herself. With Zeke it was cumulative, coming on top of weeks of draining investigative work. She couldn't blame him if all he wanted to do was to sleep.

All the same, she couldn't help thinking it was a lonely way to spend a wedding night.

Chapter 14

She awoke next morning, surprised to find she had slept for ten hours straight. Zeke was already up, so she dressed in a white shirt and navy pants she'd thrown into an overnight bag before leaving Phillip Island, and joined him in the kitchen.

When he offered her a share of the leftover pizza she pulled a face. "Not for breakfast," she said with a shudder. "I have some fruit in my bag."

"Think of the protein and carbohydrates you're missing."

She retrieved an apple from her bag, polished the fruit on her sleeve and bit into it. "I'll take my chances, thanks."

He took a deep breath. "Tara, I'm sorry about last night."

She kept her expression bland. "What about last night?"

"I was so dog-tired, I went to sleep as soon as my head touched the pillow. I didn't mean to neglect you."

Guilt welled up because it was exactly what she *had* felt but she shook her head. "It's okay, I was asleep in minutes, myself. It was quite a day."

He had plugged his phone in to a power outlet to recharge, and she started when it rang beside her. Zeke picked it up. Seconds later, the pizza dropped from his hand. "What the blazes...?"

She saw him blanch and alarm shrilled through her. "What is it? What's wrong?"

He held up a hand. "Where? When? Are you sure? I'm not putting her through this if there's any chance it's a mistake."

His eyes met her over the compact phone. For once she couldn't read the expression there. He had come to his feet and looked primed for action. But why? And against what? What didn't he want to put her through?

He braced himself against the table as if his legs had trouble holding him up. "Then it must be true. We'll be there as fast as we can."

"What is it?" she repeated as he ended the call. He was breathing as erratically as a long-distance runner at a finishing line.

He grabbed her hand. "We have to go. I'll explain on the way."

"Why can't you tell me now?" she asked, but he tugged her along, slamming the front door behind them before urging her into the car. Bill would have to wait to get his car back she realized as Zeke slammed it into gear and roared out of the driveway as if the hounds of hell were chasing them.

Sure that their rate of travel had nothing to do with the speed limit, she braced herself to hear sirens behind them, but none came. "Can't you slow down? Where are we going?"

"Ross Fine has surfaced at his wife's place. It seems he was there when Bill called, but Fine made his wife promise not to tell anyone. Luckily, she managed to get to a neighbor and call Bill back."

"Did Ross hurt her?"

"Worse, much worse. He took a baby hostage."

"Oh, no." The idea of anyone using a helpless infant for their own ends made her feel ill, but she didn't understand how it involved Zeke or herself. "You can't believe you're responsible?"

"More than you possibly know," he muttered.

There had to be something more. "That does it. Stop this car right now and tell me the rest."

He reacted almost too quickly, the sudden deceleration throwing her against him as he screeched to a halt across a driveway. When he turned to her, his face was white. "There's no easy way to say this, but the baby he's holding is probably Brendan."

She rammed a knuckle against her mouth to stifle a scream. "No, it's a cruel hoax. Brendan is dead. I held his body."

"You held a baby's body, but there's every chance it was the Fines' child, not ours." Zeke's voice was icy. Touching him, she found his body was the same.

Her thoughts whirled. "What about the DNA test?"

"Fixed by Fine while he worked at the hospital. When his wife insisted on getting one done, he used details from a test on an older child by his previous relationship, changing the name and birthdate to match their present child. It satisfied his wife at first, but recently Ross has been acting so strangely that she became convinced he had switched her dead child for a healthy one. Without telling him, she had another test done and the baby isn't theirs. Since only one other boy was born at the same time, it has to be ours."

"Oh, God." The universe spun around her and she gripped Zeke's arm. Her baby was alive. She couldn't afford to faint now, while he was in the hands of a man known to be mentally unstable. Horror rang in her voice as she said, "We must do something."

"We're about to. Ross is asking for us and we're not going to disappoint him."

He slammed the car into gear and pulled out again, the tires spitting gravel. This time they were intercepted by a police car, but as soon as Zeke identified them and explained the situation, the officer led them through the traffic, lights and sirens clearing their way.

The Fines' house was on the other side of the city, taking almost forty minutes to reach it at breakneck speed. By then, the street was blocked by a fleet of official vehicles and watched over by TV crews and some of the press Tara recognized from the airport.

"How did they get here so quickly?" she asked as they were escorted through the throng.

"Scanners tuned into the emergency frequencies." His clipped tone suggested he wasn't coping much better than she was. She slid her hand into his. He squeezed her fingers, getting her message. Whatever happened, they were in it together.

A police officer approached them with a pinch-faced woman in tow. Tara recognized her immediately, although she hadn't been sure she would. "Jenny Fine?"

The woman nodded. "I'm sorry it's come to this. If I'd only done something sooner, but whenever I suggested something wasn't right about our baby, Ross told me I was imagining things. But I'm not, am I?" Her voice wavered and her eyes flooded with tears.

Tara felt her own eyes fill. "Thank you for having the courage to speak up."

"Ross won't hurt the baby, I know him. He just couldn't stand to lose another child."

So he stole theirs. Tara bit the accusation back. It wasn't Jenny's fault and she had done all she could to put things right. Tara could barely imagine what she must be going through now. She touched the other woman's hand in wordless response.

Jenny nodded as if Tara had spoken. "I guess I wanted to believe he was ours, too, although he didn't look anything like Ross or me, or our other baby."

The police officer went on alert. "Is there another child in the house?"

Jenny shook her head. "Ross's son from his first marriage lives with his mother. Our other baby died at four months. Crib death, they said. He just didn't wake up next morning. Ross wasn't the same afterward."

"You knew Ross was sick, didn't you?" Tara interposed.

"Because his marriage had broken up, and then we lost the baby. But he was able to go back to work. He told me he's all right now."

"Obviously he isn't all right."

The police officer frowned. "That's all we need."

Jenny protested, "He isn't crazy. He loves Vaughan—I mean, your baby."

Tara's stomach twisted into knots. "Then why is he holding the child hostage?"

"He thinks you want to take him away."

"Of course I do, he's my child," Tara all but screamed.

"He's convinced himself the baby is really ours. I believed it, too, until I started reading the stories in the newspaper. We argued about it and Ross stormed out. I didn't know what to do. Then yesterday he came back, but made me promise not to tell anyone he was there. He said people were following him. I guess it was the police. When I suggested we should get some help, he started threatening me, and I ran out of the house. Tom, our neighbor, is good to me. He urged me to call the police, and promised to be there for me, when this is all over."

"You did the right thing," Tara said. It took everything

she had to be patient with Jenny, when all she wanted to do was to go to her baby.

The other woman's eyes brightened. "The irony is, I'm pregnant again and this time everything is going really well. If Ross had only been patient..."

At a sign from the officer, a policewoman shepherded Jenny away. Tara saw a good-looking man a little older than Jenny intercept them and place an arm around her shoulders. Jenny's face lit up and Tara felt a flicker of hope pierce her despair. If that was Tom, Jenny and her coming child would be all right.

Tara felt Zeke's arm go around her. "It's true, our baby is alive," she said in a faint whisper. After months of mourning, it was nearly too much to take in.

"I know." He sounded hoarse and his eyes swam. He blinked hard and martialed some resource within himself. She suspected it would be needed to get them both through this. "What can we do?" he asked the officer.

"At the moment, wait."

Zeke's anger flared. "To hell with that, my son is in there."

"I know it's hard, but our negotiator is on the job. If the other lady's right, her husband loves the baby so he won't hurt it."

"You can't be sure," Tara said fiercely. Her heart ached and her arms did, too, with the need to hold her child, warm and alive this time, not...she wouldn't let herself remember the other time. *Brendan was alive, hang on to that,* her inner voice said.

"What are his demands?"

The officer looked relieved at being asked something he could answer. Only Tara sensed that Zeke's composure was no more than surface-deep, a result of years of journalistic experience. She felt his tension radiating along the arm he kept around her.

"He hasn't asked for anything yet," the officer said. "He keeps repeating that no one is going to take his baby away."

"Has he made any threats?"

"Only implicit ones. His wife doesn't think he's armed, but we aren't taking any chances."

Tara wrestled herself free of Zeke's grip. "Listen to yourselves. 'Is he armed? Has he made any threats?' This is my baby you're discussing so calmly. We have to do something."

"They are doing something." Zeke's cold statement cut through her mounting hysteria. "It won't help to fall apart now."

His statement had the desired effect. She wrestled herself back under control. "I can't just stand and wait."

"Doing anything else could put the baby at greater risk," the officer said.

She reined in the part of her wanting to rage and scream, and struggled to match Zeke's composure. It wasn't easy but she drew strength from him, wondering who he was supposed to draw strength from. From her, she realized. She had to be strong for him, and for her baby. She straightened. "There must be something I can do?"

"The negotiators will probably want you to talk to him over a loud hailer."

"Why can't I go to the house?"

Zeke's expression swiftly vetoed any such idea. "The man is dangerously unpredictable."

"He was sane enough to organize a baby switching racket." She had never imagined that her child was one of his victims.

"He was an underling, paid to falsify records and keep his mouth shut. The real organizers probably held his past over his head to get his cooperation. Since they'd already left the country by the time Brendan was born, I don't think he was meant to be part of the scheme," Zeke said. "Ross's part in the switching scandal probably gave him the idea of stealing ours after his own was stillborn.''

Tara had a sudden vision of the small, lifeless body she'd been given to hold and felt anger threaten to swamp her. She held on to Zeke's arm as if to a lifeline, knowing it was the only thing keeping her connected to reality. Without his presence, she would have stormed the house, regardless of the risk. All she could think about was snatching her child from the kidnapper's arms.

She made herself think rationally for Brendan's sake. ''Let me talk to Ross.''

The officer nodded. ''I'll take you to the negotiators. They'll tell you what to say.''

''I know what to say. I want my baby back.''

''We have to let them guide us,'' Zeke said. ''For the baby's sake.''

It was what she'd told herself and she knew she would do what the experts recommended. She would do anything if it brought her baby back safely. She wasn't going to lose him a second time, she vowed silently.

The negotiator, a woman in her thirties, looked alarmingly unprepossessing. It was probably her job to do so, Tara accepted, but only remembering what was at stake stopped her from screaming at her to take immediate action. The woman sensed her hostility. ''It's normal to want to rush in with guns blazing, but it's invariably better to talk your way out than to shoot your way in.''

The woman's calm manner had the desired effect. ''It's so hard.''

''I know. If my baby was in there, I'd feel the same way.''

Shaking, Tara let herself be led to a police car being used as a shield between the officers and the house. Zeke positioned himself at her side as if glued there. Crouching down and motioning them to do the same, the negotiator handed

Tara what looked like a microphone. "Speak into this and you'll be heard inside the house."

Now that she was in the front line, Tara felt her throat close. "What do I say?"

"Tell him who you are. He's been asking for you."

Zeke had told her this. "What does he want from me?"

"He thinks you're plotting to take his child away. He thinks if you tell everyone that the baby is his, we'll believe him."

The microphone dropped from her nerveless fingers. "I can't agree to give up my baby."

The negotiator retrieved the handset and wrapped Tara's icy fingers around it. "You don't have to agree. Just go along for now and let him do the talking. Are you up to trying?"

Tara felt Zeke's hand on her shoulder. She looked at him and he nodded encouragement. She took a shuddering breath. "I'm ready."

"Then go ahead, but try not to say anything to set him off. If you feel tempted, hit this button." She indicated a switch on the side of the handset. "It cuts off the loud-hail."

A sense of unreality overcame Tara but she gulped in air, then hit the switch. "Ross, this is Tara McNiven. What do you want from me?"

The negotiator gave her a thumbs-up sign and mouthed the word, "Good."

Across the street, the front door slowly opened and a man's thin face appeared briefly in the opening before he pulled back. "Come closer, where I can see you," he shouted.

Tara started to rise but the negotiator held her by the arm. "You're not going out there."

"You bet she's not," Zeke muttered under his breath. "If anyone goes out there, it will be me."

The negotiator touched Zeke's shoulder. "Nobody's going anywhere."

He shook off the restraint. "Then let me talk to him."

The negotiator nodded and Tara passed Zeke the handset. He clicked it on. "Ross, this is Zeke Blaxland. I've been writing about the hospital."

"I've read your stuff. I didn't steal those babies."

"We know that," Zeke soothed. "That's why I want you to tell your side of the story."

Tara snatched the handset and rammed the off switch home. "What are you doing, taking his side?"

"He's doing exactly the right thing," the negotiator stated. "The aim is to get everybody out of this alive, whatever it takes."

Numbly Tara returned the handset to Zeke and he clicked it on. "Ross, did you hear me?"

"I heard you, but I'm not falling for it. I read the papers. You claim you're my baby's father."

"I never claimed to be Vaughan's father," Zeke returned, choosing his words carefully.

"Tell that to my wife and the police."

"I've already told them. What else can I do?"

"Ask your lady friend to tell them. Then get everybody out and leave me and my family alone."

"First you have to let the baby go, then we can talk," Zeke said.

"You're not taking my son," Ross yelled back.

High-pitched wailing reached them through the open door and Tara choked back tears. Her baby was crying and she ached to go to him. Ten months of thinking she had lost him hadn't dulled her mothering instinct. She half rose but Zeke pulled her back down. "Can't you hear him?" she asked dazedly.

"I hear him." He clicked on the loud-hailer. "The baby sounds hungry, Ross. At least let us bring you some food for him."

"There's plenty of food here but it's cold. He won't eat it."

Making a cutting movement across her throat, the negotiator waited until Zeke turned off the handset. "He can't warm the food because we cut off the power."

Tara took the handset again. "Ross, you don't want the baby going hungry, do you? At least let us bring you some warm food for him."

Zeke made a gesture of negation but she ignored it. "Ross?" she repeated, clenching her fists as the wailing grew louder.

"All right, since he won't eat the cold stuff. But just you, no one else. One more thing."

She braced herself. "What is it?"

"Have someone get you one of those statutory declaration forms from the news agent and write on it that Vaughan is my son and you have no claim on him. Sign it and get it witnessed and bring it with the baby food."

Tara's chest heaved with the effort of holding back sobs, and when she brushed a hand across her face, her cheeks were wet. He wanted her to sign a legal document denying her own child. Wasn't it enough that he had deprived her of the first few months of her baby's life? "I can't," she said.

"You'd better. I'm not giving up my son."

The implied threat was accompanied by a violent sound that made her recoil in horror from what she first thought was a shot, until she realised it was only Ross slamming the door shut. "Wait," she called, hoping he was still listening. "I'll do it."

The door cracked open. "Don't take too long. Vaughan's hungry."

The negotiator took the handset from Tara. "Good work. I'll have someone get the baby food and the declaration. As soon as they're ready, I'll take them in."

"You can't, he knows me," Tara said.

The negotiator paused. "How well?"

"He's the midwife who delivered my baby."

''Damn. Changing clothes with you won't help then.'' The negotiator thought for a minute. ''Okay, but you'll wear a bulletproof vest, and you'll do exactly what we tell you.''

She would do anything if it saved her baby, Tara knew. Anything was better than sitting here, wondering what was happening in the house.

Zeke watched her being fitted with the vest. ''I should be doing this,'' he said through gritted teeth. If anything happened to Tara, he would never forgive himself. Exhausted as he was, he hadn't gone to sleep right away last night, as he'd told her he had. Instead he had lain awake wondering what in the devil he was doing.

Putting his mother's ring on her finger had felt more right than anything he'd done in a long time. Several times since then he'd been on the verge of saying he loved her. Why hadn't he? She had made it clear she wasn't about to give up on him, so it came down to whether or not he trusted her.

Why had it been so easy to walk away from Lucy, and so hard when it came to Tara? Because she held custody of his heart, he acknowledged. She wouldn't let him get away with anything less than a soul-deep commitment, and it terrified him.

So why didn't he accept what she offered and count his blessings? Because a casual relationship was no longer enough, he accepted, or he wouldn't have been so eager to show her his house and carry her over the threshold. The truth had been right in front of him all along. He was already committed to her in every way that mattered. All he had to do was tell her.

A police officer duck-walked up to the car with a bottle of baby formula and a document, handing both to Tara. ''Should I sign it?'' she asked, sounding so strained that it was all Zeke could do not to tear the form out of her hands.

The negotiator shook her head. ''It's as legal as it's going to be.''

Tara's relief that she didn't have to sign the document was palpable. She turned to Zeke. "Wish me luck."

He pulled her to him, the unaccustomed bulk of the vest under her blouse serving as a grim reminder of what she was facing. "I love you, Tara."

He felt her shock in the stiffening of her body, and her eyes sparked questions at him. Later he would take great pleasure in answering them, he promised himself. He set his jaw, telling himself there would be a later for them because there had to be. It took everything he had to let her go.

As she started to walk toward the house, he barely restrained himself from following her. The threat to his mate and his offspring aroused his most primal protective instincts and he knew the veneer of civilization had never been thinner.

He concentrated on the house. When she reached it, the door opened and Ross put his head around it. Seeing what looked like a baseball bat in the man's hand, Zeke's tension notched impossibly higher. His muscles bunched as the instinct to take on the world for her sake seized him.

He couldn't hear what was said, but she must have asked to see the baby. Amazingly, Ross brought the child to the door and Zeke felt rather than saw the officers around him snap to a new level of alert.

He ignored them, his whole focus on Tara. She reached for the child but Ross pulled the baby back. Her hand skimmed the blanket swaddling the baby then trailed slowly away. Zeke could almost feel how much she yearned to hold her child. He shared the feeling, wanting to hold them both so much that his arms hurt.

She handed Ross the paper and he scanned it eagerly. Tara leaned across him, apparently to point out some detail, and while Ross's attention was diverted for a split second, she acted, snatching the baby and spinning around in one fluid motion.

Beside Zeke, the negotiator sprang to her feet. ''What does that fool woman think she's doing?''

But Zeke was already up and moving, closing the distance between them with the speed of an Olympic sprinter. He saw Ross hurl the baseball bat after her in fury.

As if in slow motion, the missile arced through the air, aimed at Tara's back. Hunched over to protect the baby, she was defenseless. If the club struck her... Zeke lunged across the space between them, desperate to put himself between her and the missile.

He knew he was seconds too late, but his run managed to deflect her from her course, pushing her to one side so the club caught her shoulder. With a cry of pain that arrowed all the way to Zeke's heart, she went down.

With nothing left to lose, he charged the doorway, ramming his foot into the opening as Ross Fine tried desperately to close it. With a war cry, he grabbed the man and slammed him against the door so hard it bounced on its hinges. Zeke pulled his right fist back.

Someone locked on to his arm and held it in a grip of iron. Zeke fought the hold until he became aware that it was one of the police officers. ''That's enough, let us do our job now,'' he said. Still, it took all his strength to pry Zeke's left hand loose from the man's shoulder.

Zeke spun around, bracing himself for the sight of Tara and his son on the ground, injured or worse. To his astonishment, he saw her stumble to her feet, assisted by the negotiator. She held the blanket-wrapped baby against her body as if she never meant to let him go.

The baby was crying but seemed unhurt, and Zeke offered a silent prayer of thanks as he raced to her side. She must have cushioned the baby's fall with her own body. ''Tara, my love. I thought he'd hurt you.''

''Only my shoulder,'' she insisted.

He didn't miss the pain dulling her gaze or the odd way

her left arm hung. "Your shoulder's dislocated. Somebody get her an ambulance."

"It's already here," the negotiator said. "Although by rights, we should put both of you in the wagon. What kind of stunt was that?"

"The hero kind," Tara said with an incandescent look at Zeke. "If you hadn't pushed me aside..."

Her indrawn breath of pain wrenched at him. "You're the hero, not me, although your heroics almost got you killed."

"Once I saw Brendan, I didn't care what happened to me. I only wanted him to be safe. Oh, Zeke, he's our baby. I knew it the moment I set eyes on him."

He peeled back the blanket and looked into eyes as dark as his own. Any doubts that his son lived were swept aside as he recognized traces of his own features in the small face. It was screwed up with crying right now, but the sound was music to his ears. His throat began to close. "I'll take care of him while the paramedics do their stuff," he said huskily, not sure if she would let him.

To his surprise, she passed him the baby without demur. "Brendan, this is your daddy," she said softly, her eyes filling.

His tears weren't far behind as he took the squirming child, feeling all thumbs. Someone handed him a spare bottle of warmed formula. On instinct he offered it to the baby who began to drink hungrily. At the sight, a door to some emotional wellspring cracked open deep inside him, and he knew he would never be able to close it again, or want to.

He kept one arm around the baby and put the other around Tara's undamaged shoulder, well aware that only willpower kept her on her feet. "I love you," he said again, finding that it got easier with practice.

"I love you, too," she said hoarsely, having trouble believing she had heard him. Zeke had always made love to her, but had never said he loved her. But there was no mistaking the way he looked at her now. As she swayed the negotiator motioned the paramedics forward with a stretcher. She looked at it with distaste, but pain overrode her reluctance and she let herself be helped onto it, moving stiffly, on her last reserves of energy. When she was settled, she gave Zeke and the child a look of fierce determination. "You're coming with me to the hospital."

He gave her a thousand-watt grin. "Just try and stop us."

Chapter 15

Lillian McNiven was the first visitor. She regarded her daughter with concern as she sat up in bed with Zeke on one side, protective of Tara's damaged shoulder, now reset and nestled in a sling. On her good side, she cradled Brendan as if she never meant to let him out of her sight again. He'd fought sleep for as long as he could but succumbed at last, tired out by all the excitement.

Lillian tiptoed to the bedside. "How's the patient? The doctor said you're recovering nicely."

Tara gave a tired smile. "I'm fine. Come and meet your grandson."

"I don't want to disturb him." But Lillian leaned over, her gaze softening as she looked at the sleeping infant.

Zeke rolled his eyes. "A brass band wouldn't disturb him right now."

As had most of the country, Lillian told them, she had watched the hostage drama unfold on national television, and had sat with her heart in her mouth as her daughter walked into the line of fire. Until Zeke called her from the hospital, Lillian hadn't known that the child was her own flesh and blood. She still couldn't believe that the baby Tara had thought she'd lost was alive and well. It was a miracle.

"Is he really all right?" Lillian asked.

Tara nodded. "He's fine, but the hospital wanted to keep him overnight for observation. Since I wasn't about to leave him, they gave us a room together."

Zeke's hand brushed her hair. "The rest won't do you any harm, either, my love."

Hearing the endearment, Lillian's eyebrows lifted. "Did I read the headlines correctly yesterday? You two ran away and got married? I tried to call but got no answer at your place and no one at Zeke's office knew where he'd gone, either."

Tara heard the hurt her mother tried to conceal. "You didn't miss the wedding, so don't look so disappointed." She felt her eyes brighten and knew it was at the prospect of becoming Zeke's wife for real. With his ring on her finger, she felt as married to him as she could ever feel, but with their child to consider, he insisted on making everything official. "We'll be married as soon as the fuss dies down," she said.

"In the meantime, we had to tell the papers something to get them to stop hounding us," Zeke added.

Lillian's mouth twitched. "A new experience for you, Zeke?"

He held up a hand. "As a result, I promise to be a kinder, less intrusive journalist from now on."

Tara laughed. "And pigs might fly." Her tone said she didn't want him to change. She wanted him to stay as much a crusader as ever, to go on fighting in print for the rights of those who couldn't defend themselves. And to go on loving her and their child. The miracle was almost as great as finding their baby alive. Her cup of happiness brimmed over.

"You just missed Ben and Carol and the children," she told her mother. That scene had been emotional enough to bring the house down. She had a feeling Brendan was going to be thoroughly spoiled by his relatives. By her, too, if she wasn't very careful.

Her mother dropped a kiss on her forehead. "You must be tired out. But you can have a break now. Your father plans to stop by, but not until the afternoon."

Tara said stiffly, "That's kind of him."

At the door, Lillian paused. "Don't be too hard on him, Tara. He's changed after living on his own for a while. He's not as demanding as he used to be." Lillian's gaze lingered on the tableau of father, mother and baby. "I don't think I need to explain it to you anymore."

Her vision blurred and Tara shook her head. Love didn't set conditions and it didn't vanish because you willed it to. "Do you think you'll get back together?"

"Who knows? I'll always care about him. In his own strange way, he cares about me, too. He's taking me to dinner tomorrow night."

It was a start, Tara thought. She smiled. "Have a good time."

She looked up at Zeke. "I'm staying at Zeke's place until I have the full use of my arm back." It was still hideously sore, and the pain of having her shoulder put back into place had been blinding, but the memory was fading fast. The sling was to ensure that she rested the arm and avoided the risk of dislocating her shoulder again. With Zeke finally admitting he loved her, and their baby safe by her side, she couldn't bring herself to complain about anything.

But Zeke saw the flicker of pain that crossed her face. "Would you like the doctor to give you something? I can take Brendan if he's too heavy for you."

Her good arm tightened automatically around the baby. "He could never be too heavy. Oh, Zeke, I can't believe he's real." She let her fingers trail over the baby's soft black hair. "He's so big now and we've missed so much." His first sounds, how he reacted to his first taste of solid food, discovering he could sit up by himself. All of it had taken place without her. She blinked hard.

He placed his hand over hers on the baby's head. "I know, and we can never get those months back, but we have all of the future together."

She took comfort in the warmth of his touch. He hadn't left her side for a second since she had been brought to the hospital. Without her having to say so, he had understood that she couldn't bear letting Brendan out of her sight, and had held the baby in his arms where she could see them both while her shoulder was set. She hadn't been able to stop herself from crying out at the pain, and Zeke had looked as if he wanted to hit the doctor causing it. But she had kept her eyes on Zeke and her son, knowing nothing else mattered.

He had even changed his son on a table nearby, she recalled. He had never done it before in his life, but had allowed a nurse to talk him through the process, treating the job as a labor of love. He had surprised her quite a few times lately, and she suspected it was only the beginning.

"Did you mean it when you said you love me?" she asked in a low voice.

"I'm only sorry it took me so long to say it."

"Remember what you told me. We can't get those months back, but we have the future." It had never looked more radiant.

Zeke looked at the sleeping child. "How long do you think it will take before he accepts us as his parents?"

"At this age, the doctor told me he should bond quite quickly. Even though we didn't share the first ten months of his life, there's still the blood tie. I think he knows I'm his mother." Wishful thinking perhaps, but she couldn't help herself.

"I'm sure of it." In truth, Zeke wasn't sure of anything anymore. In a day his whole life had turned upside down. He had discovered that not only was he capable of committing to Tara, nothing on earth was going to keep them apart. He had also discovered fatherhood in a big way. While holding his son and watching Tara's injuries being treated, he had felt a love such as he had never known in his life. It welled out of the deepest part of his being, and wove like an aura around the three of them. Caveman he might be, but he intended to guard his small clan as ferociously as any cave dweller in the history of the planet.

Her eyes drifted shut and he saw that she was asleep. He eased himself into a chair within touching distance of the two of them, knowing he wasn't going anywhere until the three of them went home together.

By tacit agreement, they had decided to return to Zeke's new house rather than either of their homes. Of all the places she had lived, Tara knew that this house felt more like home to her than anywhere else. Their home.

"Just as well I carried you over the threshold last time, because it wouldn't be a good idea this time," Zeke said.

Her shoulder twinged occasionally and she still wore the sling, but it was already less bothersome than when she left the hospital a few days before. Zeke had insisted on taking them to a luxury hotel suite in the middle of the city, where she and the baby could be waited on hand and foot, shielded from the media who were having a field day with the story.

She had enjoyed the hotel experience, especially of having Zeke's undivided attention, she acknowledged. He had written a wrap-up of the baby swapping scandal at the hotel and it had been published to great fanfare. If her shoulder hadn't been too sore to make love, everything would have been perfect. She consoled herself with Zeke's promise that their whole future lay ahead of them.

Another surprise awaited her when Zeke unlocked the front door. "The place is furnished," she exclaimed.

Where the large rooms had echoed with emptiness before, there was now a comfortable ambience that Tara loved on sight. In the hallway, leafy green plants flourished in pots and a vase of old-fashioned roses perfumed the air. She had always liked country style, and she gloried in the Laura Ashley fabrics and Sanderson cabbage-rose prints that dominated the living-room furnishings. A guest bathroom had been decorated to match, she noticed as she passed it. She could hardly wait to explore the rest. "It's wonderful."

Settling Brendan comfortably in his arms, he gave a pleased smile. "I know what you like, so I had a decorator come in while we were at the hotel."

"Now I know why you wanted to keep me away."

He regarded her seriously. "I never want to keep you away again. And I did want you to get some rest."

"I feel like a real lotus-eater. I've never done so little in my life." He had canceled her commitments on behalf of Model Children, telling everyone that she wouldn't be available for at least a couple of weeks. She had sighed at his heavy-handedness, knowing they would need to talk about it soon. Having him pamper her was one thing, but he couldn't be encouraged to take control of her life. At the same time, she understood why he felt the need. Proposing marriage and becoming a father were huge steps for someone who had never wanted to be tied down by anyone. She couldn't blame him for going a little overboard.

He saw the flicker of doubt cross her face. "Don't worry, I'm not planning to keep up the macho stuff forever, only until you're recovered and Brendan has adjusted to being with us, then I'll go back to being the self-centered boor you're used to."

She had to smile, knowing Zeke wouldn't do any such thing. He might regard himself as a caveman, but she could see changes that he hadn't yet noticed in himself and she loved every one of them. He was gentler, more accommodating of her feelings, probably because he was more in tune with his own.

The baby had also adjusted remarkably well. She had braced herself for tears and tantrums, and the counselor the police had sent to talk to her, had assured her it wasn't personal. Brendan needed time to get to know them and get over being separated from the people he'd known as parents for the past ten months.

"Have you heard any more about Jenny and Ross?" she asked.

He nodded. "Bill's keeping tabs for me. Ross is in custody, awaiting trial for kidnapping. He's agreed to give evidence against the organizers of the baby swapping ring, and that will help his case. They'll also take his mental problems into account."

"And Jenny Fine?"

"No charges were laid against her. The police accept that she didn't know anything about the switch."

"I hope her baby is born well and strong this time. She deserves some happiness." Knowing what she'd endured after she believed her baby had died, Tara's heart went out to the other woman.

"She should have come forward a lot sooner," Zeke said, sounding less than sympathetic. "Then you wouldn't have suffered for so long."

"It's over now. You said yourself, we have the future ahead of us."

While she settled the baby in the newly furnished nursery that opened off the master bedroom, Zeke went into the kitchen, saying he would make coffee. It was so cozily domestic that she felt as if a giant hand had enclosed her heart. What more could she possibly ask from life?

"How's Brendan?" he asked when she joined him in the kitchen.

"Sleeping like a baby," she said, then heard herself and laughed. It was tempting to creep back and check on him every five minutes, but she was trying to cure herself of the habit. The counselor had warned her that she would be tempted to wrap the child in cotton wool, but ultimately it would do more harm than good. But it was so hard to make herself stay away even for short periods.

Zeke sensed her dilemma. "Want me to check on him?"

"We mustn't. At least not more than a dozen times an hour." It gratified her to see that he felt the same way. Despite his earlier misgivings, she had seen enough to convince her that Zeke was going to be a great father.

She picked up the coffee cup Zeke had passed to her, but before she could drink, the doorbell rang. It was the first time she'd heard it since arriving at the house and the cheerless sound reminded her of a Gothic movie. Her eyes widened in astonishment.

Zeke's gaze met hers. "I'll get it changed tomorrow."

He hadn't moved. "Aren't you going to answer it?" she asked.

"Do you want visitors?"

She shook her head, knowing everyone she wanted to see was already under the roof. But the doorbell pealed again. Whoever it was wasn't going away. "If we don't answer it, that awful bell will wake the baby."

He set his cup down and went into the hallway. A man's voice she didn't recognize greeted him and she followed, curious to see who it belonged to. A tall, slightly stoop-shouldered man in his early seventies stood at the door. His silver hair gave him an air of distinction, and his craggy features looked oddly familiar, she thought.

"Greg Blaxland, meet my fiancée, Tara McNiven," Zeke said with a strange catch in his voice.

She felt her smile freeze. Blaxland? What was going on here? Habit made her offer her hand. ''What can we do for you, Mr. Blaxland?''

''I'd like to come in for a few minutes, if I'm not intruding,'' Greg said, his diffident tone at odds with his confident appearance.

She glanced at Zeke, who nodded. The man followed them into the formal living room, but seemed reluctant to sit down. Instead he paced a little, caught himself, thrust his hands into his pockets, took them out again.

He looked so ill at ease that Tara took pity on him. Zeke was obviously waiting for Greg to make the first move, for some reason. ''We're having coffee in the kitchen, would you like some?'' she asked.

The man's relief was apparent. ''That would be great, thanks.''

Zeke also seemed to welcome having something to do, as he got out another cup and filled it, adding cream and sugar at the man's request. When there were no more small tasks to busy himself with, he looked at Greg. ''Why are you here?''

The man hesitated. ''I should ask the same question you asked me when you arrived on my doorstep to tell me my daughter had died. Can't a man visit his family without an excuse?''

Family? More confusion roiled through Tara. ''Who are you?'' she asked.

Zeke's shoulders hunched as if he was in pain. ''Greg is my mother's father.''

''Your grandfather?'' She said the word he had avoided, understanding why the man looked so familiar. There was an unmistakable family resemblance. ''*You're* the man who turned Zeke away after he finally tracked you down?''

The older man looked as if he might break down, but regained control of himself with an effort. ''You don't have to remind me. I've lived with that memory every day for ten years.''

Zeke's hands balled into fists. ''You're not the only one.''

The man flinched as if his grandson *had* hit him. ''The religious group I belonged to preached the old biblical rule that if your eye offended you, you cut it out.''

''Even if the offender was your own daughter?''

''Even then. I don't belong to them anymore. I left that group soon after your visit, but it was too late, or so I thought.''

''It is too late,'' Zeke said savagely.

The man started to turn away, hunching as if against a howling gale. ''I can't blame you. But I hoped, now you have a child of your own...''

''Wait.'' Zeke sounded so bleak that her heart turned over. ''You're right, I can't do to you what you did to me.''

''Even though I deserve it,'' the man finished his thought, but sounded a fraction more hopeful. ''I've followed your adventures in the papers since you discovered your baby was alive.''

''How did you locate us?'' Tara asked.

''As it turns out, I've known one of your new neighbors for years. When she told me who'd moved in here, it seemed like an omen. I had to come, although I was far from sure of my welcome.''

''You *are* welcome,'' she said decisively. ''For our son's sake. It will be good for him to grow up knowing Zeke's side of the family.'' She used the phrase deliberately, taking satisfaction in the wonder she saw spreading over Zeke's face. ''You are his great-grandfather,'' she added.

''My wife, Angela, will spoil him rotten if you let her,'' Greg said, his voice cracking. ''She was too uncertain of our welcome to come today, but I hope you'll let me bring her over soon.''

''Whenever you like.'' Tara hoped she hadn't gone too

far, but saw from Zeke's expression that she had said the right thing, perhaps the words he wanted to say but couldn't yet.

As if reaching a decision, Zeke set his cup down. "Would you like to see your great-grandson?"

Greg's face lit up. "I'd like it very much."

Zeke led his grandfather to the door of the baby's room and they looked in at the sleeping child. Watching them watching her son, Tara's heart felt so full it wanted to burst. The one thing she had wanted for Zeke had set the seal on their future. His real family had acknowledged him at last. She was glad Zeke hadn't turned Greg away. He, too, might have regretted it all of his life.

There would probably be other relatives for him to meet, memories and, no doubt, family disputes, as well. She'd known them all in her own family, and looked forward to seeing Zeke discover them for himself. As well as the joys family could bestow. They would make him whole.

When he showed Greg out after inviting him to bring his wife the next day, Zeke's eyes were shining. "I never thought I'd see the day."

She shrugged off the sling and wrapped her arms around him, pleased to find that her shoulder gave only the merest twinge. Zeke looked alarmed. "Should you?"

"I'm fine, really." She studied him from under lowered lashes. "The doctor said I can do anything I want to, as long as I'm careful."

Her voice played on his nerves like a violin. "Anything?"

She tightened her hold. "Anything I want to."

He began to kiss her slowly, thoroughly, until her heart sang with joy and anticipation before he lifted passion-drugged eyes to her. "If you're sure?"

"I didn't break into pieces out there."

He laughed. "Bold little thing, aren't you?"

"Frustrated more likely." It had been days since the hostage crisis and she was aching for him. "Do you know how long it's been?"

His face told her he knew to the second how long it had been, but he kept his caresses gentle, arousing her, loving her, as if she were made of precious porcelain.

Wonder warred with desire inside her. "Lord, Zeke, will it always be like this with us?"

"Always," he promised, raining kisses over her face until he reached her mouth, where he staked his claim with breath-taking assurance.

When she could breathe again, she said, "I thought you didn't believe in always."

"You made me believe. For richer and poorer, good and bad, until death do us part." He lifted his head. "Tell me it's what you want, too?"

She rested her head against him. "It's what I've always dreamed of with you."

He tilted her chin up. "Just goes to show you, dreams can come true."

"Ours have, all of them."

"Not quite all. Brendan is still an only child."

But not for long, she thought as Zeke's arms came around her and his mouth found hers. Not for long.

* * * * *

INTIMATE MOMENTS™

presents a riveting new continuity series:

FIRSTBORN SONS

Bound by the legacy of their fathers, these Firstborn Sons are about to discover the stuff true heroes—and true love—are made of!

The adventure continues in September 2001 with:

BORN TO PROTECT by Virginia Kantra

Former Navy SEAL Jack Dalton took his job *very* seriously when he was ordered to protect Princess Christina Sebastiani from ruthless kidnappers. But nothing in the rule book prepared this Firstborn Son on the proper code of conduct to follow when the virgin princess managed to capture his world-weary heart!

July: **BORN A HERO**
by **Paula Detmer Riggs** (IM #1088)
August: **BORN OF PASSION**
by **Carla Cassidy** (IM #1094)
September: **BORN TO PROTECT**
by **Virginia Kantra** (IM #1100)
October: **BORN BRAVE**
by **Ruth Wind** (IM #1106)
November: **BORN IN SECRET**
by **Kylie Brant** (IM #1112)
December: **BORN ROYAL**
by **Alexandra Sellers** (IM #1118)

*Available only from
Silhouette Intimate Moments
at your favorite retail outlet.*

Where love comes alive™

Visit Silhouette at www.eHarlequin.com

SIMFIRST3

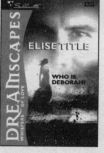
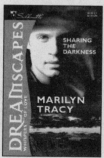

HARLEQUIN "SILHOUETTE MAKES YOU A STAR!" CONTEST 1308
OFFICIAL RULES
NO PURCHASE NECESSARY TO ENTER

1. To enter, follow directions published in the offer to which you are responding. Contest begins June 1, 2001, and ends on September 28, 2001. Entries must be postmarked by September 28, 2001, and received by October 5, 2001. Enter by hand-printing (or typing) on an 8 ½" x 11" piece of paper your name, address (including zip code), contest number/name and attaching a script containing 500 words or less, along with drawings, photographs or magazine cutouts, or combinations thereof (i.e., collage) on no larger than 9" x 12" piece of paper, describing how the Silhouette books make romance come alive for you. Mail via first-class mail to: Harlequin "Silhouette Makes You a Star!" Contest 1308, (in the U.S.) P.O. Box 9069, Buffalo, NY 14269-9069, (in Canada) P.O. Box 637, Fort Erie, Ontario, Canada L2A 5X3. Limit one entry per person, household or organization.

2. Contests will be judged by a panel of members of the Harlequin editorial, marketing and public relations staff. Fifty percent of criteria will be judged against script and fifty percent will be judged against drawing, photographs and/or magazine cutouts. Judging criteria will be based on the following:

   - Sincerity—25%
   - Originality and Creativity—50%
   - Emotionally Compelling—25%

   In the event of a tie, duplicate prizes will be awarded. Decisions of the judges are final.

3. All entries become the property of Torstar Corp. and may be used for future promotional purposes. Entries will not be returned. No responsibility is assumed for lost, late, illegible, incomplete, inaccurate, nondelivered or misdirected mail.

4. Contest open only to residents of the U.S. (except Puerto Rico) and Canada who are 18 years of age or older, and is void wherever prohibited by law; all applicable laws and regulations apply. Any litigation within the Province of Quebec respecting the conduct or organization of a publicity contest may be submitted to the Régie des alcools, des courses et des jeux for a ruling. Any litigation respecting the awarding of a prize may be submitted to the Régie des alcools, des courses et des jeux only for the purpose of helping the parties reach a settlement. Employees and immediate family members of Torstar Corp. and D. L. Blair, Inc., their affiliates, subsidiaries and all other agencies, entities and persons connected with the use, marketing or conduct of this contest are not eligible to enter. Taxes on prizes are the sole responsibility of the winner. Acceptance of any prize offered constitutes permission to use winner's name, photograph or other likeness for the purposes of advertising, trade and promotion on behalf of Torstar Corp., its affiliates and subsidiaries without further compensation to the winner, unless prohibited by law.

5. Winner will be determined no later than November 30, 2001, and will be notified by mail. Winner will be required to sign and return an Affidavit of Eligibility/Release of Liability/Publicity Release form within 15 days after winner notification. Noncompliance within that time period may result in disqualification and an alternative winner may be selected. All travelers must execute a Release of Liability prior to ticketing and must possess required travel documents (e.g., passport, photo ID) where applicable. Trip must be booked by December 31, 2001, and completed within one year of notification. No substitution of prize permitted by winner. Torstar Corp. and D. L. Blair, Inc., their parents, affiliates and subsidiaries are not responsible for errors in printing of contest, entries and/or game pieces. In the event of printing or other errors that may result in unintended prize values or duplication of prizes, all affected game pieces or entries shall be null and void. **Purchase or acceptance of a product offer does not improve your chances of winning.**

6. Prizes: (1) Grand Prize—A 2-night/3-day trip for two (2) to New York City, including round-trip coach air transportation nearest winner's home and hotel accommodations (double occupancy) at The Plaza Hotel, a glamorous afternoon makeover at a trendy New York spa, $1,000 in U.S. spending money and an opportunity to have a professional photo taken and appear in a Silhouette advertisement (approximate retail value: $7,000). (10) Ten Runner-Up Prizes of gift packages (retail value $50 ea.). Prizes consist of only those items listed as part of the prize. Limit one prize per person. Prize is valued in U.S. currency.

7. For the name of the winner (available after December 31, 2001) send a self-addressed, stamped envelope to: Harlequin "Silhouette Makes You a Star!" Contest 1197 Winners, P.O. Box 4200 Blair, NE 68009-4200 or you may access the www.eHarlequin.com Web site through February 28, 2002.

Contest sponsored by Torstar Corp., P.O Box 9042, Buffalo, NY 14269-9042.

SRMYAS2

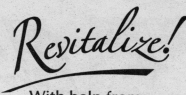